For testimonials from law enforcement,
visit Carolyn Arnold's website.

ALSO BY CAROLYN ARNOLD

Detective Madison Knight

Brandon Fisher FBI

Detective Amanda Steele

Matthew Connor Adventure

Standalone

An absolutely gripping and addictive crime thriller

GIRL ON THE RUN

She was living with a dark secret.
No one around her was safe.

CAROLYN ARNOLD

A Detective Madison Knight Mystery

HIBBERT & STILES PUBLISHING INC.

Hibbert & Stiles Publishing Inc.
www.hspubinc.com

This is a work of fiction. Names, characters, places, and incidents are the products of the author's imagination or are used fictitiously. Any resemblance to actual events, locales, or persons, living or dead, is entirely coincidental.

Names: Arnold, Carolyn, author.
Title: Girl on the Run / Carolyn Arnold.
Description: [London, Ontario] : Hibbert & Stiles Publishing Inc., [2022] | Series: Detective Madison Knight series ; [book 11]
Identifiers: ISBN 978-1-989706-74-9 (paperback 4.25 x 7) | ISBN: 978-1-989706-75-6 (paperback 5 x 8) | ISBN 978-1-989706-77-0 (hardcover) | ISBN 978-1-989706-73-2 (ebook)

Additional formats:
ISBN: 978-1-989706-78-7 (paperback large print edition 6 x 9)
ISBN: 978-1-989706-79-4 (audiobook)

GIRL ON THE RUN

PROLOGUE

In the Near Future...

Her heart is racing as she steps off the bus. There's no way they'll find her here if there's a god in heaven. The hinge point is *if*. He or She, if they do exist, forgot about her a long time ago.

Braybury is only a couple of hours' drive from Stiles, but it should put enough space between her and the people who are after her—for now. And it's a huge city with a population of seven million, so she should be able to blend into the background.

This could all be a good thing—the start of a new and promising beginning.

While people continue to disembark, she stands back, catching her breath and slipping her arms through the straps of her backpack. All these faces. She checks each one with intense scrutiny to see if any of them are familiar. Not one among them.

Maybe she actually escaped their clutches after all. A giddy elation flutters through her. She even smiles, though briefly.

The man on the street corner. Tall and muscular with a thick neck inked with the abstract markings of a tattoo that means something only to him. But his face is one from her nightmares. He's with *them*. The people she fears won't just let her walk away. They have tendrils everywhere.

But how did he find her here? She'd been careful, watching over her shoulder as she's been accustomed to doing all her life. She hadn't noticed him before now.

He smirks and starts coming toward her.

How he found her really doesn't matter. He's here, and he's onto her.

She has to run! But to where?

She glances around. Maybe if she can sink into the crowd, she'll lose him. The hope shatters with a hard slap of reality. He's already found her once, increasing the odds he'll find her again.

She sets out and bumps into a person who snarls at her.

"Watch where you're going!"

She keeps moving, her feet smacking against the pavement as she weaves through the bodies lining the sidewalk. She glances over a shoulder, and he's definitely in pursuit.

She picks up speed. Now at a fast jog.

She looks back again. He's keeping up, and the smile on his face tells her he's enjoying himself.

She begins to run, faster than her legs want to move. Her torso leaning forward, urging her limbs to follow suit.

It does no good. His long legs aid him in keeping up with her.

Skyscrapers tower over her, and buses and vehicles rumble past on the street. She feels the vibration of the subway running under her feet and wishes she could just disappear. Maybe if she can get herself into the underground labyrinths, she'll lose him.

There's a sign announcing the Richmond Street subway entrance above a staircase that sinks beneath the earth. She takes the steps two at a time. At the bottom, she looks back, and there's no sign of him.

Until there is.

Her entire body trembles. If he catches her, she's dead. She hasn't done even one thing right in this lifelife. Not that life has given her much of a chance.

More people are in the tunnels and pushing through turnstiles. Every one of them is oblivious to her plight. If they knew, would they care? Her fate doesn't affect them.

Another glimpse back, and the man is in full pursuit, rushing toward her at a faster pace.

She tries to pick up speed again, but throngs of people continually hinder her progress. She rounds a corner and leans against a door, trying to catch her breath and slow her breathing.

There's nowhere she can go. Nowhere she can hide.

She wraps her hand around the door handle behind her, and she twists. It gives.

She tucks inside. A stairwell. Maybe she will get away. Just maybe.

Before she can lock the door, it opens.

The tattooed man steps inside, never taking his eyes off her. He holds a gun in his hand, and it's trained on her.

"Gotcha." He laughs, and her entire body shudders.

"Just, please, let me go." There's no point in running now. She must be brave and face her fate, her dark future.

He's still smiling when he says, "You'll be wishing for a bullet by the time she's done with you. But don't worry, I'm sure death will come nice and fast." He reaches out and snags her arm, his grip tight and unyielding, his fingers digging into her flesh even through her jacket. She shrieks in agony, but there's no one to hear her cries, no one to save her.

CHAPTER 1

Present Day

Madison's mind had her up, out the door, and in line for caffeine at seven AM. The compensation was a heady aroma of different beverages, most of them based on espresso, served with a stream of people lined up from the counter to the door. There were at least fifteen people ahead of her. At this rate, the venti caramel cappuccino she'd dreamed of might get into her hand by noon.

She tapped a foot and stepped to the side to look around the lumberjack of a man immediately in front of her. Though at five foot five, it didn't take much height to block her view.

A twentysomething woman in a pencil skirt was at the counter rattling off an order she was reading from a tablet. At least seven drinks and as many *special* breakfast sandwiches.

Scratch noon. She'd be here all day.

One cappuccino. That was all she needed, and she'd be on her way. Simple and done. No half this, half that, a splash of this, a blend of that. She had no need for a fancy sandwich either. Stress had her stomach compacted into the size of a raisin.

The line inched forward as Pencil Skirt shuffled down the counter.

One person closer, and the wait would be worth it. The end justifying the means. Maybe if she focused on the explosion of flavor that cappuccino would deliver to her tongue, her impatience would melt away with her problems.

She closed her eyes, and the rims burned from lack of sleep, but her mind had good reason for being overactive. The Russian Mafia. Corrupt cops in her department. Dealing with Internal Affairs. The baby she'd lost… That was the big one, and it was something she still hadn't shared with all those she cared about. But she didn't have time to dwell on her loss or she'd forfeit her sanity. She was teetering on the edge already from all the conflicting emotions that washed over her—grief, relief, anger, acceptance. Her therapist would tell her to be with her feelings and process them, but she had a job to do. And a plan. All her focus and energy would go into the first three items on her list. Whenever they got sorted out, she'd tackle her lost baby.

The line inched forward again in response to another server asking for the next in line.

She looked out the window; the city was stirring to life. Pedestrians crowded the sidewalks, and vehicle traffic buzzed by in a blur of colors. Yellow taxis lined up across the street in front of Liberty Train Station, eager to pick up new fares or drop some off. So many people with somewhere to be, and based on the numerous scowls, most weren't eager about getting there. At least she had a purpose and drive, even if that light had dimmed in more recent days.

The line was moving more quickly now, and she was pleased to see she was next. She could practically taste that cappuccino.

"He has a gun!" A woman's scream filtered from outside and through the front windows of the coffee shop.

The woman shot past the window, frantic. More people followed her down the sidewalk. All of them were moving at a fast clip.

Damn. The cappuccino would have to wait.

Madison pulled her badge and held it up for everyone to see. "Detective Knight, Stiles PD! Everyone toward the back of the store."

Sleepy patrons became wide-eyed and confused as they stared at her like she had three heads. Finally, her message saturated their caffeine-deprived brains.

They scurried to the back while Madison headed to the door and tucked her badge away. Her hand was hovering above her holster, ready to draw her weapon if necessary.

She stepped outside. Vehicles were either stopped or crawling along. Men and women ran past her. *What is going on?*

Rounding the hood of a truck, she got her answer. There was a mass exodus from the train station.

Madison pulled her phone from a pocket and called dispatch. She gave her name and badge number. "Possible shooting at Liberty Station. Approach situation as if the perp is still there and armed." She hated not having details to provide, but life didn't always present things on a silver platter.

The communications operator confirmed units had already been dispatched to the scene and officers at the station were responding.

"Then you know what's going on already?"

"Uh-huh. A shooting with suspected casualties. But that's all I know at this time."

Suspected casualties… That was her cue as a detective with Major Crimes. Madison ended the call and rushed toward the station.

Sirens started up in the distance, their roar growing louder as they got closer.

Madison stopped a woman coming through the doors and announced herself as police. "What happened?"

"Someone… Gunfire." Her eyes were wide with shock, and she ran away before Madison could ask exactly where the shooting had taken place.

Liberty Station covered at least a square mile and was multiple stories. It offered a food court and even warranted its own police detail, though a lot of good that did today.

Madison stepped inside and looked behind her at the touch of someone's hand on her shoulder. She braced herself for a confrontation and relaxed at the sight of Officer Reggie Higgins, her training officer from back in the day.

"Tell me what's going on," she said to him.

"Shooting at the Just Beans kiosk. Understand three shot, two dead on scene."

"And this *just* happened?"

"Five minutes ago. If." Higgins passed her and rushed through a second set of doors, and she followed.

She wasn't that familiar with the layout of the station, having no need to grace the corridors herself. They wound through a few long hallways, their guns at the ready. Officers behind them worked to corral panicking and shocked civilians that remained. They'd be questioned, their information taken, then released. But one person in this crowd could be the shooter. She eyed everyone with suspicion.

"We need to shut this place down. No one in or out," she told Higgins. Not that it would do any good for those who had already managed to run to the streets.

"In the works."

"It could already be too late. We'll also need to stop all trains from leaving and arrivals from disembarking."

"Being handled." He glanced at her with a raised brow, a subtle reminder that he'd trained her.

She nodded.

They proceeded down a ramp to a lower level, and the aftermath was ahead of them—three bodies sprawled on the floor, surrounded by blood. From this distance, details were hard to make out, but their heeled shoes told her they were women. The Just Beans kiosk was positioned where two hallways intersected and wasn't part of the food court—thankfully, or there could have been more victims.

Madison rushed forward while bystanders, some who were screaming and crying into their hands, were ushered away by uniformed officers.

With each step she took closer to the scene, her legs became heavy. *All that blood...* She swallowed the nausea that brewed in her gut. The sight and smell of it nearly overwhelmed her senses, but adrenaline came to the rescue, painting the scene in front of her with a fictionalized brush and dulling the noises surrounding her.

Two dead with holes in their chests. One woman alive and groaning. Her mumbles were barely coherent as she said, "I've...been...shot." Her eyes fluttered shut.

Higgins called in over his radio and said, "Need an ETA on those paramedics."

"Stay with me." Madison got as close as she could to the injured woman without traipsing in the blood. "Help is on the way."

Behind the counter, two women stood, their hands in the air. Their sudden appearance startled Madison. Their uniforms announced them as employees of Just Beans.

"You're all right now too. Everyone will be—"

One of the workers collapsed, clipping Madison's words. *Ah, shit!*

Madison rushed around the counter, and the woman was in a heap on the floor. Passed out.

It wasn't long before paramedics raced toward them with a few sets of gurneys, but only two at this point would be necessary. The decedents would take a different ride.

What the hell had happened here?

CHAPTER 2

"Why am I not surprised to see you?" Detective Terry Grant, Madison's partner on the job, arrived behind crime scene investigators.

"I was getting a cappuccino across the street."

"Uh-huh. Trouble always seems to find you."

Fair assessment, and it wasn't the first time she'd heard that, not just from Terry but from others as well. Her fiancé, Troy Matthews, was one of them.

"Any word on the shooter?" Terry asked.

"Vanished into thin air. Apparently, that's possible." Madison threw up her hands. She had a very low threshold for incompetence, and losing the trail of a shooter was a prime example of that.

"Do we have IDs on the vics?" Terry asked.

Her gaze skimmed to the two mounds covered with black tarps. Officers had quickly rushed to drape them over the bodies to prevent any possibility of onlookers capturing them on video. It was sickening that such measures had to be taken. One would think humankind would have inborn sensibilities to respect the dead, but when so many didn't respect the living, it shouldn't really be a surprise. Madison hadn't gotten a good look at the dead women as she'd been distracted by the employee who had passed out. She had riffled through their attaché bags and purses, though. She noticed each women had a cell phone, and one a tablet, but she had gone straight to the wallets for IDs.

"Maddy?"

"Yeah, we do. The decedents are Dana Ridley, thirty-eight, and Morgan Walker, thirty-six." She paused there, the fact sinking in that Walker was the same age as her. That always hit home, not to mention how knowing the identities of the victims made the carnage that much more real. The bodies had once been living, breathing individuals with people who loved them. Madison continued. "Shannon Brennan, forty-one, was shot and rushed to the hospital. At this point, I'm not sure of her status or whether her injury is life threatening. Higgins is currently pulling the background information on all three women." She didn't need to say it, but the least fun part of her and Terry's job would soon follow—notifying next of kin.

Her gaze skipped to the tarps again, her mind on what was beneath them. At this point, she'd wait until Cole Richards, the medical examiner, arrived to get a closer look at them. There'd be less chance of contaminating the scene in some way. "They were just here to catch a train…" The emptiness and meaninglessness of it all. They'd simply been going about their typical weekday, then *boom!* everything changed. "Typical weekday," she mumbled more to herself than Terry. Did the women regularly commute and grab their coffee at the same time and place? Was the shooting as random as it appeared? She'd bench these questions for now, but the answers would be critical in solving this case.

Cynthia Baxter, Madison's best friend and head of the crime lab, was busy with her team of three processing the scene. They were snapping photographs and placing markers and collecting whatever could be perceived as evidence. Every square inch would be processed, and by the time they finished, nothing would be missed.

Madison proceeded to fill Terry in more. "Two workers were on duty at the time of the shooting. One was taken to Stiles General. We'll catch up with her and Brennan later. Right now, let's find out what she has to say." Madison nudged her head toward the Just Beans employee with

Officer Tendum. They were a short distance away, down a nearby hallway. The woman was talking animatedly, her arms flailing in wild arcs.

The woman stopped all movement when she saw Madison and Terry approaching.

Tendum slightly dipped his head and stepped aside.

"Hey! Where are you going?" the woman barked at him.

"I'll be around if you need me, but these detectives need to speak with you about what happened." Tendum kept his voice level and professional, and Madison was almost impressed. Almost. She and the officer had a shaky history that, at one point, had her wondering if he was worthy of the badge. And now, Madison would have expected him to introduce them to the employee and not just abandon her. Another strike against him.

"Detectives?" The Just Beans employee contorted her otherwise beautiful face into an ugly mask. She was in her early twenties with blond hair in a high-mounted ponytail that reached her waist. She wore large teal hoops that took Madison back in time to the eighties when they were all the rage, but maybe they were "in" again. Or maybe this person just wore what she wanted to, trends be damned.

"Detectives Knight and Grant." Madison gestured to where her badge was clipped on her waistband. "Your name?"

"Julie"—she knotted her arms—"Nelson." Body language closed off. Certainly a different image than the one she portrayed to Tendum. Her gray, catlike eyes leveled at Madison.

"We can appreciate that you've been through a traumatic event. If you'd like to sit..." Madison indicated a nearby bench, and Julie took her up on the offer.

She sat and leaned forward, her hands braced on the front curve of the bench seat. "I can't believe this happened."

"Can you just run us through what did?" There was no time to be sucked into an endless loop of woes and disbelief. It niggled enough that the shooter had disappeared without a trace. Even worse was the possibility that she'd passed by him on the street.

Julie slid her bottom lip through her teeth and nudged her head in the direction of Tendum. He was now about twenty feet away, his thumbs hooked into the band of his pants like he was some sort of cowboy. "I just told him everything."

"We need you to run through it all again with us," Madison said firmly. "It's procedure."

"It's a waste of time," Julie hissed. "Shouldn't you be out there finding who did this?"

Madison took a deep breath and stamped out, "Ms. Nelson, just talk and we'll be on our way."

"What if I don't want to live it all over again? It was troubling enough being there when it happened. I just want to forget about it now."

Madison's body vibrated with indignation. "Two people are dead. One was shot and might not make it. Your coworker passed out and was taken to the hospital. None of these women have the option to *forget about it*. Neither do their families. It's fair to say others are having a worse day, and asking you to answer some of our questions—even if you're repeating yourself—is a small price to pay. So, I'm going to ask again: what happened, and do you know what prompted the shooting?"

Julie shook her head, and tears beaded in her eyes. She nodded.

"No? Yes?" Madison was close to shaking the girl but talked herself back from that ledge. Julie had just lived through an ordeal. Maybe it wouldn't hurt to extend some empathy, exercise a little more restraint.

"I know some of it, I guess."

"We're listening." Madison was one millisecond away from tapping her foot.

"This guy came over and started yelling at the women in line."

"This guy being the shooter?" Just to clarify.

"Yes."

"And he just started yelling?" Terry squinted and angled his head. "All out of the blue, and about what?"

"It was because of this girl."

"Her name?" Madison asked.

"I have no idea, but she's always wearing an orange backpack."

Always...? "Okay," Madison dragged out, not sure where this was going. "Her age?"

"Early twenties, *if*, but she lifts stuff from the cooler. You know, the one at the front that's open for customers to take what they want."

Madison recalled the refrigerated bunker and nodded for Julie to continue.

"Well, this chick just helps herself, if you know what I mean."

"On a regular basis?" Terry asked.

"Yep."

"What happened next?" Madison wanted to understand how a young woman with a backpack could have triggered the shooting. She very well could be a student who commuted to Braybury or elsewhere for school.

"The women in line saw her steal and started murmuring about it. They were all in shock that she just walked over and stole, like it was nothing, and carried on. They were trying to get my attention to let me know."

"But you already knew she did this," Madison stated matter-of-factly.

"Yes, and there's nothing I can do about it. Even Bob, the owner of Just Beans, says to let it go. Obviously, it was wise advice because these women started yapping about what she'd done, and next thing I know this guy comes over all bat-shit crazy."

There was a scale of crazy, and *bat shit* would definitely score at the top. "Why do you say 'bat shit'?"

"Oh, he just raced over and was all like, 'What are you? A bunch of Good Samaritans?'"

"Just because they wanted to tell you about her stealing?" Madison was trying to make sense of what she was hearing, and it wasn't clicking together just yet.

"Uh, yeah. He claimed he was a cop, actually." Julie leveled a judgmental glare at Madison.

Madison's blood went cold. No one could be trusted. Not even in the brotherhood of blue. She, of all people, knew that well. One had rammed her car last month, landed her in the hospital, and she was quite sure the accident contributed to the loss of her baby. He and another officer were now under investigation by Internal Affairs, and Madison was sure more officers would be added to the list. The Russian Mafia was active in Stiles, and it had a way of reaching into the Stiles PD and finding the corrupt within the department. Her mission, or she'd die trying, was to bring them all down.

"He was lying," Terry said after a few beats of silence and with far more conviction than Madison could have.

The shooter had fled the station. It was as if he'd disappeared into thin air. If he wasn't a cop himself, did he have the help of some? Same now went for the girl with the backpack. Where had she gone? They'd need to speak to the officers on duty at the time of the shooting.

"I don't know about that." Julie paled. "One of the women, one with red hair, she's like, 'You're not a cop.' That's when he pulled the gun."

"And he fired right away?" Madison asked.

"No. She kept going at him, telling him he wasn't a cop, no way he was a cop. That's when he started shooting." Julie's body shook, and she pinched her eyes shut. Tears squeezed from them, down her cheeks.

"And after that…?" Madison felt for Julie's situation but couldn't afford to get weighed down by emotion.

"He ran off."

"Which way?"

Julie pointed straight across from them, past the Just Beans kiosk that was positioned where two corridors intersected.

"And you told this to Officer Tendum?" Madison asked.

"Yes, and he told others over his radio thingy." She gestured to the top of her arm, indicating where Tendum's radio was attached.

Madison pulled her gaze from the hallway. "Has this happened before—the guy coming over and acting threatening? Surely other customers would have reacted like the women did today."

"I've never seen him before."

Not exactly an answer to her question, but Madison had an inkling Julie was holding something back. "Okay, so the girl is a regular thing, but the guy isn't?"

"Him? No."

Tingles laced down Madison's arms. "But there's usually a man hanging around—what? Watching over the girl?"

Julie pointed across the way. "He stands over there. I think he's the girl's handler or something."

Handler? Madison assembled what she'd been told, starting with a young woman who regularly passed through the station *always wearing an orange backpack*. On its own that wouldn't raise any red flags. But a man watching over her on a routine basis certainly did. Putting both together, it suggested the girl was transporting something on her person, such as drugs or weapons. The handler would be there to protect her as an asset and see to it that she wasn't apprehended, that she reached her destination. But why would the girl put herself at risk by stealing? And what happened to the girl's regular shadow? "Why do you leap to him being a handler?"

"Call it a feeling."

Madison trusted feelings more than her partner did, but there seemed to be some merit to Julie's suspicions. "You said the girl steals regularly. How often exactly?"

"About two to three times a week."

Madison was trying to understand what had granted the girl with the backpack immunity, though she had a feeling it had to do with the man who watched over her—or the people he worked for. Julie had mentioned the owner of Just Beans told his staff to let the robberies go. He must have feared retaliation to allow that. She wanted to see Julie's reaction, so she asked, "Do you know why your boss never wanted you to stop her or report her?"

"She, ah, wasn't really hurting anything." Julie's gaze dipped briefly to the floor, and she pressed her lips together.

Julie was definitely afraid—and probably for good reason. The shooter had claimed to be a cop. Whether he truly was or not, the damage was done, and the integrity of the badge was called into question. It was, at minimum, a claim that intimidated. If a person accepted that he was a cop, they'd be less likely to approach a uniformed officer. They'd fear corruption. At the worst, there actually was something going on in the train station that involved bad cops. "And the guy who is normally here, the one you believe is her usual handler, has he ever come over to confront people?"

"Sure, the odd time, but it's never escalated like it had today. As I said, today it was a different guy. If it's all the same to you, though, I don't want to talk about either of those guys or that chick anymore."

"I'm sorry, but we need to know more," Madison said. "Did you see where the girl with the backpack went? What direction?"

"She had already walked away before the shooting." Julie pointed down a hallway that would have had the girl passing the shooter.

So she stole, carried on her merry way, the shooter—possible new handler—steps up and gets into the confrontation with the women. Meanwhile the girl with the backpack is long gone...? But surely, she heard the gunfire and ensuing chaos. If she was moving drugs or something equally as illegal, did she fulfill her original mission? If Madison were the girl, she'd have run. "We might need you to work with a sketch artist on the shooter, the regular guy who hangs around, and the girl." It couldn't be assumed she was innocent in all that transpired. Madison also couldn't assume that video surveillance captured their faces.

"I'll do what I have to." Julie leaned back and rubbed her arms.

"One more question before we go. Did you ever see the three women from the line before?" she asked.

"Uh-huh. They usually get a coffee in the morning. Not always at the same time, though. Thinking they probably catch the train to Braybury for work."

That made sense as Braybury was significantly larger than Stiles, which only had a population of three hundred thousand. "Okay. Thank you." Madison pulled her card and gave it to Julie. "Call if anything else comes to you, and stay in town in case we have more questions."

Julie nodded.

Madison and Terry left her sitting on the bench, and Officer Tendum approached them. They compared stories, and they lined up. One small mercy, but they still had more questions than answers. And Madison was twitching for more than a caffeine fix—she craved justice.

CHAPTER 3

"Nope, don't even start." Terry shook his head under Madison's gaze.

"Corrupt cops, Terry." Her entire body was quaking at the prospect.

"Not every cop is corrupt. You're being paranoid."

"No. You don't get to go there." Even if his accusation was somewhat on the mark, she had good reason to suspect what she did, and Terry knew it. He'd even helped her gather evidence against two officers for Internal Affairs.

"Well, it's true."

She huffed out a breath. "Whatever, Terry. Answer me this: how did the shooter get out of the station?"

"Do we know that he did?" he countered.

"What do you mean?" Her chest tightened. "Like the shooter is somewhere close, hiding in plain sight?"

He shrugged. "Why not? And the girl for that matter."

"She could be an incredible witness. She might have gotten a good look at him. Based on what Julie Nelson told us, the girl would have passed him as he headed to the kiosk."

"Until we figure out exactly what happened, what's to say she wasn't in on the shooting? You just heard an eyewitness tell us her action set everything in motion."

"Technically, it was the women in line who wanted to turn her in." She heard the implication of her words and was sliced by guilt. As if the victims were responsible for the shooting.

"All I'm saying is we shouldn't just dismiss the girl from suspicion," Terry said.

She'd considered the same a minute ago and call it gut instinct, but the girl wasn't in on what happened. "I'd say the shooter took advantage of a situation. They knew about the girl and her handler."

He didn't say anything for a few seconds. "We don't know there was a handler."

"It was something the eyewitness told us."

"Who knows?"

"You can't take some of what she said and believe it while dismissing other aspects. And even you must admit it all sounds suspicious—a young woman being watched over. She was moving something, probably drugs."

"I guess. Maybe."

"Gah, Terry. Just think about it." She glanced over to the Just Beans kiosk.

Cole Richards and his assistant, Milo, were there and had the tarps removed from the bodies.

Madison went over, not wanting to argue with Terry anymore. She also desired to get her first real look at the victims. She greeted Richards and Milo, with her eyes on the deceased.

Both women were dressed formally in pantsuits with blouses, and high heels. Likely businesswomen. Their makeup was also applied tastefully, but their faces were twisted in masks of horror.

Dana Ridley. Second in line at the kiosk counter, and a redhead. Was she the one who had first antagonized the shooter by insisting he wasn't a cop? If so, Madison admired the woman's spunk, but look at what it got her—and the others. Was she a tragic example that risking one's life, even if for a good cause, wasn't necessarily worth the sacrifice? If Ridley could go back in time, would she have made the same choice to call out the shooter, or would she have remained quiet?

Her hair was styled in a long bob, and the sheen and coiffured appearance told Madison it had seen the hands of an experienced hairdresser. It was also the fact that her driver's license photo had shown her as a brunette. Her fingernails were short but manicured and polished clear. Her clothing wasn't brand name or designer but still appeared to be of high quality.

Next to Ridley lay Morgan Walker. Her long, brown hair was fanned across her face and, in some places, stuck there with blood, like a macabre papier-mâché. Tall, easily five foot ten, she was dressed in a navy-blue suit and blazer. She had a delicate nose and pointed chin. Trim and lean. Athletic. Her brown eyes stared lifelessly toward the ceiling.

The loss of life was such a waste it twisted Madison's gut.

"Nothing easy about this. It's just all so meaningless," Richards said as he got to work on Ridley.

"Was just thinking that." It was strange standing there next to the ME and his assistant and not peppering Richards with the usual questions: time of death, cause of death, etcetera. In this case, she already had those answers.

"Oh." One word from Richards, and it had shivers lacing down her spine.

"What is it?"

"I'll conduct more tests at the morgue, but I'm quite certain this victim was pregnant."

"She was... She was..." Madison stiffened. The world around her was closing in and suffocating her. She laid a hand over her stomach, just briefly, her thoughts drifting to the child she'd lost last month. Her little secret—well, hers and Troy's. The pregnancy hadn't been planned, and during most of the time she'd known about it, Madison wasn't even excited about becoming a mother. That was something she didn't even want to speak out loud. She had no right to play victim and grieve for a child she hadn't wanted. "Ah, how far along?" She licked her lips, suddenly fearful of her stomach purging its contents, which weren't much.

"Based on some of the body changes I see, I'd say around sixteen weeks."

"It would have its fingers and toes…" Madison stopped there, swallowing roughly. She could picture the child in her mind. Its organs also would have been formed by that stage, and Ridley might have even felt the baby moving inside her.

All eyes turned to her, including Cynthia's. In that moment, Madison felt like they all knew the dark secret she'd been living with. Of course, she knew that wasn't true, but still… "My sister has three kids."

None of them said a word. Maybe they were experiencing shock at Richards's revelation—another murder victim, though unseen. Dana Ridley's unborn child. She had probably been proudly awaiting the birth of her child, like any normal woman would. If Madison had the right to grieve anything, it was the part of herself that was lacking. She stuffed down the self-judgment. "Guess on caliber size?" She fanned a hand toward the bodies.

"I'd say a nine mil," Richards said.

"Common and easy enough to buy on the street." Madison would make sure officers were checking garbage bins and dumpsters in the area for the murder weapon. The shooter may have discarded it. "Once you've done the autopsies and extracted the bullet fragments, get them to the lab ASAP. We can have them run ballistics to narrow down gun make and model and maybe see if the gun was used in any other crimes."

"You know I'll do that," Richards said.

"I do." What Richards and the others might not realize was sometimes laying out the procedural process helped ground her—especially these days when her personal life haunted her. If only she could suppress her feelings enough, maybe they'd just disappear. "When are the autopsies scheduled for?"

"I'll confirm by text, but probably tomorrow morning," Richards said. He returned to his work without another word.

While Terry's gaze went to the bodies, Cynthia's remained on Madison. Her friend had a way of reading her mind. *But no, not today. Not right now.* "Let's go, Terry. And keep me posted," she told Richards and started to walk off.

Terry caught up to her. "Where are you going?"

"I'm going to find the person who did this. That's our job." She didn't look at him as she spoke, keeping her gaze straight ahead and her steps at a fast clip.

"And you're planning to do that how exactly?"

"By starting with a visit to the station's security office to watch the shooting. I want to see this guy's face. See if we can get a still and run it through facial recognition databases. We also need to find that girl with the backpack." She stopped, frustrated, and looked at Terry. "Where the hell is the security office?"

"Come with me."

They resumed walking, just as Higgins rounded a bend and appeared in front of them. The three of them stopped.

"Tell me you or other officers have something, Higgins," she said. "A lead on the shooter's whereabouts, the murder weapon?"

"Next of kin." He winced.

"Too much to hope for something else, I guess. All right, hit us." Just asking had the acid levels in her gut ratcheting up. While the victims' suffering was over, for those left behind, it was just beginning. And it wasn't just those who knew and loved the deceased who experienced the loss. The world missed out on the advancements the dead could have brought to society. Also, to think of Dana Ridley and her unborn child—all that untapped potential.

"Ridley and Walker were married. Walker had a teenager and a five-year-old. No kids for Ridley."

"Yet," Madison pushed out.

Higgins angled his head and looked inquisitively at Terry when Madison didn't say anything.

"She was four months pregnant," Terry explained.

Higgins winced. "Ouch. That's gonna be a rough notice to deliver. Would have been their first kid."

It took all of her mental fortitude to squeeze out the fact this baby would have been Ridley's first. "The worst part of the job."

"Told you that from the start," Higgins said.

"Yeah, well, you were right." Madison felt Terry's eyes on her profile, and she was quite certain he suspected something was off with her. Though her imagination could be working overtime.

"Here's the husbands' info." Higgins handed Madison a piece of paper.

"Thanks." Madison looked at the page. Wayne Ridley and Shane Walker. Both of their worlds were about to be tipped upside down—already were, but they just didn't know it yet.

"Don't mention it, and good luck." Higgins squeezed her shoulder. She wished he hadn't. The physical contact and his obvious concern had her chest constricting. But she'd redirect the grief to determination to get justice.

"You never gave us the information on Brennan's next of kin." It wouldn't be a death notification, but whoever it was needed to be informed that Shannon had been shot and taken to the hospital.

"No need to worry about that. I've sent officers to talk to her husband." With that, Higgins walked off, and Madison and Terry continued on their path to the security office.

"Everything all right with you?" he asked.

"Why wouldn't it be? Two women are dead, a third one's fighting for her life." She wasn't going to even touch on the baby.

"'Fighting for her life' might be over the top..."

She glared at him. "Fact remains that she was shot and will need surgery."

"Fine." He held up his hands in surrender. "You still want to check the video before notifying next of kin?"

"Yep. Then we'll go break the news to the Ridley and Walker families." Maybe she was procrastinating, but it would benefit the investigation to actually see what happened. With most murders, that wasn't an option. Everything was pieced together by witness statements and the evidence.

"All right, but Winston's there from what I heard, and I'm sure everything is under control." He silenced under her gaze.

Garry Winston was their commanding sergeant, and he and Madison didn't see eye to eye. Things had only gotten worse between them when she brought in Internal Affairs. Now she wasn't just a female in his department, she was a snitch. He loved to micromanage and valued talk over action. Those were his good qualities. His bad ones were that he was old-school and chauvinistic. "Under control? If others in the department—and those in security here at the station—had things *under control*, we wouldn't be in this mess in the first place. You've got this handler standing around all the time and this girl lifting food items from Just Beans, and they what? Just watch it happen day after day and do nothing?"

Terry held up his hands. "Someone's a little punchy."

"Someone's a little tired of people getting away with doing a half-ass job."

By the time they reached the security office, Madison had calmed down—a little. Then she heard Winston's voice, and her nerves ratcheted back up again. She took a deep breath and rounded the bend.

"Here are my detectives now. 'Bout time you got here." Winston jabbed a glare in her direction.

With him were two security people, both men in their forties, and a uniformed police officer. The latter offered a grim smile to her and Terry.

"Detective Knight and Detective Grant," Winston said and raised his coffee to his lips.

She fantasized about tearing the cup from his hands and taking it for herself. *Caffeine...* Maybe if she had just a sip, she'd be less cranky and more willing to play with others. *Nah.* "Any luck tracking the movements of the shooter or the girl with the backpack after the incident?"

"The girl with the backpack?" Winston asked. "Who are you talking about?"

Obviously, he had nothing under control. Madison filled him in on what had triggered the shooting—the girl lifting product from Just Beans—and Winston motioned for the security guys to answer her question.

The one closest to her shook his head. "Not that we could find working through the footage."

"They both couldn't have just disappeared." She'd cling to that, but not far from her mind was the possibility that the shooting had been planned, intentional. If that was the case, they would have laid out an escape route. "Did they leave together?"

"He just said he didn't see where they went," Winston punched out.

She ignored his attitude. "Did you see them together at any point after the shooting, even before?"

"No."

That could have been careful planning, but the fact the shooter wasn't the regular man hanging around raised the question of why he was here today and not the other guy. What had happened to him? Was the shooter his replacement and simply more trigger happy? "We've been told there's normally a guy buzzing around Just Beans who watches the girl with the backpack, but today it was someone else—the shooter. I'll need the best stills you can provide of this girl, and the shooter, also her normal handler. You might need to check footage from days prior."

The security guys nodded while Winston just looked at her.

"Handler?" Winston asked.

She ignored Winston's question and spoke to the security guys. "Do you know who I'm talking about?"

The guys looked at each other, then shook their heads.

"You have no clue that drugs are being smuggled through the train station?" Possibly premature, a lunge for the jugular, but the leap to this conclusion was obvious to her. What else would explain a girl with a backpack being watched over by a man? She was obviously moving something, drugs being the most likely. It was hard to believe that the very people tasked with watching video surveillance never noticed her or the handler.

"No," one of them said.

"And you have no knowledge about this girl with the backpack?"

"Well, I mean she's on video around the time of the shooting this morning…" the one security guy said.

She kept pushing. "Have you ever seen her before today?"

"You know how many faces we see every day?" It was the other security guy who countered with that defense.

"I'm sure a lot. But it's also our understanding that this girl swiped food and drink from the Just Beans kiosk on a regular basis. You never witnessed that, either?" She didn't care for the security guys and had this gnawing in her gut that they were lying. Something was going on at Liberty Station and it involved a lot of compliant parties. Fear and money usually bought that level of silence, but who was behind both?

"Nothing's been reported to us."

"All right. Well, we'll need all that footage and the stills as soon as possible. Send it here." She handed each security guy one of Cynthia Baxter's cards, which her friend had authorized that she do as long as Madison let her know who she'd given them to.

"Sure." It was the security guy closest to her who'd conceded. At least he'd done her the courtesy of not double-checking her directive with Winston.

"And here's my info if you think of anything." She gave him one of her cards. "Now, if my partner and I could watch this morning's shooting…"

The video played out on one of the numerous monitors in front of the security guys.

Just Beans was center, and there was a line of five people. Then three. The girl with the backpack entered the view.

"Can you play this in slow motion?" Madison asked.

The playback was slowed, and it was clear that the girl had swiped something from the refrigerated unit and swept it into the pocket of her coat. She hadn't even done a good job of concealing the crime. Was it because she knew she'd get away with it, or was it a cry for help? Maybe she wanted to get caught so she could be freed from the life she was caught up in.

Madison pointed at the screen. "You did just see that, yes?"

After a brief hesitation, the security guys bobbed their heads. "Easy to see in slower motion," one offered.

Uh-huh. Somehow, she managed not to voice her skepticism.

The video continued, and the series of events were just as Julie Nelson had described. Unfortunately, though, the camera was positioned behind the shooter.

"Do you have another angle?" she asked.

The security guys brought up the other available angles— not that they were of much help. In all of them, it was near impossible to identify the shooter. None provided a clear image of his face which was shielded by a hoodie. He wore blue jeans and had a lanky frame, but that was about as detailed as it got from what they were seeing. Unless a look at more footage gave them the shooter's and handler's faces, Julie Nelson would need to work with a sketch artist. There was one other possibility… "How robust is your security system? Is it possible to search for people based on height or stature?"

The security guys looked at each other and smiled. "We're not in Vegas."

"Could do without the sarcasm," she said stiffly. "Two people are dead, and one is in surgery. People lost family today."

Both men turned away, but Winston had his gaze fixed on her. Was she supposed to feel bad for putting them in their place?

She went on, talking to the security staff. "We'll need you to go back in time, from before the guy went over to the Just Beans kiosk. See if you can figure out where and when he entered the train station. Maybe we'll get lucky and see his face." She was putting on an optimistic front out of sheer desire to resolve this case, but she had a feeling it wouldn't be that open and shut.

"They already tried to follow him out, but he just disappears," Winston said, stepping in for the security guys.

"That's why I asked about his *arrival.*" She took a deep breath, tried to calm her temper, but her blood was running cold. "Just send everything to Cynthia Baxter. ASAP."

"In the hall." Winston pointed a finger toward the open door.

Terry followed quickly. She set out too but, on the way, caught sight of a map of the train station. She stopped and scanned it, committing as much as possible to memory.

"Knight," Winston bellowed, prompting her to action.

She left the security office and joined Terry and their now red-faced sergeant.

"What do you think you're doing?" he barked.

"My job."

"You have trust issues, Knight, and you're going to need to get them under control."

"Or what?" she snapped back.

He shut his mouth, and his nostrils flared. There was a subtle tapping at the back of her heel. Terry and his freaking shoe. God, she was tired of always being reined in!

Seconds passed in silence, but the tension crackled around them like thunder.

"I trust when it's warranted. But something's going on here, and I don't like it one bit. And you can be certain the families of the women who were shot today won't either. They'll want answers, which they deserve." She put her hands on her hips. "We need the names of everyone who works in that security office and is responsible for watching the security video. Then, we need to pull backgrounds on every single one of them."

Winston huffed and shook his head. He looked at Terry. "Maybe you can get somewhere with her?" He went back into the room, flailing a hand over his head as his walked.

She stood there, seething. The sergeant's comment was an obvious jab at her cynicism.

"Maddy?" Terry prompted.

How dare Winston treat her like the enemy when all she was guilty of was upholding her vow to the badge? "What the hell is his problem?"

He cringed at the use of the word *hell*. He had a strong aversion to swear words and any that came close. "My guess is he's pretty pissed that you didn't call him about what happened here. I'm assuming you didn't by his attitude in there…"

"What? It's not my job to notify him of—"

"One call?"

"There was a shooting. An active situation. I had to move."

"You called dispatch."

"Ah, so his feelings are hurt that he wasn't my first call?"

"He wasn't any call."

She rolled her eyes. "Nope, I'm not being guilt-tripped here. I refuse. He steps on me and belittles me any chance he gets. You saw him in there."

"I did, and you don't normally let him get to you to this extent." He scanned her face. "Everything all right with you?"

"No, it's not, as I told you before." If he was seeking details that didn't have to do with their current investigation, he was out of luck. "Let's go break some hearts." As she said this, her own splintered.

CHAPTER 4

They say it's best to just rip off the Band-Aid. A flash of pain, and it's over. If only notifications worked like that. Rather, it didn't matter how fast the delivery went, sometimes the impact cloyed emotionally for hours or days afterward.

Madison and Terry would be informing Wayne Ridley about his wife while he was at work. One advantage was that he'd have the support of his coworkers. Terry got the door at Stiles Optical and held it for her. She thanked him and beelined straight for the front desk.

"Detective Knight, Stiles PD," Madison said, holding up her badge. "My partner and I need to speak with Wayne Ridley."

The woman at reception was in her thirties and offered a pleasant smile as they approached. It was quickly turning downward into a frown. Her brow even creased as she spoke. "Dr. Ridley is with a patient at the moment. He shouldn't be too long, but is this urgent?" Her blue eyes searched Madison's.

It was, and it wasn't. Bad news could hold for a while. For selfish reasons, Madison wanted to get this over with sooner rather than later. "Please just let him know we're here."

"Of course. If you'd like to take a seat while you wait…" She gestured to a grouping of chairs.

"Thank you," Terry told her.

He sat. Madison paced. It was her turn to deliver the notification, a responsibility she and Terry volleyed between them. Her insides were churning at the thought of telling this man his wife *and* unborn child were dead.

The receptionist kept passing them glances, trying to be discreet about it, but she wasn't very good at hiding her interest in their presence. Humans were, by nature, curious creatures.

A pair of voices came from a hallway, and the receptionist looked at Madison and nodded. Madison poked Terry in the shoulder, and he got to his feet.

A man in a white lab coat rounded the bend into the front office, followed by a woman.

"Your lenses should be in next week," he was saying to her. "We'll give you a call the moment they're here."

"Thank you."

"What we're here for." The man was smiling long after the woman walked across the lobby to the front door.

Madison knew that the man was Wayne Ridley. One, he resembled his driver's license photo. Two, the hint from the receptionist. Three, the obvious fact he was a doctor. She took a step toward him as the receptionist beckoned Wayne's attention, and he went to the counter. Madison couldn't hear all that was being said, but he looked over at her and Terry. Then he went back down the hallway.

What the...?

Madison rushed across the room.

"Detectives, please." The receptionist stood and leaned over the counter. "He's just gone ahead of you. He'll meet you in his office, first door on the left."

"Thanks." Madison hadn't met with this reaction before, and she wasn't quite sure what to make of it. Did Wayne fear their news so badly that he immediately sought out privacy?

Madison entered Wayne's office, Terry just behind her. The space was warm and decorated with a designer's touch. There was an ornate desk, a plush leather chair, and wood filing cabinets on one end of the room. The other side was less formal. That was where they found Wayne Ridley, seated on a couch, legs crossed. He appeared casual, like he was about to have a social visit with friends.

"Please, sit," he said.

Madison and Terry dropped into chairs positioned at each end of the couch.

"Can I get you anything? Tea, coffee, water?"

"No, thank you." She shot a look at Terry to make sure he declined the offer as well. *In and out as fast as possible. Drop the bomb and leave.* She internally winced at her thinking.

"I'm fine," Terry said.

"All right, what can I do for you?" Wayne narrowed his eyes for a trace of a moment. He rested his gaze on Madison.

"Unfortunately, we're here with bad news about your wife," Madison began. "Dana was killed this morning in a shooting at Liberty Station."

Wayne sat there quietly. Staring with glazed-over eyes, like his mind was a million miles away. Likely shock.

"Dr. Ridley, did you hear me?"

"Yeah, I…" He sniffled and pinched the tip of his nose.

Madison let him have a few moments and looked around the room. Framed doctorates on the walls. Photos of Dana and him captured in different places were scattered throughout the space. Wayne was obviously proud of his wife and his relationship and—Madison looked at his ring finger—he wore his wedding band. That was something a lot of men forfeited these days, as if it were somehow more masculine to go without.

"We appreciate this might be a shock," Terry said after a few beats of silence, "but we have a few questions we need to ask."

"Ah, yeah, sure. Go ahead." Wayne waved a hand to emphasize he was fine to continue.

Terry glanced at Madison and pressed his lips, as if prompting her to pick up again.

She wasn't sure where to start, and this rarely happened to her, but her brain kept kicking back the fact that Dana had been pregnant. It was like her thoughts were playing on repeat. How was this going to impact Wayne Ridley? Had he and his wife been trying for a long time, and their efforts had finally paid off—only to be snatched away from them? Would he be beyond devastated at the loss of his wife and child, or relieved on a teeny, tiny level that he wouldn't have the responsibilities of fatherhood?

"Ah, Dr. Ridley," Terry said and shot her a quick look. "Was your wife regularly at the train station?"

"Every weekday. She commutes to Braybury for work."

Madison cleared her throat. "And her work?"

He fussed with a button on his lab coat, then looked up. "She's a lawyer for an environmental firm. It doesn't pay a lot, but she loves her job."

Madison noted the present tense but dismissed it as a natural thing to do in the immediate aftershock of loss. "The name of the firm?"

"EverGreen, one word, capital E and G." Wayne was like a robot, stiff and responding succinctly, as if simply following commands.

"What train did she take?" Madison asked.

"I don't know the number, but it's the one that leaves at seven thirty."

"When does she normally arrive at the station?"

"All depends on the day. She's not the best sleeper, and she's often up before the sun. This morning was one of those early days. She was out the door by six thirty."

Madison nodded. "But that's not a regular schedule for her?"

Wayne's brow wrinkled in concentration. "I suppose she's always there by about seven. She was never one to rush around and stress about being on time, but she always was."

"There were other victims in the shooting. Do you know a Morgan Walker or Shannon Brennan?"

"Other victims? My wife—" He hiccupped a sob, pressed his lips into a tight, thin line. "She was…ah…murdered in a random shooting? A mugging?"

Madison had failed him, as she should have given him more details from the beginning. "Robbery wasn't the intent." How could she tell him that they really had no solid answer as to motive?

"I don't understand." His chin quivered.

"It's still early in the investigation, and that's about all we can say at this time. I promise you we're trying to determine exactly what happened."

"Trying? My wife is dead," he spat, his eyes becoming a raging wildfire.

"And we're very sorry for your loss," Madison kicked back with sincerity. She noted that he hadn't yet expressed any sorrow or grief about the baby. Did he not know his wife was pregnant? If it was news to him, best they hold that information until their other questions were answered. She repeated her inquiry about Walker and Brennan.

Wayne shook his head. "Never heard of either of them. Who are they? They work with Dana?"

"We don't believe so." At least from the brief report they'd obtained from Higgins—he hadn't noted that connection. If it was there, he would have told them.

He met her gaze. "If this was random, why are you looking for a connection?"

Madison debated her wording. "Sometimes things aren't always as they appear." Then she laid out the events of that morning.

When she had finished, Wayne was rubbing his forehead. He said, "One thing is certain. Nothing will bring her back."

Madison had nothing to say to that. Empathizing with him wouldn't make anything better for him. Nothing would. Death in all forms was meaningless, but also a sad fact of life. No one knew when their time was up. Like Dana and Morgan, starting off the workweek like any other—only to have their lives end abruptly.

While there was never going to be a good time, Madison decided she needed to ask about the baby. "Did you know your wife was pregnant?"

His eyes snapped to hers. "What? No. What are you talking about?"

She'd been right—he didn't know. "Your wife was several weeks pregnant."

"Ridiculous. That's not possible. We decided early on in our marriage we didn't want kids, didn't even want to chance it. I got a vasectomy." He was studying her as if seeking an explanation, and there were a couple that struck her.

Sometimes life found a way regardless, but with the new way doctors performed vasectomies, that was unlikely. Still, she asked, "Maybe the procedure reversed itself somehow?"

"Nonsense. No, it's intact, or not intact... You know what I mean."

That left the possibility that Dana had cheated on Wayne with a man who could father children. "How was your marriage, Dr. Ridley?"

"Beg your pardon?" His eyebrows sliced downward, and his features tightened into a scowl.

"Is it possible that your wife was having an affair?"

"No. How dare you—" Wayne fidgeted and squirmed on the couch, and he glanced at Terry as if Terry could somehow save him.

"I'm just asking," Madison said. "The fact remains that she was pregnant."

"Well, I don't know how." His cheeks flushed, and he raked a hand through his hair.

Hard and fast denial. It wasn't like his wife was miraculously impregnated like the Virgin Mary. "We're going to need to look into the call history and activity on your wife's phone." They'd need a signed subpoena, but she wanted to be transparent with Wayne Ridley about her intentions.

"If you think it will help. But Dana could have just got caught up in someone else's mess."

"Could be. The investigation is still very young. That's why we need all possible information available to us."

"I really don't think you're going to find anything on my wife's phone." The pain flickering in his eyes told her he was referring to an affair.

Madison hoped his faith in his wife was wisely placed, and there was an innocent explanation for Dana's pregnancy. But experience taught her not to get her hopes up too high. "We might not," she told him.

"If someone did target your wife," Terry began, "would you be able to point us in anyone's direction? Someone who had something against your wife?"

"What? No. I mean why would anyone? She was a kind soul." Wayne's voice was trembling.

"We appreciate this may be upsetting and confusing. Shocking. But we'll explore all angles and get the answers." It was essentially a promise, something cops were encouraged *not* to do, but it was one Madison planned to deliver on. She stood, passed her card to Wayne, and extended her sympathies again.

She led the way out of the store and slipped behind the wheel of the department car. She sat there shaking her head, chastising herself more than anything.

"What's wrong with you?"

"What do you mean?" She looked over at Terry in the passenger seat.

"It's obvious something is going on with you. Does it have to do with the IA investigations?"

"No."

"Then what?"

She took a deep breath, squeezing out any thoughts that threatened to implant themselves about the baby she'd lost. She shifted instead to those that focused on the Ridleys. She'd just begun to latch onto a rosy image—that of a loving couple creating a child that would be loved and cared for— and the likelihood of adultery soured the entire thing. Cheating was something she had zero tolerance for. Without trust in a relationship, there was nothing.

"Maddy?" Terry prompted.

"I'm fine"—she cringed at the word her therapist had worked hard to eradicate from her vocabulary—"but there are two women in the morgue who are not."

"Fine? If you say so." He eyed her with suspicion.

If anyone should fall under suspicion... "Dana Ridley was pregnant, and it would seem that her husband wasn't the father."

"Yep. I was in there."

"We need to find out who she was sleeping with."

"For what purpose?"

"Even you must admit that maybe the shooting wasn't random."

"I am with you on exploring different angles—what you said to Wayne Ridley in there. I'm surprised that it came from you. You're normally so black and white."

"Let's just say I'm trying something new."

"Wow." He smirked at her, and she punched him in the shoulder. Same old sideshow. Terry was more brother than partner. "Ouch." He rubbed where she'd impacted. "What? It's not like you're known for having an open mind."

"Hey, people can change."

"Well, I like it."

She shrugged it off, not needing his approval. "It is possible it was just a random shooting, but what is niggling at me is the different handler."

"According to Julie Nelson."

"Yes…taking someone's word for it. But what happened to the original handler?"

"I think it's best to focus on the man who killed two people and shot a third—handler or not," Terry kicked back.

He made a fair point. "You're right. We don't even know if the shooter was also a handler. Not until we find out what happened to the regular guy or the girl."

"I'd express surprise at you saying I'm right, but you're stubbornly clinging to a handler existing."

"It's a path I think we should explore."

"What do you suggest, then?"

"We reach out to Narcotics."

"Oh, your buddy…Detective Commons?"

"I was thinking Detective Marsh."

"*Preston* Marsh. Such an uppity-sounding name."

"Whatever, Terry. He's a good guy." Madison had met Marsh at the start of his career in Narcotics. He was five years younger than she was and came with the reputation of a being a ladies' man. He definitely had charisma, but she'd never felt any chemistry between them. "We can find out if he recognizes the original handler and the shooter. Also the girl." She lit up at that epiphany. "Maybe she's a regular at a stash house that Narcotics is watching?"

"Only one problem with that. We don't have any pictures to send him."

"I can, at least, give him the girl's general description and tell him she normally wears an orange backpack."

"Not sure that will be enough."

"Well, I'm not just going to sit on my hands. I'll also ask him if Narcotics is aware of a drug-trafficking ring operating through the train station." She placed the call and had to leave a message.

"Hopefully he calls you back."

"And why wouldn't he?"

Pain burrowed in Terry's eyes, and she read his mind.

"Because of my bringing in IA?"

"It doesn't make you the most popular person at the police station."

"The only ones who have a problem are the corrupt cops."

"Maybe. But what's his motivation to tell you he's aware of drug trafficking through the train station—assuming there is? He might think you'll start looking at him and accusing him of knowing and covering it up."

"Well, if he knows about it, he should fix the problem."

"See? That right there. You don't even know the full picture. Could be a lot more going on than you're aware of. There could be a sting planned or—"

"There are cops bankrolled by the mob. Fact. And they'd be more than willing to look the other way while the girl with the backpack, likely others too, roll in and out of the train station day after day."

"Now the mob's behind the alleged drug trafficking?"

"I'm just saying if they'll take cash from the mob, they'll take it from anyone if the price is right."

"I'm just asking that you keep that mind of yours open and be careful with the accusations."

She held his gaze, remained silent. Eventually, she mumbled, "I'll try."

He smiled. "That's the spirit. Now we just need to figure out what actually happened this morning."

"Yeah, after we ruin someone else's day…" Madison put the car into gear and set off in the direction of the Walker residence.

CHAPTER 5

A young boy peeked his head out the front door, giggling.

"We need to speak to your fath...*er.*" Madison was left speaking to a closed door because the kid had shut it in her face. She knocked again and prayed that Shane Walker would come this time instead of his son.

Though Terry was smiling at the frivolity of the child, Madison was less amused.

"Shouldn't he be in school?" It wasn't that she hated kids. She just didn't really get them—and that worked both ways with the exception of her three nieces. She was certainly better suited to the role of aunt than mother.

"He's probably all of five. Kindergarten maybe? Likely on a part-time schedule."

Footsteps shuffled on the other side of the door, and it swung open.

"Dad!" the boy was yelling loudly and dancing circles around Shane Walker. Shane kept reaching for his son's hand and failed on numerous attempts before finally latching on.

"That's enough." He spoke sternly, and the boy stood still and pouted.

Madison was certain wailing and waterworks were next and would do anything within her power to stop that from happening. "Mr. Walker, we're detectives with the Stiles PD, and we need to come in and speak with you about your wife, Morgan."

Shane stopped the staredown with his son just long enough to acknowledge Madison with a glance.

"Joel, go to your room and play. I'm not telling you again." Shane thrust a pointed finger into the bowels of the home. The boy stalked off. Shane watched after him for a bit, possibly to make sure he was following through. Then he turned and leveled his gaze at Madison and Terry. "What is it that I can help you with? You said you're here about my wife?"

Terry took a step forward. "Is it possible we could come in and sit?"

"Ah, sure." Shane appeared flustered and disheveled. His white T-shirt was tucked in on one side, hanging out on the other, and there were brown stains on the front. His cropped hair was sticking up in little spikes, and his teeth were coffee stained.

He led them to a living room that looked like a cyclone had blown through.

"Please excuse the mess," he said as he picked up some throw pillows and positioned them on the couch. "I thought it would be less stressful being a stay-at-home father." He laughed, but the expression missed hitting his eyes. "Sit wherever you can find space."

Terry was the first to do so. Madison sat beside him on the couch, just on the edge of the cushion.

"We're sorry to inform you that your wife was shot this morning at Liberty Station, and she died on scene." Terry managed to finesse the harsh truth with a touch of kindness and empathy.

"She's, ah…?" Shane swallowed roughly, his Adam's apple bobbing.

"We're investigating the event—"

"Event? I don't understand. She, ah…how?"

"As I said, she was shot."

"Why?"

"We're still trying to determine exactly what happened."

"Did you catch the shooter?" Shane's eyes were wide and wet.

"Unfortunately, not yet."

"The person who shot and killed Morgan is out there... free? Why are you here talking to me? Go get them." A rogue tear splashed his cheek, and he quickly swiped it away.

Madison stepped in. "Mr. Walker, we are very sorry for your loss, but know that we are doing all we can." Grief was like a living entity that required a target on which to lay the blame, and often that was projected on the person delivering the unfavorable news.

"Tell me what happened. Where? Oh, you said the train station?"

"Yes," Terry said, taking over again. "She was in line at the Just Beans kiosk."

"She loved their coffee. Couldn't get enough of it," Shane offered.

"A man came over, and there was a confrontation between him and your wife and others in the line."

"And he just shot her? What was this confrontation about?"

Terry shared what they knew while leaving out mention of a handler and possible drug trafficking.

"The wrong place at the wrong time." Shane sighed.

"It may simply be that," Madison said and stopped there.

Shane's gaze snapped to meet hers. "It may?"

Madison turned up the palms of her hands and shrugged. "We don't know yet what truly prompted the shooting. Do the names Dana Ridley or Shannon Brennan mean anything to you?"

Shane squinted, his forehead compressed in thought. "I don't think so. Should they?"

"As my partner mentioned, others were in line with your wife. Shannon Brennan was shot and taken to the hospital. Dana Ridley was dead on scene, along with your wife." She paused there at the knot of anguish that contorted Shane's facial features like he'd been gut-punched.

After a few seconds of silence, Shane shook his head. "Their names don't sound familiar."

"Did your wife take the train every morning?" Terry asked.

"She did. She worked at Peters, Hampton and Douglas. They're a pretty big law firm."

Shane had made quite a fast transition to past tense, but that didn't necessarily mean anything. Grief had a way of rolling in like waves, bringing with it a delicate dance of shock and acceptance. But Madison noted something else. The two women who had died were both lawyers, though at different firms. Were their careers a coincidence, or had they provided motive? Was the shooting some sort of elaborate "kill all the lawyers" movement? She'd be looking up what Shannon Brennan did for work when they left here. It was possible that somehow Morgan's path had crossed with Dana Ridley's. "Does the environmental firm EverGreen mean anything to you?"

Shane chewed his bottom lip. "Can't say that it does."

"What does the law firm your wife worked at specialize in?" Madison asked.

"Criminal defense."

There was the possibility that Morgan Walker had defended someone who wasn't happy with her work. Madison was quite familiar with such a situation resulting in murder. The client was Dimitre Petrov, the don of the Russian Mafia. He lost in court and was still in prison serving out his sentence, but his lawyer was shot down in his driveway after the guilty verdict came back. But at least justice was finally found— even if it took eight years to get there.

Shane continued. "She really pulled herself up from nothing too. She was incredible."

"From nothing?" Terry asked.

"Yeah." Shane nodded. "She had a bit of a shady past. I don't even know half of it, but she put herself through college and night classes to become a lawyer."

"We are sorry for your loss, Mr. Walker. If you think of anyone or anything else that might help us find your wife's killer, please call." She gave him her card.

Shane bowed his head. "I can't believe this is happening... *happened*. How am I supposed to break this to Joel and Leanne?"

"Who is Leanne?" Madison asked.

"Our daughter. Fourteen. Joel, well, he's five. He might be more resilient with all this, but Leanne"—his chin quivered—"she's a sensitive girl to begin with. This is going to devastate her."

Terry inched forward in his seat. "Is there anything we can do? Someone we can call?"

He shook his head. "I'd say pick her up at school, but…"

"We can do that," Terry said.

"No. I want to tell her. Don't want the cops showing up like that. I'll wait until she gets home."

Madison understood Shane's reasoning, but it could also backfire. The girl might feel like she should have been told sooner. "If you're sure…?"

"Yeah." Shane nodded.

Terry stood and laid a hand on the man's shoulder. "We're very sorry for your loss."

"Thank you."

"We'll see ourselves out," Terry added as he led the way to the front door.

Madison's steps slowed as she came upon a wedding photograph of Shane and his bride that was hanging on the wall amidst a montage of photos. The woman was a brunette with a dominant nose. She wasn't a perfect image of the photo on Morgan Walker's driver's license or the woman Madison had seen at Liberty Station, who had delicate features and a small nose. But there was the spacing between the eyes and the shape of her chin that were identical. Madison was transfixed on the bride for other reasons, though. She looked so much like someone else, a person from Madison's past— Courtney Middleton. But that was impossible. Her college friend had gone missing fifteen years ago.

"Detectives?" Shane tucked into the hall. "Is there something else?"

Madison pointed at the picture. "Your wife, Mrs. Walker."

"Ah, yes…" Spoken like, *Who else it would be?*—a valid reaction.

"She, ah…did something to her nose?" That was the most polite way Madison could think to ask.

"Yes. Crazy if you ask me. She was beautiful just like that, but getting the cosmetic surgery made her happy. And who am I to stand in the way of that? She was always touchy and self-conscious about its size."

"It's like a freaking bird's beak," Courtney said, tapping the tip of her nose.

"Come on, it's not that bad!" Madison was doubled over laughing at her friend's latest drama.

"No, it is, and one day, I'll get it fixed."

"Anything else, Detective?"

Madison blinked herself back to the present, her eyes coming into focus on the woman's face. *Courtney?* She cleared her throat. "When did the two of you meet? Where?"

Terry was eyeing her profile. She shook her head subtly.

"Comsey Park, a couple of hours from here. At a bar."

Comsey Park was west while Braybury was east of Stiles. "When?" Her entire body was shaking, and she hoped to hell it didn't show.

"Seven years ago."

She forced a smile. "Very nice. Again, sorry for your loss."

Shane nodded, and Madison and Terry left.

She slogged to the car, dragging her feet, her mind elsewhere. No way Morgan Walker was Courtney Middleton, right? Madison had to be seeing a ghost. It was assumed Courtney had died years ago—though no body had been found. Uncertainty clenched her gut. If Courtney was alive all this time, what had she been up to? And did that have anything to do with the shooting?

CHAPTER 6

Madison pulled a quick background on Shannon Brennan, interested in her line of work. "She works at a place called Spark Media in Braybury. Doesn't sound like a law firm." She went on to explain the brief theory that had run through her mind while at the Walker residence.

Terry was in the passenger seat with his phone. "Just googling…" His fingers pecked on the screen. "They're not. They are an advertising firm. Billboards and the like."

"So she isn't a lawyer like Dana Ridley and Morgan Walker were." *Or Courtney Middleton?* She wished she could just ignore the physical similarities, but they were eating away at her.

She put the car into gear and pointed them in the direction of Stiles General Hospital.

The last time Madison had seen Courtney Middleton was fifteen years ago at the Roadhouse Bar in Stiles with two other girlfriends. There had been a storm that night with a heavy downpour. Courtney had warmed up to some older guy, and there was no talking her into leaving.

I'll be fine.

Those were the last words Madison ever heard her say, and Courtney Middleton was never seen again.

"All right, you've gone eerily quiet…"

Until she could answer some questions about Courtney, she had to consider the ghost from her past might matter to the investigation. Had she changed her name and her appearance to be reborn as Morgan Walker? If so, was she running from someone? Then what had her returning to Stiles, assuming she hadn't been here all along? And that was assuming any of this applied. Courtney could very well be long dead and have nothing at all to do with Morgan Walker.

"Madison," Terry prompted.

"Just thinking about the case."

"Whatever you say. You sure were acting strange about that wedding photo. What was with all those questions? Do you know Morgan Walker or something? If so, you need to tell me. It would be a huge conflict of interest."

"I don't know her." The truth, and she hoped it would cool Terry's rant before it really heated up. Even if Morgan was the woman who had been her friend in college, Madison hadn't known her as her new identity. And any inkling to come clean with Terry was wiped out when he brought up conflict of interest. If Morgan actually was Courtney, that could get her kicked off this case, and there was no point in going there yet. Besides, there was nothing to indicate that the shooting was specifically related to Morgan Walker.

"If you say so. You made a big deal about her nose job."

"It just stood out to me. Okay? Are we done with the inquisition?"

Terry held up his hands in surrender. "Where are we going?"

"Stiles General. I want to talk to the other Just Beans employee, Tanya Murray, and see if Shannon Brennan is out of surgery."

"Can give it a shot, I suppose."

"Fine," she snarled. "Where would you have us go?" She was on edge before—her natural state of being since losing the baby—but seeing Courtney's face was really messing with her mind. More than ever, she felt the need to retreat and erect a wall.

"Now I know something's eating at you."

"Eating at me?" She scoffed with laughter.

"Here we go, picking on my wording again."

"You make it easy." She pulled into the lot for the hospital. Hopefully Terry would let the whole thing about Morgan Walker go.

"We have no record of a Tanya Murray being admitted." The nurse, a rotund woman with black-framed glasses, gestured to her monitor with her hand.

"And Shannon Brennan? She should have been. Came in with a GSW." Gunshot wound, but that was all Madison was aware of. She still had no idea how severe Brennan's injuries were. No news would indicate she was still alive.

The nurse pecked on her keyboard, the keys clacking loudly. "Yep, yep. I see her, but you won't be."

"Excuse me?" Madison snapped. "Why not?"

"She's still in surgery. And once she's out, you won't be going near her today. Talking to her won't do you no good anyway. She'll be friends with the Easter Bunny by then." A small, amused chuckle.

Madison gave the nurse her card. "Call the minute she's up and alert."

"Sure, darling." She put the card on the desk, which was cluttered with paperwork.

"Don't lose that." Madison pointed at her card.

"No worries there. Might look like a mess, but old Mary knows what she's doing, and everything you see is organized and catalogued." She tapped a finger to her head.

Madison turned away and rolled her eyes. She leaned in toward Terry. "We'll check back first thing in the morning."

"What? You don't trust someone?"

She narrowed her eyes at him. "Hardy-har."

"Using my line again." Terry shook his head.

They left the hospital and its funky smells behind and brought up the home address for Tanya Murray. She lived in the east end of the city, the least glorious and most notorious for its high crime rate.

Murray's place was a two-story semi-detached house with a crooked front porch, peeling paint, and yawning shingles that begged for retirement.

Madison knocked and was answered a second later.

"I'm coming!" Footsteps hurried toward the front of the house. Two deadbolts *thunked*. The door opened with a *swish*. A woman in her forties was standing there with cash clenched in yellow, nicotine-stained fingernails. The odor of whiskey and stale beer oozed out of the house, but the woman was the one who pulled a face. "Who are you?"

They displayed their badges.

"Detectives Knight and Grant. And you're Tanya Murray," Madison added.

"Uh-huh." Her eyes were round and beady like a rat's.

"We need to speak with you about what happened at Liberty Station this morning," Madison said. "We'd like to come in."

"If you need to." Murray stepped back to allow them room to enter. Her stance faltered a bit, and given that the house smelled like a distillery, it was a safe conclusion she'd been drinking.

Madison and Terry followed Murray to the dining table that was off the kitchen, and each of them dropped into a chair.

"I see you're feeling better," Madison said.

"I am. Thanks."

"Were you expecting someone?" Madison jacked a thumb over her shoulder. There had been the hurried steps and the cash in hand.

"What? Oh, just thought it was the pizza I ordered."

Madison's eyes drifted to a crumpled, greasy takeout bag on the counter, and Murray followed her gaze.

"That, I should have thrown out." She shot up and went about doing just that. "When I'm stressed out, I turn to food."

Not that anyone could tell, given the woman's willowy frame.

There was a banging at the front door. Probably that pizza.

"Just a minute." Murray slipped away with the cash clutched in her hand.

Madison used her absence to look around. She discovered a stack of envelopes on the counter and decided to do some snooping. She had a few precious minutes—if that.

"What are you…" Terry didn't finish and shook his head.

She turned up the edges of the envelopes, shuffling through them. Most of them were collection notices.

"What do you think you're doing?" Tanya Murray set the pizza box on the counter and snatched the envelopes out of Madison's hand. She stuffed them into a drawer and slammed it shut. "They are none of your business. Think it's time for you to leave."

Madison squared her shoulders. "Not going anywhere until we speak with you about this morning."

"Do that, then, but keep your nose out of my personal affairs."

Madison returned to the table and sat down where she had before.

Murray slid the pizza box onto the table and sat. She lifted the top and pulled out a slice. Strings of melted cheese stretched, refusing to let go of the rest of the pie. Madison was practically salivating at the smell and the image on the box. It was from Tony's Pizzeria, *the* best pizza place in Stiles.

"What do you want to know?" Murray asked, speaking around a mouthful of food.

"Run us through what happened. From the beginning," Madison said. "What prompted the shooting?"

"Well, the shooter was hopped up when he came over. He started yelling at the women, they gave it back to him. He didn't like that." Murray gave the brief and light recount, as if doing so from a detached standpoint, like she hadn't been present for the traumatic event herself.

"What made him come over?" she countered.

Murray took another bite before responding. Her eyes darted around as she chewed. Was Murray afraid of something, someone? Julie Nelson, her coworker, hadn't wanted to talk much about the girl with the backpack. Was the same true for Murray?

"Ms. Murray," Madison prompted.

"I ain't no mind reader, and I'm not really sure what happened. All right? I was busy making up a coffee order, and next thing I knew, there was yelling and gunfire." Murray was making Madison work to pull out every word from her.

"What was being said?"

"I didn't catch it all."

"Think. Hard." Madison wasn't about to let her slide.

"Something about him being a cop? Listen, I don't really want to get involved in any of this." Murray set the rest of her slice on the lid of the box.

"No one wants to be involved in this type of thing, but you are, and what you saw and heard could go a long way in catching the killer." Madison chose that last word intentionally, hoping it would make clear the dire reality. The man who had pulled that trigger wasn't just a shooter; he had murdered two women, injured another. "Can you tell us what the shooter looked like?"

"I didn't get a good look. As I said, I was busy."

"I'm sure something about him stood out. Tattoos? Birthmarks? An accent?" Madison was nothing if not persistent.

"He was wearing a hoodie, low, and it shadowed his face."

"Age?"

Murray licked her lips and rubbed her arms. "In his twenties. Maybe thirties. It's hard to tell these days."

"Good. What else?"

"That's it! I don't know anything else."

"Have you seen him before?" Terry was the one to ask this, and it had Murray leveling her gaze at him.

"I don't think so."

Julie Nelson had said the same thing. "Before he came over, where was he?"

"I have no clue."

"And the girl with the orange backpack… What was her role in all this?"

"Her role? I don't know."

At least Murray wasn't questioning the existence of the girl with a backpack. That was a start. "You see this girl before?"

"I might have."

"Huh, we heard she makes it a habit to lift food from the refrigerated unit," Madison said.

Murray hitched a shoulder. "Don't know."

"How long have you worked for Just Beans in the train station?"

"A few years."

"And in that time, the girl never stole a thing?" Madison couldn't mask her disbelief. How could both Just Beans employees have such different stories? One of them had to be lying, but who and why? And did the answers to those questions have anything to do with the shooting?

"Not that I saw."

The line was drawn. Murray didn't want to talk about the girl anymore. *Too bad.* "We're aware of a man who often hung around the girl with the backpack." Spoken like a verified fact when all they truly had at this point was Julie Nelson's word.

"News to me."

Madison leaned forward. "Is it?"

Murray's shoulders sagged, and she wet her lips, her gaze dipping to the abandoned pizza slice. "Maybe I saw some guy buzzing around her once or twice, but I didn't really pay much attention to him. And he wasn't who did the shooting. That guy looked entirely different."

Either Murray was obtuse and ignorant, or she was smart and doing her best to protect her own interests—whatever they may be. "All right, what about the women in line? You recognize any of them?"

"Yes."

"They usually get their coffee at the same time, all together?"

"Within the same timeframe."

"And that would be?"

"Around seven in the morning."

"But they're not usually in line together?" Madison wasn't entirely sure where she was headed with the questioning, just that she had a sense these questions needed to be asked, like they'd have relevance as the investigation continued.

"Never really paid attention."

"Okay." They could find this out for themselves by watching hours of surveillance video. Madison stood and put her card on the table. "Stay in town, and call when you feel like talking."

Murray licked her lips and stared defiantly. "There's nothing more to say."

Madison waved over a shoulder as she headed for the front door.

"Thank you for your cooperation," Terry said.

Wow. Really?

Outside, Madison turned to her partner. "That woman didn't cooperate—at all. She's either afraid of something or hiding something. Maybe both, but I'm going to find out."

"How did I know you'd be saying that?"

She eyed up his shoulder for a punch but didn't hit him. "We're going to pull Murray's background, and Nelson's. See if there's anything there. Neither of them wanted to talk much about the girl with the backpack. Actually, it's time we pull backgrounds on everyone close to this case, including the security staff from Liberty Station."

"Sure. We should probably get subpoenas signed off for the phone records of Morgan Walker, Dana Ridley, and Shannon Brennan."

"I'll leave that to you."

"Of course you will. It involves paperwork."

"And a meticulous eye for detail, which you're so good at."

"Flattery doesn't work on me."

"Of course it does." She laughed.

He flashed a smug smile and slid into the passenger side of the department car.

She got into the driver's seat and put the vehicle in gear. In the silence, her mind veered away from the kiosk employees and right to Courtney Middleton.

What really happened to you?

CHAPTER 7

Madison and Terry arrived back at the police station, coffee in hand and food in their bellies—burgers picked up at a drive-thru. Cynthia and the rest of the crime scene investigators hadn't returned yet. Terry got to work on the subpoenas, and she started pulling backgrounds.

None of the security staff from Liberty Station had a criminal history. If any of them were getting paid to look the other way, it would be in their financials, and until she had a solid legal reason to go there, they were untouchable.

The records on Julie Nelson and Tanya Murray were clean too. Nelson had never been married, and Murray was divorced. Very bland, ordinary things.

Next, she printed out the reports on the Ridleys, Walkers, and Brennans. None of them had a single blemish.

When Madison finished, she snuck in a glance at Terry. Their desks were butted against each other, no divider or partition to afford privacy. He was focused on his monitor and clicking away on his keyboard. He'd have to enter every minute detail to support the subpoenas for the phone records. The approval should come fast and swift—after all, two of the histories belonged to murder victims—but it was the upfront part that was tedious.

With him occupied, she had time to satisfy her own curiosities. It was thought all this time that Courtney had met with a bad fate, but what if she had planned to run away? What if from there she assumed the name Morgan Walker?

The report on Morgan showed a complete background including the maiden name of Gardner. If Morgan was indeed Courtney Middleton, creating such a convincing background wouldn't have been an easy or cheap task. Where had she gotten the money for that *and* law school? Also at what point had she assumed the identity of Morgan Walker and what made her start over—if she had? After all, Courtney had come from a loving family. Madison knew her parents, Phoebe and Bruce. She'd been to the house many times for dinner and popped over during the holidays. The Middletons had always come across as kind, loving parents. Possibly a tad protective of their daughter, but that had been the viewpoint of Madison's college self. Had it been the quest for freedom that had Courtney running away—that is, if she had?

Madison keyed Courtney Middleton's name into the computer. She wanted to read the investigation file again. She'd done this before years ago, and she doubted it would offer much in the way of any new information now.

The lead detective on the missing person case was Detective Burrows. He had left the Stiles PD before Madison joined the ranks. She read over the notes, and everything was pretty much as she remembered it. There weren't many details.

Detective Burrows had inquired about the man Courtney had last been seen with, but he never made any headway. Madison hadn't been much help. All she could provide at the time was the name Scott. It was a miracle she'd remembered that much considering all the tequila she'd consumed.

It turned out Scott was a new face at the Roadhouse Bar, and he'd paid in cash that night. No one saw him leave, so no one could attest as to whether he'd left alone or with Courtney.

Madison could accept the crowd's ignorance. It had been after mid-semester exams, and everyone needed to blow off some steam. At that age, it meant consuming as much booze as possible.

If Scott had taken Courtney, there was no proof, and now any trail would have long gone cold.

If only I had stayed with Courtney... She took a deep breath. *Would things have turned out differently?*

After years of holding out hope, Madison's optimism had turned to acceptance. Courtney was gone and most likely dead, or she'd met with an even worse fate. But was any of that the true story?

The more Madison thought about the Walkers' wedding photo, the more convinced she was her friend and Morgan Walker were one and the same. The eyes, the shape of the jaw...that nose. It was unmistakable.

Shane Walker said they'd met in Comsey Park at a bar. What was Courtney doing there? Madison could push Shane for more information about his wife, but even he'd said she had a shady past he knew little about. That right there only brought more suspicion.

Madison could turn elsewhere to get some answers, possibly even hunt down the retired detective from the case. He could remember something that wasn't noted in the records. Then there was always the Middletons. Madison could visit them and ask some questions. Would any of that shed light on the shooting in the train station, or just satisfy her personal curiosities?

"All right. I'm finished up here," Terry said. "All the subpoena requests are off."

"I'm out of gold stars." She smiled.

"Hardy-har. You know it wouldn't kill you to help me out with this sort of thing more often. Or even once."

"As I said before, I have you, and you're so good at it." She batted her eyelashes.

"Whatever. So what have you been up to?" He was around their desks and looking at her monitor before she could close the window on the Courtney Middleton investigation file. "Who is...?" He leaned in. His need for glasses wasn't in dispute, his vanity still fought against it. "Courtney Middleton?" He pulled back. "What does she have to do with our investigation?"

"It's nothing." She closed the file.

"But it is something."

"I pulled everyone's backgrounds—the coffee shop employees, the security guys at the train station, the victims and their husbands. Nada."

"Why are you ignoring me?"

"I'm not. Talking to you right now."

"Do you know this Courtney Middleton person?"

"I did once. Yes." There was no harm in admitting that much.

"And…?" He raised his brows.

"She was a friend of mine in college. She went missing partway through our second year."

"Why are you looking into her now?"

"Oh my God, Terry." She threw her hands in the air. "Enough questions." Yet she was the one with the nickname Bulldog because of her tenacity.

He didn't say a word, blinked slowly. She could feel his mind working.

"Terry, I'm asking you to just let this go."

"I've never heard you bring her up before. So why are you now?" He tapped a finger to his chin in dramatic fashion and paced. "She has something to do with the shooting maybe? Oh—" He stopped talking, his eyes widening. "You went on about Morgan Walker's nose job. You think Morgan is Courtney Middleton."

She huffed out a breath. "Maybe."

"No, you do. It's written all over your face. You have this determined look in your eyes, your jaw's sitting slightly to the right because you're concentrating. But we have enough on our plate without you chasing a ghost."

"I agree, and we don't even know if I'm right or if any of this relates to the shooting."

"And we can't ignore the conflict of interest that arises if Morgan is your old friend."

"There's that. But I'm trusting you to keep quiet about this, and we don't know they are the same person anyway. I could just be seeing what I want." Only she didn't want this—at all.

"If I see it's jeopardizing the case, I'll need to say something."

"I know." She sighed. Her partner and his moral high ground. Something she both respected and disliked—when it was working against her. "I promise I won't let it, but I also bet you that Morgan Walker is Courtney Middleton." *There, I admitted it.*

"Officially?"

"Sure." The usual twenty-dollar wager was made, and a handshake sealed the deal.

"Just please don't let it interfere with the progress of the case. You have a way of becoming obsessed sometimes."

Her earlobes heated with anger. "Obsessed or driven? And Courtney was a good friend of mine. Regardless of this case, I want to know what happened to her once and for all."

He jabbed a finger at her. "That right there could get you into trouble."

"I just need answers." She paused, suddenly overwhelmed by the unfairness of how Courtney may have shown up after all this time, only to be dead. There was no chance for a reunion or reconciliation. No closure. But how to prove whether Courtney was Morgan? It would involve comparing the DNA from the body in the morgue to her friend's. And where was she getting that exemplar? DNA wasn't attached to the missing person report. When Courtney had gone missing, it had been a different time. She shook aside her thoughts. "But you're right. Finding the shooter takes priority. Speaking of that endeavor, I haven't heard back from Marsh."

"Give the guy two minutes."

"He's had more than that."

"It's an expression."

"I know that. Just like I know something is going on in that train station that has both kiosk workers afraid to talk. Even has the owner willing to look the other way while the girl with the backpack steals from him."

"And what makes you so sure that it points to an illegal underground operation."

"Not just any operation. Drug trafficking. If you think about it, it makes perfect sense. There isn't much security with train travel, certainly not like there is with flying. That would make it rather easy to smuggle and transport whatever you wanted to another city or state. Customs checks would only get involved at the country's borders. Even then the protocols are probably rather light." She jumped up from her chair.

"Where are you going?"

"I'm going to see if anyone in Narcotics is in."

"Can't you just wait for a call back?" Terry followed, mumbling. "Just try not to piss off anyone over there, at least not too much." His mouth was in a straight line, his eyebrows raised, but his expression cracked into a smile.

"I'll do my best." Not that she was worried about being the diplomat. She was wired for ferreting out the truth, not for a pleasant bedside manner or playing well with others.

She hustled to the warren of cubicles that belonged to Narcotics, and not a soul was around. She pulled out her phone and called Marsh. Landed in voicemail again, where she left another message, stressing the urgency even more this time. She ended the call but held on to her phone with a tight grip. "We need to return to the train station," she said to Terry. "Time to talk to the police officers who were on duty."

His eyes narrowed. "Just remember to play nice, and please promise you won't accuse them of being corrupt or taking bribes."

"No promises." And that was the best she could do. She tended to run with first impressions, and those were based on instinct and intuition. They were more reliable than the versions that came after overthinking. Excuses and justifications entered, tainting reality. The truth was, if the officers were regularly assigned that beat, and there was something illegal going on in the train station, they were either blind or they were paid to look the other way.

"Crap." Terry dragged himself along the corridor behind her, his arms dangling long and making her think of the last time she was at the zoo, looking in on the orangutan exhibit.

She stifled a laugh at the imagery but delighted at the reprieve of a jovial thought amid the rest of them that were so dark and full of death.

CHAPTER 8

It was four in the afternoon when Madison and Terry got to
Liberty Station, and judging by the parking lot, the place was
still crawling with police. Madison parked beside Sergeant
Winston's SUV and groaned internally. She wasn't in any
hurry to face him again. He'd have a million questions and
attempt to micromanage her to the point she'd wish for
death. It was rather surprising he hadn't called her ten times
already. He always sought her first impressions, which he'd
hold against her if she was wrong. And *sometimes* she was.
He hadn't even asked about her opinion this time when
they'd spoken at the security office. She had no idea what
prompted the change, which was a little unsettling.

She'd called Higgins on the way over, and he told her the
officers on duty at the time of the shooting were still on
scene and set to clock out at seven. That left her and Terry
plenty of time to question them, and the officers could still
get home in time for dinner with their families—assuming
they had them. Higgins told her that he'd get the officers to
the Just Beans intersection of the station, and he'd arrange
for other uniforms to cover their posts.

Ahead of them, Madison could see two officers twenty
feet or so away from the coffee kiosk. They were talking,
their heads angled toward each other, like people do when
they're sharing secrets. The hairs rose on the back of her
neck. Maybe Terry was right, and she saw corruption even

when it didn't exist, but better to be prepared than caught unaware. Giving people the benefit of the doubt made one vulnerable—something she tried to avoid.

The immediate area around the kiosk was cordoned off with tape and monitored by a solo officer who stood off to the side, away from the other two officers who were waiting to be interviewed.

"Officers," she said, and their conversation immediately stopped. They claimed their individual space about a foot or so apart, straightened their postures, and waited.

She and Terry introduced themselves, though the officers did not.

The names on their uniforms gave her their last names—Galloway and Morris. Both were in their mid-twenties, she guessed, with athletic builds.

"Higgins said you wanted to talk to us?" This from Galloway, presumably the leader of the two. He squared his shoulders and met her gaze. Eye contact could be a good thing, but there was a challenge housed in his.

"Where were you guys at the time of the shooting?" she asked.

"Doing the regular rounds." Galloway put his hands on his hips. A move to intimidate, or perhaps to overcompensate for lack of confidence. But Madison was less interested in his body language and more interested in what he had said.

"Regular rounds. So, you have places you have to be at certain times of the day?" If that were true, then maybe the shooting had been planned and was only staged to look random—a stretch, but an angle to consider, nonetheless.

"That's right," Galloway said.

"And it's the same routine every day?" Her heart was starting to pick up speed.

"Yep." Galloway sneered and rolled his eyes as he turned to look at Officer Morris.

Madison took a deep breath and tried to calm her temper. "Just to confirm, the regular rounds had you on the other end of Liberty Station at the time of the shooting?" She'd been told earlier that was where they had been, but she wanted to hear it directly from them. She looked at Morris for the answer, curious if he had a voice at all.

"That's right," Morris responded and went on to tell them what entrance they'd been near at seven that morning.

Madison nodded. She recalled the map of the station in the security office. The area Morris indicated was at the other end of the station. The shooter getting away could have just been a simple matter of him being aware of the rotation and where the officers would be posted. It didn't mean these officers were corrupt and paid to look the other way. Still she wanted to see their reaction to the suggestion. "Are you aware that drugs are being trafficked through the station?"

Both officers looked at her, at Terry, back at her, then each other.

"News to us if that's the case," Galloway said.

"No one is paying you to look the other way?"

She could feel the heat of Terry's glare on her, but she refused to acknowledge him.

"Answer me," she pushed.

"No, of course not." Morris's brow wrinkled, distressed.

Galloway's mouth set in a frown. "Where do you get off accusing us of—"

"You wouldn't be the first officers to take money on the side."

"Let's go." Galloway flailed a hand and flicked Morris's arm.

"I never said you were excused, Officers." Madison peacocked her posture.

"We don't need your permission. You're not our sergeant."

With that, Galloway walked off. Morris eventually followed, but seemed hesitant and tossed a glance over his shoulder as he left.

"Making friends all over the place," Terry mumbled.

"What?"

"Thought you were going to be nice."

"Hey, I never promised anything."

"You can't just go accusing them of things like that. You attack people, they're going to put up a wall. When will you realize this?"

"I'll just bulldoze the wall down."

Terry shook his head. "It doesn't always work that way."

"Fine. It's possible they don't know about a drug-trafficking operation."

"We don't even know for sure that there is one. The shooting could have been made to *look* like there was something else going on. For all we know, everyone was in on it and there wasn't even a guy who is normally standing over there." Terry pointed toward the wall where Julia Nelson had told him the regular "handler" stood. "And we're assuming that if there was a man, he was a handler. Then that makes the shooter his replacement or something else altogether?"

"That I don't know."

"Finally. You admit there are some things you don't know."

She shoved him in the shoulder.

"No need to get physically abusive."

She narrowed her eyes at him.

"What?" he rushed out. "I'm just saying until we can confirm drugs are being run through the train station, it's a suspicion at best. Think about it."

She took a deep breath, studied his face. "Something has to explain that girl with the backpack and the handlers standing around."

"*Men* standing around. Just assumption and rumor they are anything else."

"Gah." She looked up at the ceiling. Her partner could be infuriating at times. "I'm confident there is drug trafficking going on, but regardless, it seems we're both steering away from the shooting being random. As such that would suggest that at least one of the women was the target."

Terry seemed to consider, bobbed his head side to side. "Okay, I can give you that."

Again, her mind slid to Courtney Middleton. Maybe finding out what Courtney had been up to all these years was more valid to the investigation than she'd first thought. Her phone pinged with a text message, which she read and shared with Terry. "Richards saying he's starting the autopsies tomorrow at nine."

He nodded.

"Madison." Cynthia was hustling down the ramp toward them, holding something in her hands—a piece of paper by the looks of it.

"What do you have?" She helped close the distance, Terry stepping in time with her.

"Thought I'd look at some surveillance video while I was here. Got this." She gave Madison a color photograph of a man leaning against a wall.

"Who is this?"

Cynthia pointed to the wall across from the Just Beans kiosk and drew her finger from there toward a small unit mounted on the ceiling—the camera that captured the picture. "Just a quick scan of the past two weeks revealed this guy often stood in this area."

"The regular handler," Madison said, turning to Terry. "You wanted some proof. This work?"

Terry smirked. "Could be anyone."

"Wow. Seriously?" And yet people called *her* stubborn. To Madison it was obvious they had their answer about whether something was being moved through Liberty Station. The most likely thing being drugs. Julie Nelson said the man often stood across from the kiosk, and now Cynthia had just confirmed that, but why there? Did it coincide with the boarding and disembarking of trains to specific destinations? "Was he there at predictable times?"

"Not sure about that. As I said, I just scanned through some footage quickly. I can definitely take a closer look at the video once I get it back to the lab and join up with the rest of the team. I already let them go on ahead of me."

"By the way, I gave your card to the guys in security," Madison said with a smile.

"Yeah, they told me that."

"Do you have any stills of the shooter or the girl with the backpack?" Madison asked. "We did see her face on the video from this morning's shooting. A snapshot of that could go a long way."

"You think she was in on what happened?"

"I don't." Madison was quite certain the shooting had been orchestrated to take advantage of the cops' rotation, so why not the girl's habit of stealing?

"Okay. I'll get the pic of her to you. Still don't have a clear one of the shooter."

Madison was hoping for better news—more immediate results—but would have to take what she was given. Not that it would stop her from asking questions. "Did you get much evidence?" She jutted her chin toward the kiosk and the bloodstained floor.

"Collected and photographed a lot. It's hard to say what will factor into evidence and actually get you closer to the shooter."

Madison nodded. "Let me know if you find any predictability as to when this guy"—she held up the photo—"stood near the kiosk. Also if anyone else stands out on the footage, like the girl."

"You'll need to be more specific there."

"Possible runners. We think drugs might be being moved through the station."

"You," Terry said. "*You* think that."

"Not sure how I'm supposed to pluck that out… Young people with backpacks?" Cynthia looked at her skeptically.

Madison supposed her friend had a point. "Whatever you can do. Use your judgment."

"Always." Cynthia smiled at her. "You doing all right?"

"Ah, yeah. Why wouldn't I be?" Madison wasn't sure what had warranted the question, then she remembered Cynthia's scrutiny when Richards had brought up Dana Ridley's pregnancy.

"You just look drawn lately."

"Wow. Thanks. You look like shit too." Not that Cynthia ever did. She turned heads wherever she went. She had long, dark hair and a contagious smile that could be as predatory as a lioness. Two months ago, Lou Stanford, another detective with Major Crimes for the Stiles PD, took her off the market and put a ring on it—even went through with the vows. Madison had gotten close before. She was only a pro at getting engaged. Twice now, but she hoped this time with Troy stuck. Actually, she was quite sure it would.

Cynthia grinned. "Only you could say such a thing and live."

"You know I'm joking. You always look amazing."

"Right. Well, I'll accept the compliment, but we need to talk, because something is going on with you." Cynthia glanced at Terry, saluted teasingly, and walked back up the ramp.

Madison laid a hand over her stomach. Her friend had a way of reading her and knowing when something was wrong. She was so talented at it, it practically bordered on clairvoyance.

"What was that all about?" Terry asked.

"Nothing. She gets things in her head sometimes." *Sort of like you do*, she thought but refrained from saying so for fear he'd continue with an interrogation of his own.

Madison put her gaze back on the photograph, actually taking a closer look this time. Twentysomething, and he was perched against the brick wall casually, one leg bent, and holding up a cell phone. But he wasn't looking at the screen. He was looking over it as if the phone was just a cover for what he was truly interested in. He had dark hair and was wearing blue jeans and a black, ribbed sweater, the sleeves rolled up. His face was shadowed by facial hair, obscuring his features. But there was something about his hands, the way he was holding his phone... No! It was the tattoos on his forearms. Her insides froze, and her breathing slowed. "I know who this is!"

CHAPTER 9

Madison couldn't get her legs to move fast enough. She was confident she'd seen that man and his tattoos before. Not that she was thrilled about where this might take the investigation.

"What do you mean you know who that is? How? From where?" Terry was easily keeping pace with her, but he made an actual habit of running in the mornings—*by choice*.

"Enough questions, Terry." Her entire body was quaking as wild theories galloped in her mind. *Please be wrong.*

"Madison. Talk to me."

"Fine, but you're not going to like it." She kept moving. "You are aware of my little spying mission on Russian mob affiliates at Club Sophisticated?"

"Yes, of course. You were looking for something to prove corrupt cops were in bed with the mob."

"That's right." Club Sophisticated was a favored haunt of the mob and their lowlife friends, but there was nothing to prove the Russians owned the place. For a time, she had skulked around the place at night, in the back alley, dressed in black and hiding beside dumpsters and garbage bags to snatch photos. She'd found more than she'd bargained for, though. The Russians kept a house in north Stiles registered in the name of Roman Petrov, the Mafia's founder. Roman had supposedly died twenty-some years ago. If that wasn't enough shock, one of his cousins, Tatiana Ivanova, was in town, and she came with the reputation of a skilled assassin.

They reached the department car and got inside. She peeled out of the lot.

Terry gripped the ceiling bar. "Where are we going?"

"My house. I have pictures there of that guy."

He didn't say anything for a few beats, then, "Maddy, I'm going to need more. How does your surveillance of the Russians tie into the here and now, to this assumed handler?"

"If he's who I'm thinking of, he works in the kitchen at the club," she said, splitting her attention between him and the road. "He came out the back one night for a smoke break, wearing a half apron. He held the door for Tatiana. If I'm right and he's the girl's regular handler, then whatever is going on at the train station is most certainly connected to the mob. And we know they run all sorts of businesses to make and launder money. Drug trafficking is entirely plausible. Though something new for them. As far as I know."

"Maybe slow down."

"Slow down? Not going to happen. I know they're mixed up in this somehow..."

"You don't *know* anything."

"Let's say I'm going to prove it then." But she and the Russians had a long history. They'd tried to kill her more than once. Last month, she was convinced, was the latest attempt. And the fact that this Tatiana woman was in town didn't help Madison's nerves. Something was about to go down. Madison just hoped it wasn't going to be her.

"All right, so let's say the guy from the club is the one from the security video, and he's a handler. It doesn't mean all of this is connected to the mob."

"I'm not necessarily saying the murders are."

"Well, last I knew, that was our case. Two dead, one shot..."

She glared at him. "We need to find this guy. It might get us closer to the girl."

"You're sure that's all this is, and you're not still seeking retaliation on the mob?"

"I'm not going to dignify that with an answer." She had a lot to retaliate for, as Terry knew, starting with her grandfather's murder by the son of a mob accountant. Also the reason she became a cop and was determined to root the Mafia out of Stiles.

"Okay, maybe this guy is caught up in drug trafficking, but I don't think he's in any way involved with what happened this morning."

"Me neither. I think we're likely looking at two very different things here. The shooting and a drug-trafficking operation."

"Presumably."

"You really need to fight me every inch of the way?"

"I'm just trying to keep your mind open."

"Uh-huh." She glanced at the photo, now in the console where she'd put it. Maybe she was blowing this out of proportion, and it wasn't the same guy. Besides, it was early in the investigation, and there were still a lot of angles to consider. They'd only scraped the surface so far.

She pulled into the driveway of the Craftsman bungalow that Troy owned and she called home for the better part of a year now. They were planning to buy a new house together, but life kept interfering and delaying their efforts.

Hershey, her chocolate Lab, rushed to the door to greet them. He was wagging his tail vigorously at the sight of her, and she rubbed his head and buried her fingers in his fur. He let out a pitiful moan—actually, happiness to see her—and then took his wriggling body over to Terry.

"Hey, boy. Hey." Terry was grinning, so at ease with dogs. He was why she had Hershey in the first place. Terry had gifted him to her at Christmas three years ago, presenting the little guy with a red bow around his neck. As far as gifts went, this one kept giving.

She left Terry and Hershey at the door and went to the second bedroom, where she and Troy had a computer and a desk. She opened the bottom drawer, pulled out the thumb drive labeled *CS*—for Club Sophisticated—*March 2*, and popped it into the computer.

She shuffled through the images, searching for ones of the tattooed man on his smoke break. It didn't take her long to find what she was after. The man had his phone in hand but was looking over it at Tatiana, his tattoos visible. She lifted the photo that Cynthia had given her and held it next to the screen. "Terry, get in here," she called out.

His footsteps padded down the hall, Hershey with him, and both entered the room.

"That's him."

Terry bent down and squinted, his gaze going between the printout and the screen.

"You seriously need to get glasses."

"I can see just fine."

"Sure, if you're right on top of whatever you're looking at." He thrust a pointed finger at the screen. "Focus!"

"Argh, Terry."

"Fine. Yes, it could be him."

"What do you mean *could*? It is him."

"The guy in the photo Cynthia gave us has a lot of facial hair."

"All right, but can you dispute the stature and this…?" She zoomed in on the tattoos on his forearms in the digital photo. "They are three-headed dragons. Russian." She'd learned from her research that dragons played a dominant role in Russian folklore, and they had at minimum three heads, sometimes as many as seven or nine. "And that"—she jabbed at the printout—"is the same design."

"More than one person could have—"

"Seriously?"

"Sure, this could be him." He smiled. "I see it."

"Hallelujah." She popped out the USB drive, returned it to the drawer, and flicked the screen off, leaving the computer on. "We'll feed Hershey, let him out to do his business, and then take off."

CHAPTER 10

Club Sophisticated might have been open to the public, but they scrutinized everyone who passed through the door. Eyes burrowed into Madison and Terry—both the patrons' and the employees'. She walked, taking each step slowly and deliberately, her hand never far from her holster in case it became necessary to draw her weapon.

One mercy was, for six PM, there weren't that many people there. But that was also a negative. There'd be fewer witnesses should something go down.

Her phone pinged with a new text. It was probably Troy acknowledging the message she'd sent before leaving the house. It had just been to let him know she'd taken care of Hershey and there was no need for him to rush home. She'd also told him she was assigned the Liberty Station shooting and to expect her home late. But now wasn't the time to check and confirm that the text was from him. She had to keep alert to her surroundings.

She and Terry reached the counter and pulled their badges to show the bartender, a bulked-up behemoth of a man. He took two steps back, and she hadn't even said a word. She held up the photo from the train station for him to see. He barely glanced at it.

"We believe he works in the kitchen here. We need to speak to him."

"Don't know who that is." His voice carried the flavor of a Russian accent.

"I'm quite sure you do. I've seen him here before. Might not be able to make it out in the picture, but he has tattoos on his forearms of three-headed dragons."

"Know nothing about it. Or him." His mouth contorted like he'd tasted bile.

"All right, fine by me. If that's the game you want to play, I'll get a warrant to search the place and come back with more of my friends."

"You think that's going to scare me?" He laughed.

She peacocked her stance. "I think it should encourage you to cooperate."

"I don't like the police. No one here does."

"Aye!" A man on a barstool several feet away raised a shot glass.

Madison couldn't force the bartender to talk, and maybe she'd been foolish to think she'd make any headway here. After all, she'd felt it before and was feeling it now—there was something off with this place. It might not be proven on the books to have ties with the mob, but she was sure it did. But she was here, and she wasn't leaving without some answers. Damn the big baboon standing between them and the guy with the tattoos. "Tell you what," she said. "We'll be in touch with the owner here, thank him for having such a cooperative—and talkative—bartender. I'm sure he'll be pleased to know you're helping the police."

He glared at her. "But I'm not."

"You're not?" She looked at Terry and shrugged.

"I know what you're doing here, and it's not going to work."

"No, then try me." She leaned toward the counter, closing the space between them. Her five foot five against his six-something. "What's it going to be…Igor?" She read his name off the tag on his shirt. And of course it would be Igor, or Boris…or something similar.

He grunted. The gears in his brain working—either that or he was constipated. "He works here," he pushed out through clenched teeth.

"Name?"

"Vlas."

Sounded Russian. "Last name?"

"Nikitin."

"Where's he live?"

"Why should I tell you? You want to find out, you come back tonight and ask him yourself."

"Not going to work for me, Igor."

"It's gonna have to." Igor cracked his knuckles and nudged his head to indicate she should look behind her.

She glanced over her shoulder. Two goons had their hands inside their jackets, likely reaching for guns in shoulder holsters. "All right." She tapped the counter. "But I'm going to remember this, and don't expect a good review on Yelp." She turned, flashed a big, fake smile at the goons, and left the bar.

On the sidewalk, Terry wiped his brow, then rubbed the back of his neck. "Why is it you always need to play with our lives?"

"They're not going to do anything to us."

"Ha. This coming from someone who had a Russian hit man sicced on her."

"And lived to tell about it." The words kicked out more on bravado. She'd never forget. That hit man had almost killed her more than once. He'd even kidnapped her sister, Chelsea, to draw Madison out at the end of last year. And it was never far from her mind that this Tatiana woman was in Stiles. Was she here to finish the job the other guy failed to do?

"So far, but someday your luck might run out."

He had no idea how it already had and that the cost had been her and Troy's unborn child. Her partner also had no inkling that she was partially relieved not to be a mother. She struggled enough on her own without subjecting a poor kid to her life decisions. And she did tend to take risks—not because she had a death wish, but because she saw her goals for justice as being of the utmost importance. Putting bad guys in jail was her legacy.

She slipped behind the wheel of the department car and keyed *Vlas Nikitin* into the onboard computer. His background came up. "Criminal record. No shock there. Vlas served two years for drug possession." She paused, looked over at her partner. "Maybe not so big a leap from possession to dealing."

"I want more before we just assume there's a trafficking operation in the train station. *And* that it's entangled with the mob."

"Of course you do," she said drily and looked back at the screen. "Have his address and know exactly where that is." Madison had lived in Stiles her entire adult life and was familiar with every square inch of her city.

She took them several intersections over and pulled down Walnut Street, looking for number 1802. This was still considered the downtown area, and it was a rough neighborhood. There were a lot of low-income housing options, and several apartment buildings had been built in just the last few years. Number 1802 turned out to be one of the latter. She parked at the curb in front of the lackluster brown-brick structure, not wanting to get involved with parking in the underground garage.

She and Terry got out of the car. "He's in apartment five-oh-two," she told him.

It was a secured building, again likely due to the crowd attracted to the area. They stepped through the exterior door into a foyer but wouldn't be getting any further until they were buzzed past the locked doors. She tapped the intercom button for Nikitin's apartment three times in a row.

Terry held out his hand to stop her. "Maybe give him a chance to answer."

She pushed the button again. Just because. He shook his head.

"He's not answering." She pushed the intercom for apartment 222. Completely random.

A woman answered, and there was a screaming baby in the background.

"Stiles PD, Detective Knight, ma'am. Please let me into the building."

Click.

Terry chuckled, and she smacked his arm. "I'm failing to see what's funny about what just happened."

He rubbed where she'd impacted him. "No need to make up for lost time."

She reached out to hit another number. Terry flinched.

"Just stop pushing random numbers. It rarely works. People are too suspicious these days."

"Probably a good thing, but fine. You tell me how you plan to get us inside. Oh—" Before she'd moved in with Troy, she lived in a secured apartment building, and Terry would regularly gain entry without calling up first. "You're actually a pro at this."

"Maybe *pro* is taking it a little far. But the trick? You wait for someone to show up and go in with them."

"We don't have time to just stand around and—"

The exterior door opened, and a thirtysomething man joined them. His arms were looped through the handles of shopping bags, and he was fiddling with a keyring. He barely paid them any attention, stuck a key in the lock, and opened the door.

Terry grabbed it for him and didn't get a thanks for his trouble, but they had access.

The three of them got on the elevator, and Madison could feel the smugness radiating from Terry. She was in for an "I told you so."

The man got off on the second floor, hardly worth even getting on the elevator, and Terry turned to her.

"See? Easy-peasy."

"We got lucky."

"You called me a pro. There's no taking it back."

"I obviously overestimated the skill involved."

"Uh-huh, well, you thought we'd be standing around waiting forever, but people are coming and going all the time. If there is a wait, it's usually a short one."

"Why do they even bother securing buildings if tenants are going to let anyone walk in off the street?"

"Not all tenants. That mother wouldn't unlock the door for you." He smirked.

"Very funny."

The elevator dinged their arrival, and they went down the hall to apartment 502. She banged on the door.

"He's really going to want to answer now." Terry rolled his eyes.

"Mr. Nikitin, Stiles PD," she said, ignoring Terry. "We need to speak with you."

"And if he was going to answer, he's certainly not now."

She shot him daggers. "Seriously? What's up with you right now?"

He shrugged.

She leaned in toward the door and listened. Not a sound. She pulled her head back, knocked again, pressed her ear right up against the door. Nothing to hear, but she smelled a distinct odor. She recoiled in disgust. When it came to this particular scent, she had the nose of a hound. "Blood. We need to get in that apartment."

CHAPTER 11

It felt like it took forever, and then some, to get the building manager moving, but Madison and Terry were finally going inside apartment 502.

"I should make you give me a warrant," the manager mumbled, making his hesitation known for the umpteenth time. And mumbling was the best it seemed he could do. There wasn't yet one thing he'd said that was clearly discernible. He pushed the key in the lock and turned the handle.

"You should just be happy we didn't bang the door down." She was tired of his bellyaching, when technically they would have been within their right to force the door open, given the circumstances. Her phone rang, and caller ID told her it was Troy. She'd completely forgotten about the text. She hadn't even checked it. It would be easier to shuffle him to voicemail right now, but she'd make it quick. "You got my message?"

"I did. You get mine?"

The manager swung the door open, and the stench of death greeted her.

"Troy, I'm sorry, but I've gotta go." She hung up without another word and pocketed her phone. He understood the demands of the job and, per her text, that she was working a new case. What she hadn't told him was some of the evidence was leading her to the mob. But she would tell him—in person.

She and Terry stepped inside the apartment. The manager moved to follow. She turned and held up a hand. "You need to stay in the hall."

"What? No, that's not acceptable."

"Only option. Believe me, you'll be glad you did." She gave him a pointed look, but he didn't back down.

He nudged out his chin. "What isn't an option is you shutting me out here."

Mumble, mumble, mumble... "If you don't back down, I will have no choice but to bring you in for obstruction." She stiffened her posture, and the manager seemed to shrink some.

"Fine," he huffed out and made a dramatic show of walking backward into the hall.

She turned to the apartment and gagged on the strong smell of blood. If there wasn't a dead body at the end of the trail, it would be surprising.

The space was compact and open concept. The kitchen was off to the left as she entered, the living room straight ahead with a window that looked over the street. To the right was a short hallway with a bathroom and a bedroom. The latter was where her nose took her.

A man's body, presumably Vlas Nikitin, was supine on the bed. He was tucked beneath the covers, which were soaked in blood. Spatter also marked the walls and the floor, like an artist had fanned a loaded brush.

"Found the DB," she said, swallowing down bile.

Terry stepped up next to her. "I'll call in Richards and Crime Scene."

"Yeah, sure. Leave me with Winston."

He smiled and pulled out his phone and started making the calls.

Winston answered on the second ring, and she filled him in and requested that he get uniforms on scene to cordon off the area immediately. He said he would and that he'd be there shortly himself.

Goody...

She kept her distance from the body, not so much because of the sight or smell now, but because she didn't want to contaminate the scene. She let her mind take in what was in front of her, filtering the blood out of her vision, just focusing on what the scene was telling her.

Terry pocketed his phone. "Penny for your thoughts?"

"Oh, Lord." She turned to face him and rolled her eyes.

He was smiling, his obvious attempt at inserting joviality had worked but its effect was fading quickly.

"He was killed in bed, probably in his sleep. Looks like he was shot, but I'm not seeing bullet casings."

"The killer took the time to clean up."

"Seems that way. So, a professional? Let's run with Nikitin having been a handler for a drug operation *and* one belonging to the mob, no less."

"All right."

"Were the Russians unhappy with his work? Or did the shooter from the train station take him out? Just listen to me, Terry," she rushed out when he looked like he was about to interrupt her. "I think it's the latter. Think about how meticulously planned this morning's shooting must have been. The timing was perfect. The cops were on the other side of the train station. Now this guy, Nikitin, who normally frequented the station and was connected to the girl with the backpack, has been murdered. I think the shooter took him out to take his place, to *look* like her new handler. But who in their right mind would take out someone connected to the Russian mob?"

"If what you're saying actually happened, maybe the shooter didn't realize the mob had their hands in the trafficking or were connected to Nikitin. Heck, we don't even know for sure." Her partner, devil's advocate until the very end.

"No. The shooter knew about Nikitin, the girl, and how she often steals from the Just Beans counter. He exploited a regularly occurring scenario as a smokescreen to hide what was really going on."

"If that's true, he may also have known that the women were regularly there for coffee."

"Yep. And to me that means one or all of them were targeted. But who and/or why?"

"If only we had a solid lead on the shooter himself."

"Well, let's say he took out Nikitin. Is he going to stop there? Is the girl safe? If she was involved in the orchestration of the shooting, her usefulness is up now. Either way, she could have gotten a good look at the shooter."

Terry paled. "She could be seen as a loose end to silence."

Madison nodded. "We need to get to her before the shooter does."

"We could be worried about her well-being for nothing. A girl like that isn't going to speak out. She'd be used to keeping her head down."

Chatter from the building's hallway had Madison turning. A uniformed officer was approaching them.

"Just wanted to let you know we've got the apartment door and the entrance to the building covered," the officer told them. "We'll make sure no one gets past."

"Start organizing a door-to-door canvas too." Madison was less impressed with what they had done and more interested in getting answers.

"Thank you, Officer," Terry said.

The officer dipped his head and left, and Madison's phone rang. Caller ID told her it was Marsh from Narcotics. *Took him long enough!* "Detective Knight," she answered formally. "Are you aware of a drug-trafficking operation running through the train station?"

Terry turned to face her and popped his eyes. He was always reminding her she could catch more bees with honey, but *honey* was in short supply.

"No, I'm not aware," Marsh said, guarded.

"Well, something's going on there."

"As I said, not aware of anything."

Madison filled him in on the shooting, the girl with the backpack, and Nikitin, including the fact that he was now dead.

"Huh. Could be she's a runner."

"We don't have her picture yet, but once I get it, I'll shoot it over to you. But she's blond, about twenty, and is often seen wearing an orange backpack. Could you keep an eye out for her? Maybe she'll show up at a stash house you're watching…?"

"Worth a try. I'm guessing based on all you've told me that if drugs were passing through the station, they'd pause operation after the shooting. Lie low for a while. I'll talk with Detective Commons about this too."

"Whatever you can do."

"Yep. Leave it with me, and send over the picture of the girl as soon as you have it." He ended the call before she could say more.

She put her phone in her pants pocket. "Marsh is going to help us out." After saying that, her thoughts turned dark. Marsh had said *they'd pause operation,* so where would that leave the girl? Would the mob blame her for what had transpired? The mob would be out cash and their ring at risk of exposure, all because her stealing was used as the trigger for the shooting. Would they see the girl as a liability to be cleared from their ledger?

CHAPTER 12

Madison's stomach was rumbling from nerves and hunger. She kept telling herself she'd get something to eat soon—whenever that would be. It was after eight o'clock, and she and Terry were still at Nikitin's apartment building.

Sergeant Winston had popped by and left swiftly. He probably had a television show to get home to watch. Cynthia and Mark Andrews, from her team, were processing everything in Nikitin's apartment from prints on doorknobs to his garbage for any possible evidence. Cole Richards and his assistant, Milo, were held up with another DB across town, but they would be here as soon as they could.

Madison was in the middle of knocking a second time on the building manager's door when it opened.

The manager stepped back, without a word, and let them inside. Madison's eyes immediately began to water at the strong smell of a litterbox. Still, that was better than blood.

The space was cluttered with furniture and bric-a-brac, something one would expect from an older person who had lived in the same place all their lives. This building was less than five years old.

A gray cat came around the corner meowing loudly, and it rubbed against Madison's leg. She looked down at the strip of hair now clinging to her pants leg and frowned.

"Sorry about that." The manager scooped up the cat. "This is my little furball, Monkey. He likes to say hello to everyone."

"Is there someplace we could sit?" Madison's eyes traced to the couch in the living room, not sure she'd be sitting down herself. If the cat left behind that much hair by merely swishing past her, then the couch probably had enough to brush.

"Right through here." The manager led the way and dropped down at the end of the couch. There was a steaming mug on a table next to him, which he lifted for a sip. "Tea. It calms my heart."

"We can appreciate it must come as quite a shock that your neighbor is dead," Terry said.

"Dead? With all of you guys crawling around, it's more than that." He scanned Madison's eyes as if he were trying to read her mind.

"All we can say at this time is that his death is suspicious." Next of kin was to be the first notified, but Nikitin had none from a quick look at his background. Still, she'd hold back on the details.

"Candy-coating. I know what I'm seeing, and this is a murder investigation."

"Beyond police activity, why jump to that assumption?" Madison was hoping to learn something about Nikitin—his lifestyle and his character. Had the manager said what he had because he could imagine Nikitin's dealings making him enemies?

"Just putting everything together." The manager leaned back and crossed his legs at the ankles. "Forensics next door, police officers knocking on everyone's door in the building, and you here questioning me."

"What can you tell us about him?" Madison asked.

"You're going to need to be a little more specific than that."

Impatience was starting to build inside of her. "Okay, let's start with something simple. Was Vlas Nikitin a good tenant?"

"Always paid his rent on time, always in cash."

"Is that the usual way people pay in this building?" she asked.

"Meh. Fifty-fifty."

"Did Nikitin stick to himself, or have you ever seen him with people—friends, a girlfriend maybe…a boyfriend?" *In the name of keeping an open mind…*

"Quite sure he had a girlfriend over from time to time."

"Do you know her name?" If they could find her, they might gain insight into Nikitin, including what had him at the train station so often—if it was, in fact, overseeing drug runners.

"Nah." The manager took another sip of his tea and set the mug down on the table.

"What did this woman look like?" The skin was tightening on the back of Madison's neck as stress moved in.

"Young, say maybe twenty. Attractive." He tossed out a shrug. "Long, blond hair."

The description was vague but could fit the girl with the backpack. Could it be that she was Nikitin's girlfriend as well as a drug runner? If she were the latter alone, it wouldn't make sense that she'd have been to his apartment for business purposes. Drugs were usually stored in stash houses and picked up by the runners there. "Did you see them being affectionate with each other?"

"Sure. I saw them holding hands before and caught them kissing once down by the mailboxes."

Whoever this twenty-year-old woman was, she *was* more than friends with Nikitin. It only made Madison want to find the girl more.

"What about any friends?" Terry asked before Madison could say anything further.

"For the most part, I'd say he stuck to himself."

They didn't have time of death yet, but she'd seen her share of dead bodies and would guess Nikitin had died in the last twenty-four hours. "Did you happen to see if anyone visited Mr. Nikitin yesterday or today?" A reach, as his apartment was on the main floor and Nikitin's was on the fifth.

"Can't say that I did, but it's not like I live next door to the guy."

Madison nodded. "Did Nikitin ever give you reason to suspect he was into anything illegal?" She'd done enough dancing around the point.

"No. I wouldn't think so, but people who follow the straight and narrow don't normally get themselves knocked off either."

Guess he's still convinced it was murder…

The manager went on. "He always came across as a really nice person. If we met in the hall, he'd always say hi and ask me how I was doing." A twinge of pain fluttered through the man's eyes.

"One more thing before we go," she started. "Does the building have security cameras?"

The manager's expression turned grim, and he shook his head. "Too much money. The board wouldn't approve them."

Huh… Madison gave him her card. "We may be back with more questions, but if there's anything you think we should know after we leave, call me."

"Will do. If I think of anything."

Madison had the feeling she wouldn't be hearing from him.

CHAPTER 13

It seemed clear whoever this Nikitin person had been, he had secrets, and he was good at keeping them. After all, the building manager hadn't suspected he was up to anything illegal, but Madison was quite sure it was just a matter of time before she had proof that he had been.

Madison and Terry went back to Nikitin's apartment, and Cynthia came toward them.

"There you are."

Madison's phone rang, and it was Troy. She held up her index finger to Cynthia to wait a second and answered. "Still really not a good time. I'll be lucky to get home before morning."

"All right, well, Hershey and I will be here."

She imagined them snuggled on the couch, and jealousy wormed right through her. "I'll get home as soon as I can. I promise you that. But right now, I've got to go."

There was a second or two of silence, then Troy said, "Go get 'em, Bulldog."

Bulldog—his favorite nickname for her, and she'd never warmed up to it. "Yeah, yeah. Love you."

"Love you too. Stay safe."

She put her phone away and caught up with Terry and Cynthia, who had gone down the hall to the bedroom. They were standing off to the side, and Cynthia had a plastic evidence bag in hand.

Cynthia held up the find. "Bullet casings. I found them under the bed."

The hairs rose on Madison's arms. A hit person with the mob wouldn't leave such evidence behind. Neither would a true professional unless they didn't care about being tracked or linked to multiple crimes. "What's the caliber?"

"Nine mil." Cynthia put the bag in an evidence collection kit, which resembled a toolbox.

Madison looked at Terry. "Same size bullets used in the Liberty Station shooting. Coincidence? I think not. I think the shooter from this morning came here and killed Nikitin, as we theorized earlier. Any sign of drugs?"

"Just a trace."

"Why not lead with that?" She bugged her eyes out at her friend.

Cynthia looked at Terry and shook her head. "She's never happy."

"What—"

"Meth. Just a trace, as I said. Nothing to prove he was moving drugs or selling them himself."

Not that a handler would do either. His job would be to oversee the logistics and that deliveries got to where they needed to go. A trace was all they needed as far as Madison was concerned. It confirmed that Nikitin was in the drug world, and it had her thoughts going crazy with theories— none of them particularly pleasant. Primarily, the mob seeking retaliation.

"You'll also want to know that Mark and I found two burner phones in the nightstand drawer," Cynthia offered.

Madison smiled.

"Why are you...?" Cynthia angled her head.

"You are looking a little scary at the moment." Terry pointed at Madison's grin.

"That's further proof Nikitin was up to no good. Also, there is absolutely no way the mob is behind Nikitin's murder. If they'd been here, if they had killed him, they'd have taken the phones with them to cover their tracks. You have the casings and the phones... That's enough to tell me that whoever killed Nikitin wasn't with the mob. The most likely candidate would be the shooter from this morning."

Terry shrugged. "There might not be anything incriminating to find on the phones, and as for the casings, maybe the mob doesn't care. There might not even be prints or anything on them."

"Urgh." Sometimes he could be so infuriating. "I know Nikitin worked for them."

"Here we go… How do you *know*?"

She stiffened. "I just do." There was no sense defending her intuition or her instincts; it would be a waste of breath.

"Someone call for me?" It was Richards, Milo trailing behind him.

"Unfortunately," Madison grumbled.

"Way to make me feel special." The ME smiled at her, and she returned the expression.

Their relationship had met with a bit of a rocky patch a bit ago, but at least all seemed to have been forgiven. "I didn't mean it that way…"

"I know, but if people keep turning up dead, I'll never get any sleep."

"Guess that's the job." *Dead bodies, disrespect, and lack of gratitude…*

"Well, I've got to go. Tonight's my shift, and I promised Annabelle I'd be home," Terry said, making eye contact with Madison. "I can call a cab."

Annabelle was his wife, and he was probably referring to his turn for baby duty. Their daughter, Danielle, was nine months old and a fussy sleeper.

"Five minutes, Terry," Madison said.

"We can't solve all this in one night. Be reasonable." He met her gaze and scowled.

He always got cranky when he didn't eat, but then most people did. She would certainly appreciate a bacon cheeseburger about now, but the job came first—not her needs. Not the needs of the living when the dead were counting on her. "Just stay to hear what Richards tells us?"

"Fine."

"I assume the room and areas surrounding the body have been processed and photographed thoroughly?" Richards asked Cynthia, who nodded. He then snapped on a pair of gloves and made his way to the body. "Let's see what I can determine at quick glance. Three gunshot wounds to the torso and neck, likely fired in rapid succession."

They'd have to follow up with the officers and see if any neighbors had heard anything. Her guess would be no, as a call hadn't been made to 911. But she couldn't see the tenants in the building going out of their way to talk to the police. "Don't think anyone heard the shots. The killer must have used a silencer."

"Sam will be able to tell from looking at the slugs," Cynthia interjected. Sam, full name Samantha Reid, worked in the lab and specialized in ballistics.

"Time of death?" she asked Richards.

"Hmm. Based on rigor alone, I'd say within the last twelve to twenty hours."

"That's quite a spread." She'd have loved a more precise window.

"Best I can do until I conduct more tests back at the morgue."

Madison looked at the time on the alarm clock. *10:10 PM.* Next, she looked at her partner, ashamed that even basic math skills escaped her.

"Between two and ten this morning," Terry said without meeting her eye.

"Bet he was killed before the shooting at the train station at seven to prevent him from showing up there. The shooting wasn't a random incident," she affirmed. "It was planned. Terry, you wanted your hard evidence. I believe we have it."

"Looks like it," he admitted.

"Cyn, we need a pic of our shooter as soon as you can get it," Madison told her. "More urgent than ever. Maybe someone in the building will recognize him."

"First thing come sunrise, I promise I'll see what I can do. Even if it takes a hundred hours of watching surveillance video."

Madison nodded. "In the meantime, we need to find out if anyone in this building saw someone around Nikitin's apartment during the hours of two and seven this morning, though probably before that, seeing as the shooter was already at the station by then. But just to cover the bases."

"Something the unies should already be doing," Terry pointed out. "And I really need to go."

"True, and fair enough. I'll take you." The canvassing officers would have been asking about the last twenty-four hours, so that would cover the TOD window. "Once we get the shooter's picture, though, maybe we should come back. Someone might be able to confirm that he hung around. After all, the shooter had to find out where Nikitin lived to kill him here."

"Somewhat risky really," Cynthia interjected. "Anyone in the building could have seen him. Why take him out here, and how did he even know where Nikitin lived?"

"He could have followed him, or the two knew each other?" Madison tossed out a couple of possibilities. "As for why Nikitin was killed in his home, his killer probably didn't want him found right away. He wanted the freedom to do what he had to do this morning."

"*Had to do*," Terry repeated and blew out a deep breath. "I just can't shake all the trouble the shooter went to in order to muddy the investigation."

"He did go to great lengths to cover himself," Madison said. "I'll say it again. This morning's shooting wasn't random. Those women—or at least one of them—was indeed targeted." Her eyes widened. "Shannon. We have to get someone to watch over her immediately. Just in case she was the target and the killer returns to finish the job."

Terry placed the call.

Richards continued with his work, and Cynthia organized bags of evidence she'd collected in her case. Madison listened to her partner. As he spoke, it sank in just how complex this case truly was. Who was the shooter, and what was his motive?

CHAPTER 14

It was just after eleven when Madison pulled into her driveway at home. She'd picked up a bacon cheeseburger from a drive-thru along the way and scarfed it down so quickly her stomach didn't even know what hit it yet. She found Troy and Hershey cozied on the couch in front of a sitcom. Her and Troy's schedules didn't typically allow a lot of time for sitting around, so when it happened, it was treasured.

Hershey padded over, moaning, his entire body quaking with happiness to see her. Troy gave her a huge kiss that made her lightheaded. Not bad when they'd been together for over a year. By this point, previous relationships had lost their magic—not so with this one and she didn't think it would ever happen. Troy certainly knew how to make her swoon, even though she'd done her best to resist him at first. But he was six foot three with an incredible muscular build, including six-pack abs, and she was made of flesh and blood. Turned out he wasn't just gorgeous either, he was also loyal. Win-win.

"Did you get something to eat?" Troy raised his eyebrows. It was no secret that sometimes she let self-care slide. For her, the job always came first.

"Yep." *Just don't ask me what...* She took her coat and shoes off and changed into pajamas—because she could. Not that she'd be in them for long. Before first light, she'd be up and at the police station.

A text came through from Richards to let her know the autopsy on Nikitin was scheduled to take place after those for Ridley and Walker.

"Come, tell me about your day." Troy patted the couch for Madison to sit, but Hershey jumped up, beating her to it. "Hey, Champ, down you go."

"He's all right." She squeezed onto the other end of the couch. "You already know how my day went."

"I know a bit, and I can tell by the hour and that look on your face it wasn't a good one."

"You can say that again. This morning's shooting is looking like it was a targeted hit."

"Oh really? The news is saying something about suspected drug trafficking at Liberty Station."

"That's hit the news?"

"What I just said." The smallest hint of a smile, an expression Troy rarely parted with. But who cared if he didn't smile much when he looked as good as he did *and* was trustworthy?

"Maybe that will get Narcotics' ass in gear."

Hershey got up, turned himself around, and dropped his head in her lap. She stroked his soft, velvety ears. Madison told Troy more details about the shooting. It was a real benefit that he was also with the Stiles PD as the leader of a SWAT team. It certainly came in handy for talking out cases without having to stress much about confidentiality.

"Marsh wasn't aware of anything going on?"

"Nope. We still don't know for sure, but I'd bet there is."

"Don't just make a leap…"

"You sound like Terry now." Troy had always been more prone to do his due diligence first, whereas she tended to jump without thought to landing.

"Maddy, even if drugs are being moved through the train station, it doesn't mean Marsh or others in Narcotics are turning a blind eye."

"I know." She sighed and went on to share what happened to Nikitin, the steps that led her there, and the suspected involvement of the mob. There was a time, in the not-so-distant past, when she would have left those details out of the recap. After all, for most of her life she only trusted herself, but it could also be chalked up to a "rogue cop" mentality when it came to the Russians. But for good reason. Her issues with them were personal. If it wasn't for their existence, her grandfather might still be alive.

His brow pinched with concern. "But you think Marsh or others in the unit are being bought off. To make it worse, the mob is behind this drug-trafficking operation."

"No doubt in my mind about the mob. Now whether Marsh is taking money to look the other way, that I don't know. But I am confident Nikitin was tied to the mob."

"In that case, you really need to watch your steps and your back."

"I will. I promise."

He peered into her eyes, the green of his electric. "I don't need to remind you about Tatiana Ivanova?"

"Nope."

"All right, then." Spoken as if it were all settled.

"And if I don't watch my back, what are you going to do about it?"

"You might be sorry." He got off the couch. She squealed and jumped up.

Too slow, and he caught her, tossed her over his shoulder, and carried her to their bedroom. There he dealt out the "punishment" in advance for not taking his advice.

When they'd finished, they were both heaving for breath and sweating. She moved to her side of the bed. "If that's what happens when I don't watch myself, I need to take chances more often." She laughed as he tickled her sides. She swatted him away, and he let go of her.

In the span of a few seconds of silence, her mind went right back to the investigation and thoughts of Courtney Middleton.

"Someone's thinking too hard over there." Troy's voice cut through her thoughts, and she turned to face him.

He was lying on his side and watching her. Those green eyes were back at it again, piercing into her brain.

"It's just the case," she eventually said.

"The mob involvement?"

"Yes and no." She shouldn't be eager to poke her nose into the Mafia's affairs again, but she'd be lying if she claimed she didn't want to. They deserved to pay for all they did and had done.

"Something's weighing on you."

"Courtney Middleton." She sat up, putting her back against the headboard and pulling the sheets over her chest.

"Who is Courtney?"

"She was a college friend of mine. She disappeared fifteen years ago. As far as anyone knew, she was dead."

"I sense a *but* coming."

She flashed a brief smile. "That's because you're a detective."

"Should just accept that praise, but you're rather easy to read."

"Hey." She batted a hand at him.

"You are, you always will be, and it's one of the things I love about you. I know what I'm getting, even if it scares me," he added with a small grin.

"Very funny." Despite his tease, she warmed at the sincerity of his words. So many people found her inability to conceal her feelings a weakness. She'd finally found a man who appreciated that about her. "One of the victims from this morning was Morgan Walker. I'm quite sure she is who I knew as Courtney Middleton."

He shuffled to a sitting position. "Some people look alike."

"No, it's more than that."

"If you really think this woman is your college friend, you should take yourself off the case."

"I can manage my feelings. There's no conflict of interest."

"Thought we just talked about you and your feelings…"

"Believe me or don't, but I can handle this case."

"Have you told Winston?"

"No, and before you get on me, it's not a proven fact yet. It's just my gut telling me Morgan is Courtney."

"Then listen to it." Tossed out there, nonchalant, like it was a no-brainer.

She touched his arm and brushed a hand to his cheek. "One of the many reasons I love you."

He leaned in and kissed her. She was the first to draw back.

"Stop distracting me, would you?"

"Sorry. Not sorry." He laughed.

A most lovely sound.

"I am sorry about the loss of your friend," he said with seriousness.

"Thank you, but it's not like I've been a part of her life for the last fifteen years. I thought she was long dead." Her friend showing up was unsettling, probably made even worse because she had been murdered—shot in cold blood. And now the evidence was pointing toward a planned killing. *Was Courtney the shooter's target?* She suspected that question would continue to bounce around her head until she had the answer. "Terry thinks I'm seeing what I want or making it up. But whatever."

"Tell me the story. What happened to her?"

Madison told him about the bar and Courtney's assurance she'd be fine.

"And not a word all these years? Yeah, I can understand why it would be a shock to find her dead this morning. And under an assumed name."

"Here in Stiles, no less. We went to the University of Stiles together, but apparently, she met her husband in Comsey Park."

"Sounds to me like you need some answers, like what brought her back to Stiles and when. And why she changed her name."

"That's just the tip of it. And did either of those things result in her getting gunned down to…day?" She yawned in the middle of the last word.

Troy stroked her short hair. "Maybe it's time to get some rest."

"How am I supposed to sleep?"

"You lie down, close your eyes…"

She nudged him in the shoulder. "Brat."

He was smiling, but it didn't last long. "You need your sleep. You're no good to the case or your friend if you're dragging yourself around like a zombie."

His comment took her back to Richards's remark about never sleeping. "That's my normal state. How I function." *The job…*

"Uh-huh. Try something new. Take care of yourself." He tapped a kiss on her forehead and rolled back over to his side of the bed. He was breathing deeply within seconds. She was quite sure he was already dreaming.

She got up and put on her pajamas again, not a fan of sleeping nude, and got back into bed, tucking herself fully under the covers. She stared at the ceiling and listened to both Troy and Hershey snoring. Unbelievable. She hugged the edges of her pillow around her ears, hoping to muffle out the noise. Even if it worked, she was sure she'd still be left staring at the ceiling. Her mind was awake, and it longed for answers.

Tomorrow she'd be sure to get some.

CHAPTER 15

Madison opened her eyes and lay there with her hand fisted against her heart. The dream she'd just had took her back to the Roadhouse Bar and Courtney. It had been great being with her friend again, bathing in the warmth of her laughter and taking delight in her sense of humor.

Courtney had told her, "I'll be fine," and touched her arm to stamp home the reassurance.

Madison responded with, "You're sure?" Then she glanced at the older man who had stolen her friend's attention.

Courtney was smiling. "Absolutely."

That was when Madison woke up. No chance to warn her friend or ask her anything. The dream was just a replay of what had happened in real life. The joy at seeing Courtney again quickly faded and was replaced with heartache.

Madison pulled herself from bed, feeling much like the zombie that Troy had mentioned last night. He had already left for work, and she had just enough time to take care of the morning rituals before heading out the door. Bathroom, shower, care for Hershey.

She was at her desk by eight, sucking back a coffee she'd picked up on the way to the station. The bagel she bought was sitting on its wrapper, only missing a few finger swipes of cream cheese—all her stomach could handle.

Terry wasn't in yet but should be any minute. She had pulled all the backgrounds on the husbands of the victims so they'd be ready to go as soon as Terry arrived. She was most interested in Shane Walker, but he, just like the rest, didn't have a police record. If one of these men had killed their wives, it would be their first criminal act. Without a picture of the shooter's face, it was possible one of them were hidden behind the hoodie. Then there was the possibility they were looking for an unknown third party. Regardless, it was obvious the shooter didn't have an aversion to killing, even if that meant taking out innocent people to cover his tracks. That, though, could be the desperate act of an unhappy spouse, lover…whomever. It was also possible that the shooter had been a hired gun.

Grr! Too many uncertainties. Just like where was he now, and where was the girl? Also, how did she tie into the shooting at the train station—or did she? It looked to Madison like she'd been used to muddy the investigation.

She had just finished reading the background on Russell Brennan, the last husband on her list, when Terry walked in holding a humongous coffee.

"Morning," he mumbled and pressed the cup to his lips.

"Rough night?" Rhetorical. He was barely coherent and had dark shadows under his eyes.

He grumbled something, and she guessed he was telling her off under his breath in his own PG-fashion.

"Knight, in my office. Now." It was Sergeant Winston bellowing from down the hall.

She rolled her eyes and got up. "Let's go."

"Hey, he didn't call my name. Just yours."

"What happened to us being partners and you having my back?"

"It engages when I've finished this." He held up his coffee.

"Fine. But I'm going to remember this." She pointed a finger at Terry and went to Winston's office. She ducked her head inside. "What's up?"

"Come in, and close the door."

So much for a casual and fleeting meeting. She did as he requested and sat across from his desk. As usual, it was covered with stacks of paper that never seemed to dwindle in height. She crossed her legs and leaned forward to give him the impression she was open to communication. Even if she'd rather be anywhere else.

"This came to my attention." He handed her a newspaper. "First headline."

She looked down. "Shooting at Liberty Station has Stiles PD Digging into Drug Operation." She let go of the paper over his desk, and it slapped down to its final resting place. She didn't know where the journalist had gotten a whiff of this, but she didn't really care either.

"That's it? You're just going to toss it aside?" Winston picked up the paper. "Did you talk to this reporter? Tell him your suspicions?"

"Nope. I'm dead bodies, not drugs." A cold way of putting things into perspective, but she wanted to nail home her point.

"Huh. Would have figured differently. I got a complaint…" He went rummaging through the papers on his desk. "From Officers Galloway and Morris. They are saying you accused them of looking the other way while drugs were trafficked through the train station."

She said nothing.

"Is that true?" he barked.

"I asked if they were aware of it, that's all. How they took it from there is on them."

"Huh." He clenched his jaw. "You've always had a problem with diplomacy."

She moved to get up, not about to sit there any longer for a verbal lashing.

"Don't go anywhere." Winston took a deep breath, and his cheeks turned bright red. "Vlas Nikitin."

"What about him?"

"Tell me what you know."

She shoved back into the chair. He hadn't seemed too interested in the entire breakdown last night when he'd popped on scene for all of five minutes. She had been relieved then, but it was obviously premature. "Quite sure he has connections to the Russian mob." *Might as well really raise his blood pressure...*

"Dear Lord." Winston huffed and looked at the ceiling, back to her. "What is it with you and them? You see them everywhere."

They are *everywhere...* She clamped her mouth shut. Anything she had to say now would come out heated with anger. Holding back was something she was working on, though she was not always successful at pulling it off.

"Nothing? You're just going to sit there and say noth—"

"I follow where the evidence in a case takes me. It led to Nikitin." The words erupted out of her.

"And how did you know where to find him? I never got that much from you last night." He raised his brows, deep creases lining his forehead.

You didn't exactly hang around that long! "I had seen him before. Back when I was staking out Club Sophisticated."

He sat back. Frowned. He'd know that time period coincided with her exposing the corrupt cops and the current IA investigations.

"Listen, I'm not asking for clearance to go knock on the mob's door yet—"

"Damn right you're not!" He scowled. "Nor would I approve that. Just stay away from them, you hear me?" He stared her down.

"Sure."

"You can be so infuriating, Knight. Just promise that you'll keep me in the loop on your steps in the investigation."

The same old conversation they had all the time. "Would you prefer we gab or that I solve cases and lock up the bad guys?"

"Some detectives manage to do both," he pushed back. "Stanford, Sovereign, the others in the department."

"Good for them." She wasn't going to say anything to sully their reputations by pointing out how much higher her close rates were than theirs. Lou Stanford was Cynthia's husband of two months, and Toby Sovereign was her ex-fiancé.

"Where are we standing with this investigation? The chief wants answers."

Chief Andrea Fletcher was Troy's sister. "She knows how to reach me," Madison said.

"Urgh. Right, all in the family, but there is a command structure. She recognizes it. Why can't you?"

"Is there anything else?" Her earlobes were hot. This entire meeting felt like it was called just so he could berate her, and she had better things to do. Like her job.

"Answer my question." He leaned forward and clasped his hands on the desk.

"Fine. Evidence is pointing me toward believing the shooting was planned—by whom or why, I don't know yet. But the investigation has also revealed the real likelihood that there is a drug-trafficking operation working through the train station." She paused when he grunted, then picked back up. "I'll know more once the lab has had a chance to examine the burner phones collected from Nikitin's apartment. Also there was a trace of meth found there."

"Trace? Then he must be dealing," he said sarcastically. "And then there's that girl with the backpack…"

"Yes, and we're doing what we can to find her. She is a material eyewitness." She wasn't going to waste her breath telling Winston that in addition to being an eyewitness, the girl was probably in danger. He'd accuse her of being irrational or making that call based purely on emotion.

"And today's plans?"

"Attending the autopsies, speaking with Shannon Brennan, who should be available to talk to us now… Then a visit to each of the victims' husbands." They had yet to meet Russell Brennan, as officers had notified him of his wife's condition, but she wasn't getting into every teeny detail with Winston. She gave him a pressed smile, fake as they come.

"All right. Sounds like we're getting somewhere."

Spoken as if we've done nothing but sit on our hands and the case is weeks old...

"You can go. But keep me posted." He dismissed her with a sweep of his hand.

She didn't hesitate and left immediately. She swung by her desk and grabbed her coat. "Let's go," she said to Terry while she was on the move.

"Great. Now you're in a mood." He stood and put on his jacket.

"Takes one to know one."

"Hardly got any sleep last night."

At least he didn't go so far as to actually blame his child, even if the onus was implied. Madison had little tolerance for how some parents had a rash of excuses all built on their kids and how hard it was to be a mother or father. And maybe it was, but don't put the entire burden on the kids. "I'm sorry to hear that. Really I am." She was being sincere, but she smirked.

"You're only sorry because you have to put up with me."

"Somewhat. Yeah. No, just joking. We'll get through this day one step at a time."

"Can the first one be a stop at Starbucks?"

To do that, she'd have to pass the morgue, which was now housed in a building only a short drive from the police station.

"Don't even think of saying no," he added.

"Sure. Absolutely."

"Okay then. We might get along today after all."

"Hope so, because we have a killer to catch, and I could use your help."

"What?" He stopped walking. "Whoa. Miss Independent wants my help? Mark it on the calendar."

"Could you bench the sarcasm?"

He shrugged. "Fine, but you admitting that you need help..."

"Terry. Let's not make a deal of it." She gestured for him to start walking, but she was the first to resume doing so.

He caught up quickly. Tired or not, she bet he ran his miles on his treadmill this morning. Some people made her sick. Running was her least favorite exercise. Why would anyone choose to do so of their own free will?

"What if I want to…you know, make a deal of it?" he asked.

"Then forget shotgun. You'll be riding in the trunk."

CHAPTER 16

Madison and Terry were five minutes early for the autopsy, a small miracle given the line at Starbucks.

"You just made it," Richards said. "I was getting ready to lock the door."

It wouldn't be the first time she'd barely made it on time. She walked farther into the morgue, and her insides were turning to ice despite the warm drink in her hand. Richards allowed food and drink in the room as long as whoever was consuming it kept a healthy distance from the bodies. And she had no intention of getting too close.

Her gaze traveled over three autopsy tables, their occupants all draped with white sheets except for their feet that hung out at the bottom. Shannon Brennan had no idea how lucky she was to be alive.

Tremors ran through Madison's body just trying to guess which one held Morgan Walker. When she saw her face today, would she still think Morgan had been her friend Courtney Middleton?

As she got closer, she ruled out the table to the far right. Those feet belonged to a man. That left one of the other two. "Who are we starting with?"

"I'll work left to right." Richards pulled back the sheet and revealed Dana Ridley. Her body had been cleaned and prepped—the external examination already conducted. "The decedent Dana Ridley, thirty-eight years old. She was killed by a gunshot to the heart. Death would have been immediate."

One tiny blessing.

"As I suspected on scene, Ridley was expecting."

Madison laid a hand on her stomach, thinking once again about her unborn child—the one that never got a taste of life outside the womb. All due to the Mafia, corrupt cops, and her own refusal to rest after the accident. Or a combination of all three? The doctor told her it might be none of those things but blaming someone else, even herself, felt better than no explanation at all.

"The pregnancy came as a surprise to the husband," Terry interjected.

"Sounds scandalous."

Madison stiffened. "Could be motive in there somewhere." Something she really had zero tolerance for was disloyalty. She'd been hurt by it in the past, and that was probably why she tended to sweep a brush of judgment over all who strayed. She turned to Terry. "We'll need to take a closer look at Wayne Ridley. He might have acted like he had no idea about Dana's pregnancy, but it could have been just that—an act. Maybe he did know about the baby *and* her affair…"

Terry nodded. "Jealousy. Motive old as time."

She put her attention back on Richards. "What else do you have for us? Caliber confirmed?"

"Yes. Nine mil. The fragments will be collected and sent to the lab for ballistics testing."

"Anything else?" she asked.

"Nothing else external to share. Moving on…" He covered Dana Ridley again and went to the second slab. She held her breath, tried to prepare her mind to focus, to be objective…

Richards pulled back the sheet.

If this wasn't Courtney Middleton, Madison truly was seeing a ghost. Her legs buckled, and she almost upset her cappuccino.

Terry reached out. "You all right there?"

She held up her free hand. "I'm fine." She cleared her throat. "Continue, please," she said to Richards.

He hesitated and kept his gaze on her. Eventually, he said, "Morgan Walker, thirty-six."

Same age as me... Just another thing that made it possible Morgan was Courtney. Madison swallowed roughly and brought her mouth to the lip of her cup.

Richards pressed a gloved fingertip to one of the wounds. "She was shot in the chest. The bullet pierced her lung, causing it to collapse. She would have taken a little more time to die than the other victim but wouldn't have suffered too long."

Victim... How she hated assigning the label at the best of times, always giving preference to names. This time, though, it was even worse. Tears pricked her eyes, but she quickly blinked them away. She hadn't broken down in the morgue before, and she wasn't about to now. But seeing the woman lying there lifeless, nothing but a shell, was almost too much. She had to rein herself in and detach emotionally. She cleared her throat.

Richards continued. "Again, whatever I can pull from her will be forwarded to the lab."

Madison looked at the dead woman again. She was more certain than ever—Morgan Walker was Courtney Middleton. But if she said as much to Richards, it would most certainly get back to Winston, and she'd be off the investigation. Surely, there had to be some means she could use to confirm identity without involving him. DNA would be indisputable, but how to get the exemplars? She believed where there was a will, there was a way. What that was in this case, she just didn't know yet.

Cynthia had Morgan's purse in evidence. Maybe Madison could get a lipstick tube from which to extract a DNA sample, but where would she get something to compare it to? But, no, she couldn't go that route with the lipstick. It could still end up getting back to Winston and land her friend in trouble. She had to think of another way.

Richards put the sheet back over Walker and moved down the line to the table with Vlas Nikitin. His body had been cleaned and prepped for autopsy as well. He looked so young and innocent in death, even with those dragon tattoos. She felt a pinch of sadness for him, but it got buried beneath her judgments. The mob, drug trafficking. Those lifestyle choices didn't promise a long life, and he would have known what he was getting himself into.

"This victim was shot with nine mil rounds," Richards said, his words cutting through her thoughts. "The fatal shot entered his throat and traveled to the back of his neck, where it severed his head from his spinal cord. He would have been paralyzed and incapacitated immediately, and death likely came swiftly. Though he might have been aware for a little while."

Madison tried to squeeze out how horrifying that would be from her mind. "Have you narrowed down time of death yet?"

Richards nodded. "I'm going to adjust my original estimate slightly. Somewhere between three and six AM."

Madison faced Terry. "This definitely could be the shooter from the train station. He takes out Nikitin and then proceeds to Liberty Station." She held his gaze, daring him to contest her, but he nodded. Why was it whenever she was expecting a fight, he just let it go? No one could say he was predictable unless it was to say he was *unpredictable*. She continued. "We need to find this guy before more people end up in the morgue." Her mind skipped to the girl with the backpack—possibly on the run, and all alone without police protection. How long could she outrun the shooter and/or the mob? They were only twenty-four hours into the investigation, and Madison felt like she was trudging uphill.

Richards replaced the sheet over Nikitin and returned to Ridley. He worked through the autopsies one by one, and Madison and Terry hung around for a while, but nothing else useful to their investigation came up. They saw themselves out, asking Richards to keep them informed if he found anything they should know.

In the parking lot, Madison called Cynthia.

"Why am I not surprised you're calling?" Cynthia's smile traveled over the line.

"You just know me. Listen, I need some answers from you."

"Of course you do. I mean why else would you be calling? Just to shoot the shit? I know you far better than that. It's all about getting to the point."

Madison couldn't help but smile at that. Her friend had her pegged perfectly. "Have you looked at Nikitin's burner phones?" She wanted more proof about the kind of person he had been. The innocent image in the morgue wasn't how she'd envisioned him in life—at all. Nor did it balance with his blemished police record.

"Just about to do that now. Wish me luck."

"Can you look at them while I hold the line?" She'd been patient enough, hadn't she? It was going on noon…

"How about I call you back when I have something to tell you?"

Madison pressed her lips together before she could say something she'd regret. She had no right to be pushy. Madison wasn't her boss, and Cynthia was already overworked and overstretched. There was no need to add more pressure to her friend. "Okay. Call me the second you get something— or nothing. Just call. Oh, and don't forget to keep me updated on the video. We really need a picture of the shooter. You did say you'd do your best to get that this morning." *Just a gentle nudge…* "And the girl too." It was surprising how long it was taking to get that in her hands.

"Madison," Cynthia said, her voice firm and authoritative and tinged with exasperation. "I know what I'm doing, and I know what you're after. Once I have it, I'll forward it along. Just give me time to work."

Terry was watching Madison, his eyes holding judgment, and it had her feeling a bit self-conscious. Maybe she was being a little pushy.

"Thanks, Cyn," Madison said.

"Don't thank me yet." With that, Cynthia hung up, but Madison was rattled by the lack of confidence in her friend's voice. Or was Madison reading too much into the response?

Madison held up her phone. "Cynthia will get back to us as soon as she has something."

"Imagine that." Terry laughed.

She shook her head, and they got in the car and decided their next stop would be Shannon Brennan at Stiles General. They hadn't heard any more about her, so that was likely good news. She was still alive. At least for now.

CHAPTER 17

Madison and Terry were directed to Shannon Brennan's private room at the hospital. A police officer stood guard at the door.

"Anyone come by to see her?" Madison asked him.

"No, ma'am. Well, only her husband, but he has clearance."

Ma'am… She cringed at that address, feeling much older than thirty-six. "It's *Detective*. Anyway, continue to keep an eye out for anything or anyone suspicious."

"Absolutely, ma—uh, Detective."

They walked into the room, and Terry leaned in toward her ear.

"You just couldn't let it go, could you?"

Shannon Brennan had her eyes shut but either sensed their presence or heard their footsteps. She opened them a sliver, squinting under the glare of the fluorescent lights.

Madison held up her badge then tucked it away, not even sure if Shannon would be able to make it out. The woman wiped at her eyes and then opened them fully.

"Shannon Brennan, we're Detectives Knight and Grant with the Stiles PD. We'd like to ask you a few questions about yesterday."

Shannon struggled to sit up straighter, and Terry helped her with the incline of the bed. Tubes fed into her, connecting her to two machines. One was likely a saline solution to keep her hydrated and her sugars up, and the other probably offered a morphine drip.

Madison's gaze hooked on the blood pressure and heart rate monitor with its colored lines and constant readouts. It was hard to believe that just a month ago she'd been tethered to one of these herself. An overwhelming sadness was starting to slink into her bones, but now wasn't the time to surrender to the emotion. In fact, no time was a good time.

"Please tell us the events that led up to the shooting," Madison said. "You were in line for coffee and then...?"

"Wow, it's such a blur." Shannon rubbed her forehead. "It's just so overwhelming, but at the same time it feels like... I don't know, like a dream? Definitely surreal. But I am lying in a hospital bed."

Shock was understandable, as was a lapse in memory due to the trauma. After Madison had been struck and landed in the hospital, waking up days later, she felt the same way. At least Shannon hadn't lost days of her life, only hours.

"Just do your best to tell us what you remember," Terry told her when Madison didn't respond.

Shannon twisted the sheets in her hands and didn't look at him or Madison for several seconds. "I was just getting a coffee. I was about to board the train to Braybury that left at seven thirty. I had plenty of time too." She shook her head, and her breathing sped up, her chest rising and falling more rapidly. The machine kicked up the digits on the screen. Shannon squeezed her eyes shut briefly. "This girl came along, and she stole an apple and an orange juice, and just kept walking. Me and these other women in line started talking about what we just saw. I mean, we were in shock. Who does that?" She shook her head in disgust at her own question. "It was so brazen."

Madison found it interesting that for regularly being in the train station Shannon had never crossed paths with the girl before. "So you never saw this girl before, either in the station or stealing from Just Beans in the past?"

"Not that I ever noticed."

She supposed that was possible and maybe the girl usually swiped from the kiosk later in the day. But while on thoughts of the girl, it had Madison wondering again why a drug runner would risk drawing attention to herself. Was it a silent cry for help?

Shannon continued. "We were trying to get the attention of the ladies behind the counter to let them know what this girl did. Next thing I know, this guy is in our faces, all hopped up. He says he's a cop and that we should all mind our own business. But then this one woman in line, she wanted to be a hero, and she's like, 'You're not a cop.' She demanded to see his badge. He reached into his pocket and came out with a gun." Her eyes filled with tears, and she sniffled. "That's when he started shooting." She plucked a tissue from a box on the side table and dabbed at her face.

"You suffered a traumatic experience," Terry empathized. "You have every reason to be upset. But we need to know absolutely everything you do, to help us find the shooter and hold him accountable."

Her partner always had excelled at playing good cop; her, not so much. Sometimes she got lucky with pulling it off, but it took loads of effort. "Did you get a good look at his face?"

She bunched the used tissue in her hand and rubbed her temple. "It was just so shocking."

"As my partner said, we need to know what you do," she said firmly. "Anything, no matter how small it might seem, could help."

"Do you really think I'm in danger?" Shannon countered. "You have an officer posted at my door…"

"We do, and that should give you even more reason to tell us everything you know." Madison was one second from tapping a foot.

"All right. I do remember he was wearing a hoodie. Black. Also he had on blue jeans. I don't know. Is any of this helping you?"

Madison resisted the urge to tell her they got that much off the security video. If she got smart with Shannon, it could cause her to shut up. They had to find out if the woman knew something they didn't. "Just stick with that. What else? Did he have an accent?"

"I didn't notice an accent. So he's probably from around here somewhere."

"Any tattoos or birthmarks, skin imperfections?" Madison asked.

"Actually, I think he had a little cherry birthmark right here…" She put her fingertips to the base of her throat.

The man had been wearing the hoodie so that it shadowed his face. Had his neck been visible? She supposed it was possible. Still, she challenged Shannon. "And you could see that even though he was wearing a hoodie?"

Shannon frowned, nodded. "He didn't have it zipped tight to his chin. I saw the birthmark when he was firing the gun."

So when she was being shot at, she took the time to notice something like a birthmark? It sounded questionable, but time had a way of slowing down during such tragic events. *Moving on…* "What can you tell us about the women who were in line with you? Have you ever seen them before yesterday?"

"They looked somewhat familiar. I think maybe they take the same train I do."

"So you never met them? Knew their names?"

"No."

She handed Shannon her business card. "We appreciate your cooperation. We might need to come back and ask you more questions. In the meantime, do you know where we would have the best chance of reaching your husband?"

"My husband?" She shifted her position and grimaced as pain must have fired through her. "Why would you want to talk to him?"

"Just being thorough," Madison said dryly.

"Do you think he has something to do with what happened?"

"Why don't you leave us to do our jobs?" She plastered on a tight smile. "Where could we find your husband, Ms. Brennan?"

"He's probably at home. He was here a lot of the night, and I told him to go get some sleep."

Now, was that so hard?

"Take care," Terry said as they left the room.

"Does it get exhausting being so nice all the time?" Madison raised her eyebrows.

"Why don't you try it and let me know?"

"Hardy-har." She smiled, but his comment hurt. She was a nice person; it just didn't manifest in the form of kissing up or tiptoeing around people. And while Shannon Brennan may very well just be a victim like the other two women, there was one very distinct difference. She was alive. Was that luck, or was there more to it? Sometimes Madison wished she was a little less suspicious of people.

CHAPTER 18

Shannon and her husband, Russell Brennan, lived in a middle-income neighborhood where the houses were spacious, but they all looked alike. Garage doors took up a good chunk of the front faces, leaving the structures begging for better curb appeal.

Madison rang the doorbell, and footsteps padded toward them within seconds. The door cracked open, and a man in his late thirties, handsome and sporting a few days of whisker growth, greeted them. No need to ask his identity, as he closely resembled his driver's license photo. For someone who was sent home to get sleep, Madison would say he had no problem doing just that—he looked rested. Considering that his wife was in the hospital recovering from being shot, that was suspicious.

Russell eyed them with curiosity and hooked a brow. "Yes?"

Madison and Terry took out their badges, confirmed his identity, and she made the formal introductions. She added, "We're the detectives investigating the shooting that took place yesterday. We would like to come in and ask a few questions."

"Ah, sure."

They stepped inside to a cramped entryway about five foot square. There was a closet to the left and a staircase leading to the second story on the right.

"Did you find who was responsible?" Russell asked.

"Not yet. Do you have a place where we could sit?" Madison peered through a doorway past the closet. "Maybe in here?" She flicked a finger toward the living room.

"That's fine." He led the way and dropped onto the couch.

Madison and Terry sat in a couple of chairs that bookended the couch. No hair tumbleweeds on the cushions or any sign the Brennans had a pet.

"You haven't found this guy, and you've got a cop posted on her hospital room. Is my wife still in danger?"

"We believe she may be," Madison said. "What is your relationship like with your wife, Mr. Brennan?" They had a lot on their list today, and it was best to get right to the point. If he was to be considered a suspect, then it was better to know now and get on with things.

"How was… my…" He was stuttering, and his discomfort wasn't a pretty sight.

"I'm going to guess that you two had your problems. Is that correct?" She could feel her partner staring at her— him and his apprehension about offending anyone. But sometimes insults could jolt people into talking on impulse. That was when the truth came out.

Russell looked at Terry. "She really doesn't beat around the bush, does she?"

"No need to get upset, Mr. Brennan. It's just a question," she said.

He crossed his legs and clasped his hands on his knee. "What I don't understand is what my marriage has to do with what happened. It was some random shooting by a drug dealer, was it not?"

"And what makes you assume that?" Madison asked.

"Between what Shannon's told me and what the news is saying… But then you do have her hospital room guarded. Do you think there was more to what happened? That it wasn't random?"

"We're still investigating," Terry said, beating her to a response.

"Huh. Then it isn't in my head. You are looking at me as a suspect."

Madison jutted out her chin. "We're looking at everyone who had a relationship or connection to the victims."

"Good. But don't look at me! The man who shot my wife and killed those other women is off doing who knows what. Isn't it your job to catch this guy? And yet you're here interrogating me like I had something to do with all this." His cheeks were growing a brighter red with every word he spoke.

"Did you?" She fired off the question quickly.

"No!" he snapped.

"All right, then you should have no problem telling us where you were yesterday at seven AM," she said.

"I was here."

"Can anyone else confirm that?"

"Ask Shannon."

"She wasn't here, so that doesn't work."

"I don't know what to say, but I didn't shoot her and anyone else."

Madison would let it sit for now, and they didn't have any proof against the guy. He did get heated with his defense, though. "All right."

Russell flailed his arms in the air as if to say, *Finally!*

"Now, we still need you to tell us what your marriage was like," she stated.

He hefted a deep breath. "You want to know… Okay, well, it wasn't all a bed of roses. We had our problems, our disagreements, but we worked through them."

His admission felt far more credible and authentic than if he'd said they were like honeymooners. Every couple had their ups and downs, given time.

"What sort of problems and disagreements?" Terry asked.

"Nothing big. What movie to watch, where to go for dinner, coming to an agreement on what couch to buy."

"There's never been anything more serious that has come up, such as an affair?" What he had shared with them didn't exactly live up to his "wasn't all a bed of roses." It was very minor stuff.

"No. But, actually, I think the biggest argument we had was about moving from Braybury to Stiles."

Terry nodded. "You were against it?"

"Yeah, I had to leave my good-paying job and come here where the market isn't that great for a graphic designer."

He could have commuted too, but she asked, "Why did she want to move here when she works in Braybury?"

"She said she wanted to live in a smaller town. And now she has to take the train into the city every day. Only reason I caved was because she makes more money than me, and if she was good with making the commute, who was I to argue?"

"But if you could turn back the clock, you would?" She wasn't getting the impression that the marriage was particularly a warm one, but had Russell Brennan shot at his wife and killed the other women and Nikitin? Being unemployed he would conceivably have time on his hands to plan the shooting.

"You think?" he pushed out, drenched in sarcasm. "My mind's going numb trying to look for work."

"When did you move here?" Terry asked.

"About eight months ago."

"Your wife, she works for Spark Media, right?" she said.

"Yeah. They're an ad firm."

As they'd discovered from a quick internet search. So Shannon wasn't a lawyer like the two dead women, but did that have any relevance to the investigation? "What does your wife do for them?"

"Ad exec. She attracts new clients by proposing different marketing strategies."

"All right. Well, thank you for your cooperation today, Mr. Brennan. We may be in touch again with more questions. In the meantime, I'm going to give you my card. If you think of anything else you'd like to tell me, call any time of day."

"You say that like I'm hiding something from you," he seethed.

She got up and pressed her card into his palm. "Not at all." There was this niggling in the back of her brain about Russell's innocence, but if he'd set out to kill his wife, why wasn't she dead? Surely, Madison's suspicions had her skepticism working overtime. Regardless, they had to do their due diligence. When she and Terry were at the door, about to leave, she added, "We will be requesting your financials."

He blanched. "What for?"

"Just procedure, Mr. Brennan," she said stiffly.

"Well, if you come at me again, I'll be calling a lawyer."

"You absolutely have that right."

She and Terry stepped outside, and Russell slammed the door so hard the front porch vibrated under her feet.

"You could have gone a little softer in there. Maybe you wouldn't have pushed him to lawyer up."

Another difference between her and Terry—lawyers didn't scare her. In fact, she used to date one. "I just get a bad feeling about the guy. I think there's a lot more going on in that marriage than he told us."

"Something big enough to have him fire on his wife and kill two other people he didn't even know?"

"Huh." She spun around and banged on the front door.

It swung open. "I told you I'll be calling my lawyer."

She held up a hand. "Just one more question... Actually, I want to show you two pictures." She brought up photos of Dana Ridley and Morgan Walker on her phone and, in turn, asked him if he recognized either woman.

"No, I don't," he said through clenched teeth.

"Have you ever heard your wife mention the names Dana Ridley or Morgan Walker?"

"No. Now please leave my property!" He slammed the door again, and Madison made her way to the sidewalk where Terry was standing.

He gestured toward the house. "What was that all about?"

"It was what you said—that he didn't know the other women. We hadn't actually asked him about it specifically. As it turns out, he didn't."

"Rules the guy out to me."

"I'm not rushing there. And he has no alibi."

"Okay, if Russell Brennan is behind the shooting in one way or another, why isn't Shannon dead?"

A few seconds ticked by.

"There you go," Terry declared. "He's off our suspect list."

"Come on, Terry, you know I'm not that quick to let go. But I am moving on…for now."

"Hallelujah."

She was tempted to punch his shoulder, but it was too public here. Terry really was the brother she didn't have. He called her out and challenged her. He plain drove her crazy. What more could she ask for in a partner?

CHAPTER 19

Madison was just pulling in front of the Ridley house when her phone rang. Caller ID told her it was Cynthia. She parked the car at the curb and answered. "Tell me you've got something for me."

"Actually I thought I'd just call and say, 'Hey, how you doin'?' Because we have all the time in the world for idle chitchat." Cynthia laughed.

"Cut that out." Madison was smiling and put Cynthia on speaker. "Terry's here too."

"Hey, Terry. Going to start from the top. Nikitin was involved with something. We have the trace of meth found in his apartment, and while I can't say for sure he was trafficking drugs, there were text messages on the burner phones that were rather cryptic. Basically they seem to be confirming different drops."

"Did you track the numbers?" Madison asked.

"Since I wasn't born yesterday, yes, I did. Didn't lead me anywhere. Probably other burner phones."

Madison smacked the wheel with the heel of her palm. Was it too much to hope for a true break in this case before more people turned up dead?

Cynthia went on. "There were a couple other numbers in the call history of the phone—one I wasn't able to track and another one."

A sliver of hope wormed through Madison. "You were able to trace one?"

"Yes and no. One of those numbers belonged to an incoming call at ten AM Monday morning, which went unanswered..."

"Yes, because Nikitin was dead."

"Right. Well, I was able to track the number, and it pinged in the warehouse district. Now, though, it's off the grid."

"Well, I know where the warehouse district is..." And for good reason, as the Russians used to run one of their business fronts there, a place called Homeland Logistics. The area ran along the lakeshore.

"Let's not dwell on why."

Madison had almost lost her life at Homeland Logistics to two top Mafia enforcers, and if it hadn't been for Terry's suspicions leading him there and the efforts of SWAT, she'd probably have died. "When did you track the phone?"

"Just five minutes ago."

And the signal was gone already! Still five minutes might as well be an eternity considering they didn't know who to look for on the other end either.

Cynthia continued. "Now here's some news I know you'll be interested in. I've had Mark working through the Liberty Station video, and he found where that girl with the backpack normally enters the station. Now he's also watched to see what times and days Nikitin was posted near Just Beans. It always seems to coincide with trains that were destined for Toronto, Canada."

Stiles was located in the northern United States, so the leap across the border wouldn't have been a far one, and traveling by train may have been less risky than driving there. "They are running meth out of the country..." She looked at Terry, and he nodded.

"He was also there when trains arrived back from Canada," Cynthia added.

This was an interesting discovery, but there were other things Madison wanted. "Send over the location where the girl usually accesses the station. I'd like to try to retrace her steps. Also, could you send the girl's photo over?" Madison thought she'd been patient enough on that front.

"As soon as I hang up."

"Ah, before you go, any luck getting a clear image of the shooter's face?" Madison felt she'd given Cynthia and her people plenty of time to find one.

"She always has to push for more, doesn't she?" Cynthia was obviously addressing Terry with that statement. Madison turned to him, and he was wise enough not to respond. Cynthia said, "In answer to your question, still working on it. Ciao." And with that, she was gone.

"A hit and run," Madison mumbled as she'd been hoping for more.

"You realize how much footage needs to be watched and analyzed to even see if they can get a shot of his face?"

"Suppose you're right…" Madison's phone pinged with a message, and a quick check confirmed it was Cynthia with the photo of the girl and the entrance she normally used. Madison fired off the photo to Marsh, then turned the car off and got out. The Ridley driveway was full of cars. "Wayne must have family and friends here with him."

"And yet you accuse me of speaking the obvious."

She narrowed her eyes at him.

"I can't even imagine losing Annabelle or…Danny."

"Now imagine losing Annabelle, only to find out that she was pregnant with another man's baby." Madison truly felt for Wayne Ridley, but she couldn't lose her objectivity.

"God, the guy must be wrecked."

"Yep, but we need to keep an open mind."

"Just don't go as hard on him as you did Russell Brennan. Otherwise, it might be best you stay in the car."

"I'll be nicer. All I can promise." Honestly, she'd be whatever the situation called for. After all, Wayne Ridley's potential motive couldn't be ignored. He very well could have found out about Dana's pregnancy and/or affair and took matters into his own hands.

"Even that would be an improvement," Terry said. "I swear Russell Brennan expected you to pull out cuffs any second."

"I wasn't *that* bad."

"Yeah, you were."

They reached the door and didn't need to knock or ring the bell. It opened wide, and a woman with gray hair pulled into a soft bun was standing there. Madison would peg her as somewhere in her sixties and guessed her to be Wayne's mother, given the shape of her chin, which looked a lot like his. "Yes?" the woman said.

Madison flashed her badge. "Detectives from Stiles PD to speak with Wayne Ridley." She bit back the urge to say *ma'am*, considering it might not be a welcome address at any age.

"Is this really necessary right now? He's been through an awful lot."

"Exactly why we need to speak with him again. We have some questions pertaining to our investigation into the shooting." Madison smiled softly at the woman.

The woman's eyes roved over Madison, then Terry. "All right, but please don't stay long." She let them inside and told them she was Karen Ridley, Wayne's mother.

There were eight people in the house. No young children, but men and women around Wayne's age, so either friends and siblings or a mixture of both. There was also one silver-haired gentleman, who Madison surmised went with Karen Ridley.

"I'll get Wayne," Karen said and padded down the hall.

Shortly after, Wayne was walking toward them. "Detectives? Did you find who did this to Dana?" His eyes were bloodshot, and his face pale.

Madison didn't sense anger, just raw grief, and it had her heart aching at the sight of him. But she had to keep perspective. "Unfortunately, not yet, but we're working the case in earnest. Is there somewhere private we could talk?" She flicked a glance toward the side room that was full of his friends and family.

He led them to a small office with a desk, computer, bookshelf, and a loveseat. He gestured to the latter as he dropped into the chair behind the desk.

"This might seem a little insensitive, but how was your marriage to Dana?" Madison hadn't intended to be quite that gentle, but there was a tangible energy around him that just oozed heartbreak. At the same time, she couldn't let herself get blinded by it or distracted.

"I thought it was good. Guess I was a fool." Tears welled up in his eyes, and he pulled a handkerchief from a pocket and blew his nose.

A wounded ego could ignite motive for murder. "How long were you married?"

"It would have been our eleventh anniversary next month."

She resisted the urge to offer condolences in this moment and sat up straighter. "You really had no idea about her pregnancy?"

There was a twitch in his cheek, like he'd been physically struck. "None. I didn't even think being a mother was important to her."

"Some women need to be mothers." At the statement, guilt coiled through her. Her sister, Chelsea, was that way and had been blessed with three girls. Madison, though, didn't have any true desire to have children. It was like she missed that part of the assembly line. At least that was how it felt sometimes. Like she was faulty in some way. And then when she got pregnant only to lose it, there had been a sense of relief, like everything would go back to the way it was. Only it hadn't. She was more solid in her stance that she didn't want a kid. She hadn't been able to tell this to Troy, fearing it would destroy him. He had been so happy when she'd told him she was pregnant, and he was devastated by the loss.

"If Dana was that way, she did a good job hiding it from me. Though it seems she led a double life, so what do I know?" His chin quivered, and a few tears splashed his cheeks.

Madison glanced away, honoring his space for the moment. She knew exactly what it was like to be betrayed in such a way, having found her first fiancé, Toby Sovereign, in bed with another woman.

"Did you have any idea that your wife was having an affair?" This from Terry when she never spoke.

"No… Well, not until…" Wayne bit his bottom lip. "Maybe I should have seen the signs. She worked all sorts of crazy hours. Said that something came up at work. Now I know that she meant it literally." He pulled back his lips in a feral scowl. "I went through her emails on our home computer after you told me she was pregnant. She was linked to EverGreen's server so she could work from home if she wanted to."

Madison's heart was breaking for the guy. The pain, even though it had happened to her the better part of ten years ago, was still rancid enough that it could be conjured to memory rather easily—and she was now in a stable, trusting relationship. "What were these emails, and who sent them?" she prompted.

"David Klein. He was Dana's boss. She went on and on about him too. I really should have known." He clenched his jaw and balled his fists.

Anger was one side of the betrayal equation, revenge or acceptance were on the other side. She needed to determine whether Wayne was lying to them. If he was, did he act on his rage? "And the context of these emails?"

"Let's just say they were sexually suggestive." He looked from her to Terry, back to her. "They were having an affair." He said it in such a way it was like he was trying the words on for the first time.

Terry leaned forward. "Have you spoken with him…since finding these emails?"

"No way. What is there to say? Besides, I'm either going to say something I regret or do something... like punch him in the face." His cheeks warmed bright red, and his breathing was heavier than a second ago.

Madison believed his claim and admired the restraint, but she was curious about something. "Why not come forward and tell us about these emails? Why wait for us to come talk to you again? It's possible that this David Klein is behind her murder."

Wayne slumped in his chair. "I was afraid that you might figure I had more motive. I'm the chump who was duped. What's to say I didn't already know about the affair long ago?"

True enough... "But you didn't?"

"No," he spat.

At least he was coming clean with them now. "All right. Just for the record, where were you yesterday morning at seven o'clock?"

"You think I killed my wife and the other women?"

"The other *woman*. There was only one other victim who died besides your wife." *Morgan Walker, a.k.a. Courtney Middleton?* "Please, answer my question," she pressed when he'd said nothing for several seconds.

"I was here getting ready to go into work, and no one can— Oh, I waved to our next-door neighbor on my way out."

She got the details on which neighbor. "And what time would that have been?"

"Around eight."

"Okay. Thank you." She went to get up.

"Please find who did this to Dana. I'd like to think if she were still alive, we could get past the pregnancy and the affair..."

He is a bigger person than I could be... "Again, we're sorry for your loss, Mr. Ridley."

She and Terry left the house. "Before we leave the area, we should just check in with the neighbor." She pointed to the house across the street that Wayne had indicated.

"You really suspect Wayne Ridley? He's destroyed."

"Aren't you always telling me we can't go by a gut feeling?" It felt good serving that back.

A few minutes later, they were loading into the car, Wayne Ridley's alibi verified. The neighbor even mentioned they hadn't seen him leave before that, so it wasn't like Wayne could have left, committed the murders and returned, only to leave again.

"I think we can rule out Mr. Ridley." She felt confident in that statement, but the fact did remain that Dana had violated her husband's trust and she was dead.

Terry did up his belt in the passenger seat. "Probably a safe bet."

"I'm not betting another twenty." She smiled at him and entered the name David Klein into the onboard system. "Just pulling up the background on Klein. Oh—"

"I don't like that *oh*."

"You shouldn't. Klein is married." She looked from the screen to Terry. "Dana could have gone to him after getting pregnant and threatened to go to his wife to expose the affair."

"If she did, this guy could have motive for murder."

She nodded. Could they finally have a solid suspect?

Time for a road trip…

CHAPTER 20

Madison was pulling the department car into the underground parking garage in Braybury at four thirty. In the building above her and Terry, EverGreen was on the tenth floor.

"I don't know how people live here." She got out of the car, her nerves somewhat shot. People were in swarms everywhere—on the sidewalks and in vehicles on the road.

"I'm quite sure this building is zoned for commercial, not residential."

She potshot him in the arm.

"Hey. I think it's nicely tenderized, thank you very much." He narrowed his eyes and rubbed his arm.

She laughed. He always complained—when she hit him *and* when she refrained for a while. There was no pleasing him.

They took the elevator up and stepped off into a lobby made of marble and chrome. A nameplate on the front desk announced the receptionist as Rhonda. She wore a headset and spoke cheerfully to whoever was on the other end of the line. A second later, she was thanking her caller and saying goodbye.

Rhonda smiled at them. "How can I help you?"

"Rhonda, we need to speak with David Klein." Using the woman's first name fostered a sense of familiarity and would likely have her more eager to accommodate Madison's request.

"Sure, do you have an appointment?" Her brow tightened, as did her voice. It was apparent Rhonda suspected they didn't. Though by this point in the day, she was probably watching the clock for the minute it struck five.

Madison held up her badge, covering *Stiles*. She didn't want to get into a jurisdictional debate. She just wanted to speak with Klein. If it became evident that he was the shooter or responsible for hiring a hit man, then she and Terry would go through the proper channels by coordinating with the local PD. "We don't, but we're Detectives Knight and Grant."

"I'm sorry, but without an appointment, I can't do anything."

"We're here with news about a loved one," Madison rushed out. It was a dirty play but also the truth.

"Oh." Her eyes widened in shock, then dulled in empathy. "Let me get him for you."

A few minutes later, they were seen to a conference room and told Klein would be with them shortly. Business must have been good. Everything in the office thus far seemed high-end and expensive, and that held true in here. There was a large table with twelve leather chairs surrounding it, and expansive windows provided views of the city below.

Madison paced, watching the clock on the wall tick closer and closer to five o'clock.

"Detectives?" A handsome man entered the room at four fifty, just five minutes after she and Terry were taken there. The man was bald, but he pulled it off. He smelled heavily of cologne, but instead of it being displeasing, it was rather pleasant. "Rhonda said you're here about a loved one? Did something happen to my wife?"

"Please sit," Madison said to him and closed the door. Then she took a seat next to Terry and across from David Klein. He had an aura about him that suggested he was the kind of man who was used to getting his way, but she wouldn't be falling for his charms for one hot second. "We're here about your employee, Dana Ridley."

Something danced across his eyes, and he drew back, softly swiveled in his chair. *A motion to self-soothe?*

"You may have noticed that she hasn't been at work for a couple of days?"

"Honestly? I've been buried in work and out of town."

That didn't mean he and Dana hadn't been seeing one another. Maybe they just weren't in contact every day. Or maybe Wayne Ridley had misinterpreted the emails? "What was your relationship with Mrs. Ridley?"

"She was my employee."

"And that's all?" she pressed.

"Yes."

"Are you sure you don't want to give it a little thought? We do have her phone and can see her communication history as well as read her emails." They still needed legal clearance to do that, but it would eventually come through.

"Fine. We might have been seeing each other, but it was nothing serious."

"How's that even possible? You're both married. That makes your affair serious right there."

"It's not how it might seem. She isn't happy with Wayne, and I'm not happy with Lisa."

"Get a divorce then," Madison spat. "That's not an excuse to step out on her." She felt so blessed to have found Troy; women could throw themselves at him and he wouldn't pay them any attention. She'd seen it. But he had been married before, and his wife had cheated on him with his best friend. He held the same zero-tolerance policy as she did when it came to cheating.

"Why are we even talking about this? You wanted to talk about Dana, fine, but my marriage is off the table. Oh— Wait, why do you have Dana's phone? Why are you here?" He swallowed roughly. "Did something happen to her?"

"She was shot and killed yesterday morning at Liberty Station in Stiles." She could have laid it out with more tact, but she found it hard to feel for an adulterer. Besides, it was always best to present the news without any fuss.

"She's…" He ran a hand over the top of his head and stared into space. His eyes became wet, and fat drops dripped from his lashes. He wiped them away. "Who? Why? Did she… er…suffer?"

"Death was immediate." *Unlike with Courtney Middleton…* Madison was confident Morgan Walker had been her friend. She added, "We're still investigating the who and why, and it's led us to you."

"Me? Whatever for? I didn't kill her. Did you talk to her husband?"

"We have no reason to suspect him at this time," she deadpanned.

"This is ludicrous. Why would I kill Dana?"

"She was about sixteen weeks pregnant." She dropped the bomb and sat back in her chair, clasping her hands in her lap. Thoughts of her lost child attempted to squeeze in, but she shut them out. Maybe she should make an appointment with Tabitha Connor, her therapist, and talk out her feelings.

"I'm still not seeing how that points to me."

"So, the pregnancy isn't a surprise?" Terry interjected, suspicion lacing his voice.

"It is, but I'm not the father."

"Mr. Ridley can't have children," she pushed back.

"Me either. I fixed that years ago. I'm not exactly the fatherhood type."

No kidding. Surprisingly, she hadn't said that out loud. Chalk that up to her getting a bit better at restraining her knee-jerk impulses. Though she did say, "Pardon me if I'm having a hard time believing a guy who cheats on his wife."

"A bit of a slap in the face, don't you think?"

She shrugged. "Where were you yesterday morning at seven?" She felt nothing for this man—not even pity. Her barricade to keep out her personal feelings was fully engaged.

"I was here."

"That early?" she countered.

"Yes. And I can prove it to you."

"How's that exactly?" It took self-control not to lay out an accusation that he was with yet another woman.

"There's a security system in the office. I can show that my code was logged in at six yesterday morning. I swear I didn't hurt her."

"She wasn't hurt. She was *murdered* along with another woman. A third was shot and injured." She wasn't about to sit there and let him minimize the crime.

"Not just Dana…" His eyes widened.

"Do you know a Morgan Walker or Courtney Middleton?"

Terry brushed his foot against hers under the table. She shoved out her chin, ignoring her partner and fixing her attention on Klein.

"Neither name sounds familiar."

She pulled up Morgan Walker's driver's license photo on her phone and held her screen for him. "Look familiar?"

He studied the image and shook his head. "Never saw her before. I wish I could say that I did. I mean if it would help you figure out who killed her and Dana." A *V* formed between his eyebrows. Sadness.

"What about this woman?" Madison showed him a picture of Shannon Brennan.

He shook his head. "Don't know her either."

"Does the name Shannon Brennan mean anything to you?" Terry asked.

"No. But I thought you said two dead, one injured. Dana was one victim. But you've mentioned three other names…?"

"We're going to need that report from the security system, Mr. Klein." She ignored his question and settled back in her chair. "We'll wait."

Klein left the room and returned with the printout, and it confirmed what he'd said.

Madison got up and pulled out her card. She went through the regular spiel and then requested to see Dana's work area.

Her space was a small, windowless corner office. Klein wouldn't let them take Dana's laptop, telling them it was property of EverGreen and would contain proprietary information. Same went for giving them access to her email. They still had whatever Dana had downloaded to her phone and home computer. Otherwise, Madison was quite sure Dana's passwords would have changed by the time she and Terry returned to Stiles.

It was five thirty when they were leaving the office. On the elevator ride down, Terry was the first to speak.

"Who got Dana Ridley pregnant if it wasn't her husband or Klein?" he asked.

"That's us taking both men's word that they can't have kids."

"You want to subpoena medical records? I don't think we have enough to support a judge signing off on that for either of them."

She shrugged. "So we find something."

"If it's there to be found."

"What I meant."

"Okay," Terry dragged out. "Going back to the pregnancy. Who's the daddy?"

The elevator dinged its arrival in the parking garage, and they unloaded.

"Another lover? Maybe we'll be able to identify that person once we get into her phone. Or maybe even her personal emails. Who knows?"

"Tomorrow then? By the time we get back to Stiles, it will be almost eight."

They still needed to revisit Shane Walker, but he could wait until tomorrow. She doubted he'd be able to shed more light on his wife's past—even he had said she was secretive about it. And could she really come right out with her suspicion that she thought Morgan was her friend Courtney?

"Madison?" Terry prompted.

"Ah, yeah, tomorrow. On one condition. We start bright and early. I'd like to see if we can backtrack the girl's steps around the same time of day she would have been there."

"How did I know you'd want to do that...particularly the *bright and early* thing?"

"Because you know me." She smiled at him for that, but she wasn't happy about how the days in an investigation melded together and flew by so fast—especially when there wasn't a lot to show for their efforts.

CHAPTER 21

Cynthia had sent an email to Madison last night, and it had her up early this morning and at the police station.

After watching days' worth of video, Cynthia had confirmed that Brennan, Ridley, and Walker were periodically in line at Just Beans at the same time but not consistently. That supported it was likely only one of the women who was the target, and the others, collateral damage. Cynthia had also said that in the footage she watched she saw the girl with the backpack steal a few times, but no fuss had been made on those occasions. And it wasn't when Brennan, Ridley, and Walker were in line.

A hunt for a clear picture of the shooter was still underway, but Madison had the girl's photo on her monitor while she waited impatiently for Terry to get there.

Round face, wide-eyed with a small mouth. All of nineteen, twenty, maybe? The young woman had blond hair that reached her shoulders, and she was of athletic build, trim, and estimated by Mark to be five foot five—the same height as Madison, as it turned out. Cynthia would be running the girl's face through recognition software in case she was older than she looked and had a record. In the meantime, Madison didn't intend to wait around. She had every intention of getting to the girl before the shooter or the mob did. The girl was a loose end, no matter how one looked at it. Someone had killed the Russians' handler, Vlas Nikitin, and they'd be after blood. The shooter might want to take her out because she got a good look at him.

Terry arrived carrying a tray with two Starbucks cups. "This is for you." He extended her one.

"Caramel cappuccino?" Though the sweet aroma wafting under her nose gave it away...

"You know it."

"Thanks."

He went to set the tray down on a corner of her desk but struggled due to all the papers that were fanned across its surface. "You are the least organized person I know."

"Not as bad as the sarge, and I know where everything is."

"Tell yourself that." He ended up putting the tray on top of a stack. He plucked his cup, took a sip, and pointed at her screen. "The girl of the hour. Ready to see if we can find her?"

"Past ready." She turned her monitor off, slipped into her jacket, and grabbed her cappuccino.

Madison drove her and Terry to Liberty Station in record time, her foot to the floor.

"You don't have to kill us," he griped, holding on to the oh-shit bar above his head as she took a corner.

"You're making a big deal out of nothing. I have everything perfectly under control."

She parked in the train station's lot, and they headed toward the door where the girl usually entered. She looked around.

City views. High-rises. Lots of concrete. Pedestrians weaving their way down the sidewalks. Vehicles driving past, horns honking in the distance. Not as bustling as Braybury but chaotic enough.

Madison took a sip of her cappuccino, savoring the richness and sweetness of it on her tongue before swallowing. "Just a guess, but I doubt she owns a car. That leaves public transit."

"Unless she lives within walking distance..." Terry pressed his lips and bugged his eyes at her.

"Okay, that is a possibility. Either way, she frequently entered Liberty Station at this point, so someone had to have seen her. Maybe even where she came from. And I bet these guys are here every day at this time." She pointed to a string of cabs lined up at the curb. "We'll split up. You do some, I'll do some. Just show the drivers the girl's picture, and see if any of them recognize her."

"Okay, but it feels like a bit of a crapshoot."

"Do you have to fight me at every turn?"

He shrugged. "It keeps things interesting."

"Whatever you say…" She smiled, drank back the rest of her cappuccino, and tossed the cup into a recycling bin outside the doors. She started walking toward the curb and looked over her shoulder when she didn't hear Terry's footsteps. He was standing there, his cup tipped back. "Don't take all day, Grant."

He scowled at her and chucked his cup.

She went to the first taxi in the line and proceeded with the questioning. She repeated the process several times. After flashing the girl's face for the umpteenth time, Madison was taken to the past when she'd flashed Courtney Middleton's picture around, asking if anyone saw her. Not that she'd been a cop then.

"Never seen her," the latest cabbie told her. "Wish I could help the Stiles PD." He tacked on a pleasant smile.

"Thank you for your time." She tapped the window frame and drew back. His response matched the rest so far. No one recognized the girl, let alone knew her name or where she was from.

After about a half hour of questioning numerous drivers, Madison and Terry convened on the sidewalk.

"This is a waste of time," he mumbled.

She stubbornly refused to entertain that he may be right. "We need to find this girl, Terry. You do realize how important that is."

"I know it's very important to you."

"She's a material eyewitness, and she's in danger."

"Possibly."

She didn't really have the energy to run through it all again, but she would *one* more time. "Her handler was murdered, and I suspect that she was also Nikitin's girlfriend."

"Speculation. And I think you might be blowing things out of proportion when it comes to the girl's welfare." He peered into her eyes, like he was trying to read her mind.

Thankfully he wasn't quite as good with that skill as Troy or Cynthia, or he'd have seen the truth: she might be projecting Courtney's situation onto the girl with the backpack. A case of not being able to save Courtney, while Madison stood a chance of helping this girl. "Think about this. The mob's not going to be too happy to find out Nikitin's dead. I'm sure they didn't appreciate the news article about the drug trafficking either. They're going to want their hands on the girl—and the shooter, for that matter. The incident probably stopped whatever they had planned for Monday morning. The Mafia may even think the girl killed Nikitin." She waved a hand. "Who knows what they might think, but I believe the girl's in real danger. And if it's not from the mob, it's from the shooter."

"And both the girl and the shooter are in danger from the mob? I have that right?"

"That's right."

"How do you know the girl isn't safe and holed up in a stash house being told to hang around until the heat dies down?"

Madison didn't know *for sure*. She had her gut feeling, though. She turned at the sound of air brakes on a public bus that had just come to a stop down the street. She hustled toward it and the small gathering of people at the bus stop. She flashed the girl's photo to them as they lined up to board.

"Let them get on the bus." The driver, fifties, dark skin with deep lines around his eyes, was glaring at her.

"Stiles PD," she replied, unfazed, and continued what she was doing. But all for naught. No one had seen the girl. Maybe she should just let the notion go of ever finding her. Then she had a thought. She stomped up the stairs to the driver and showed him the picture of the girl. "Do you recognize her?"

"Lady, get off the bus, or pay and sit." He tapped the pay station. "We take credit cards. And I have a schedule to keep."

Madison pushed her screen closer to his face. "Just take a look, then I'll leave."

He sighed and leaned in, squinting.

"Do you recognize her?" she repeated, pushing, but he wasn't the only one in a hurry.

"Ah, yes I do. Something happen to her? Why are the poleeece lookin' for her?"

"We believe she may be in danger. Do you know her name or…?"

He frowned and shook his head.

"What about— Oh, does she get on at a certain stop as a matter of routine?" The epiphany hit, and she ran with it.

His eyes widened and brightened. "Uh-huh, yes, she does." He went on to tell her right where that was.

"Thank you. Have a great day." She got off the bus, hearing the murmurings and complaints of passengers about how they were going to be late for work, but even if they were, the investigation appreciated their sacrifice.

She and Terry had their next stop.

CHAPTER 22

The location the bus driver gave Madison took her and Terry to an area on the outskirts of downtown that was mostly residential. Detached houses were lined up for a mile about a block from the stop, but immediately in front of them were multi-story, multi-use buildings. Some were entirely dedicated to commercial, while others had businesses on the ground level with apartments above them.

She and Terry stood on the sidewalk looking around.

"You realize she could be coming from anywhere within walking distance of here? And she's young. That could be a big area. Heck, she could even take another means of transportation here, then board the bus to the train station."

If that's what the girl did, then maybe Madison didn't need to worry about her. The girl knew how to cover her tracks. "She's a drug runner, not a trained spy."

"Assumed," he said, not about to let her have it for one second. "Why don't we pass this location along to Narcotics and let them take it from here?"

"We've been through this."

"Oh, right. But I'm thinking it has more to do with you feeling a responsibility toward the girl for some reason. Any idea what that might be? Because if you don't, I do."

"This isn't about Courtney Middleton."

He pressed his lips. "If you say so."

She pushed out her chin. "I do. Now, let's just do our jobs."

"I agree. Let's find the shooter and put his butt in jail."

He made it all sound so simple. She was exhausted trying to get through his thick skull that they needed the girl as much as she probably needed them. She went to the first person walking down the sidewalk and showed them the girl's picture. Terry eventually followed her lead and asked other people.

No luck for several minutes, and Madison backtracked to where a man was lifting a rollup security gate protecting the front of a pizza joint.

"Excuse me," she said to him.

The man stopped what he was doing, dropped his arms, and looked at her. "Yeah?"

"Stiles PD, Detective Knight. Do you know this girl?" She held up the picture, quite certain she was going to be met with the same response she'd heard so far—he didn't know her, and he'd never seen her. If so, she'd finally concede to Terry's wishes and stop her efforts to find the girl. At least for now.

The man leaned in, looked at her screen, and held out his hands. "Could I…? My eyesight's seen better days."

"Uh, sure." She gave him her phone, and he studied the picture.

He flushed. "Did something happen to her?"

A swell of excitement bubbled in Madison's stomach. "You know her. What's her name, and where can we find her?"

He shoved the phone back at Madison. "You don't answer my question, I don't answer yours." He pulled out a jangling key ring, stuck a key into one of the deadbolts, and twisted. *Thunk.*

"No, please." Madison put a hand on the man's shoulder and withdrew it under his gaze. "We believe she may be in danger." She made sure to make eye contact with the man when she spoke, and his eyes shadowed. How did he know the girl—and how *well*? He was in his fifties while the girl may be twenty, but perhaps she frequented his pizza place.

His eyes softened, and his gaze was full of concern.

"What is her name, and where does she live?" Madison was desperate to get some answers.

He opened his mouth and closed it, as if hesitant to answer.

"It's obvious you care about the girl, and I'm being serious when I say she's in danger. Possibly even her life is on the line." Maybe if he realized the severity of the situation, it would drive home the urgency that they talk to her.

"So, she's not in trouble with the police?"

A loaded question, since technically she was a drug runner, but that wasn't Madison's concern. Her motive in finding the girl was to make sure she was safe and to see if she had any insight to offer regarding the shooter. "She's not, I promise you." The second the vow was out, she regretted it, as it might not be one she could keep.

"Her name is Kayla Fleming." The sentence came out rushed, on a single breath.

Madison flagged down Terry for him to join them. When he stepped up next to her, Madison continued. "This is my partner, Detective Grant."

The man gave him a once-over.

"And your name, sir?" Madison asked.

"Roger Hart."

"What is your relationship with Kayla?" Madison asked.

"She's one of my favorite customers, but she also happens to rent her apartment from me."

Madison let out a deep sigh. The random questioning of strangers was finally paying off. In the least, they had the girl's name, and they were soon going to have where she lived. Hopefully all of that would be enough to get to the girl and protect her. "And where is this apartment?"

The man pointed above their heads. "Unit 2B. You get to it through there." He pointed to a doorway to the side of the pizza shop.

"Thank you." With that, Madison was off, Terry following.

"Surprised we got anywhere with all this."

"You don't say?" She laughed. "And yet you call me skeptical." She continued up a set of stairs. On the landing there were two doors. One was labeled 2A, the other 2B. She knocked on the latter one.

There were no sounds coming from inside. Madison leaned in and sniffed.

"What are you doing?" Terry hissed, sounding mortified.

"Seeing if I can smell blood." She drew back and straightened up. "Good news is, I don't. But we're going to need in her apartment." She went back down the stairs to ask Hart for assistance.

She pulled on the handle of the pizza shop, and no give. She put her face to the glass. Hart was in there, moving around in the back in what was likely the kitchen. She banged on the window.

He gave no indication he'd heard her.

She knocked again, putting more urgency into the rapping.

Finally.

Hart stopped moving and poked his head through an opening in the back wall. He pulled something from his right ear—an earbud. No wonder he hadn't responded earlier.

He unlocked several deadbolts and opened the door just wide enough for her and Terry to step inside. He had this sort of panicked glaze to his eyes, like he expected bad news. Was it because of what she'd said earlier, or did he know the people Kayla Fleming was caught up with? Maybe he was involved somehow himself. Legitimate-facing business fronts were often used by the mob to launder money. But he seemed far too cooperative if he was tied up with the Russians.

"Did you find her at home?" he asked.

"There was no answer, but we need to get into her apartment," Madison told him.

"Not going to happen"—he crossed his arms—"without a warrant."

"Did you forget the part where we think she might be in danger?"

"No, but you're not hearing what I'm telling you. I need a warrant before I can let you in her apartment. Otherwise, that would be a violation of the landlord-tenant act."

She pulled out her phone. "Fine, you need one, we'll get it for you." She called a judge who was usually good about issuing verbal warrants. "Be just one minute," she told Hart.

Five minutes later, she hung up from speaking with the judge.

"So?" the man asked, the implication obvious.

"We have verbal authorization from Judge McKinley to enter the residence of Kayla Fleming. I would be more than happy to provide you with the number to his office for you to verify this for yourself, but every minute that passes puts Kayla in more danger." She might have been ramping up the urgency more than it deserved, but she was so close— literally on the girl's doorstep—and they were hitting a wall. Enough was enough.

"Fine, I'll let you into her apartment, but not without me standing right there." He gave a glance over his shoulder toward the kitchen, and stress oozed off him. He had probably come in early to prepare for the lunch crowd and the rest of the day ahead, and now all that would have to wait. But it didn't *have to*…

"You obviously have a lot to do here. I'm guessing you came in early to get some things done, right? Let us go up alone. If you can't trust the Stiles PD, then who can you trust?" The last question had her feeling hypocritical, given her recent brush with corrupt cops.

The man rubbed his arms, seeming to hesitate. Eventually, he shook his head. "I'm going up with you."

"Suit yourself. That's fine." He might be wishing he'd stayed behind. After all, they had no idea what might be waiting for them.

CHAPTER 23

On the way back up to Kayla's apartment, they got more information from Hart. He bought the building three years ago, and Kayla had been living there for the last year. She paid her rent in cash but always on time. Kayla was an excellent tenant, and he wished they were all like her. Madison would push him more on his thoughts about the girl in a bit, but she had a feeling if Hart was bulldozed, he would stop talking.

"Here you go." Hart stepped back from the now-open door for 2B.

"Thank you," Terry said, while Madison took a step into the apartment.

"Stiles PD," she called out. "Kayla Fleming, if you are here, please make yourself known."

The space was compact but functional, and Kayla kept it neat and tidy. Somehow observing this humanized the girl even more. What got her into running drugs in the first place? It was unlikely just the money. So often these young women had nowhere else to turn, and these organizations gave them a sense of belonging, of family—no matter how delusional that was. Again Madison wondered if Kayla's stealing from the Just Beans kiosk had been a cry for help so she could escape the drug ring.

Madison walked slowly through the apartment, listening closely. It was whisper silent. Kayla was either dead and couldn't respond, or she wasn't home. The latter was confirmed just a few moments later, and it put a knot in Madison's chest. She turned to Hart.

"How well do you know Kayla?"

"Not too well. I mean you've probably noticed the age difference between the two of us."

"That means nothing when it comes to friendship." Her mind often went straight to the inappropriate, but she wasn't sensing that with Hart.

"Suppose that is true. She's a kind girl who is always generous with offering a smile and a greeting. Good tipper, too, when she comes down for a slice."

"When did you see Kayla last?" Terry asked.

Hart tapped a finger on his chin. "I'd say probably sometime over the weekend. It's all kind of a blur."

"So not anytime this week?" Had Kayla gone on the run straight from the train station after the shooting? Or had she found out Nikitin's fate? Madison imagined that when he didn't show up at Liberty Station, she would have gone looking for him—especially if she was also his girlfriend.

"No. Definitely not."

"You ever see anyone come to her apartment? Friends, a boyfriend maybe?" Madison asked.

"I didn't stalk her."

She wasn't sure why he'd leaped there. "Never suspected that you did. Was just curious if you had noticed."

"No, I can't say that I have, but Diane might have seen someone."

"And Diane is…?"

"She lives in 2A."

"All right. Thanks. We'll speak with her," Madison said. "But first, we'd like to take a closer look around Kayla's apartment."

His face darkened. "You really think Kayla's in danger, huh?"

"Why we're going to all this trouble, Mr. Hart," she said.

"But who is she in danger from? Should I be concerned that she's not at home?"

"Is she normally home at this time of day?" Madison countered.

He pressed his lips and shrugged. "I'm usually pretty busy getting things set up at the shop to notice much of anything. And I don't live here. I live down the block."

Madison nodded.

"You never did answer my question." He leveled his gaze at her.

She was hoping he'd forgotten his question, because she didn't really want to scare him by providing the answer. No one responded calmly at the mention of the Russian Mafia. And probably for good reason. They killed without remorse and were rarely held accountable—nowhere close to what they deserved.

"Detective?" he prompted.

"We believe Kayla may be caught up in a drug-trafficking ring." She'd leave the mob out of it.

He scowled. "You lied to me. You are here to arrest her."

"I never lie," she replied firmly. It was a matter of principle, and she was insulted at the accusation. She might stretch the truth at times, if it was to get justice in the end, but she *never* lied. "We are not interested in finding Kayla to arrest her. We just want to make sure she's okay. And until we find her, we can't assume that she is. She's gotten herself involved in a bit of a mess."

Hart pinched his eyes shut for a moment. When he opened them, they were full of tears. "Well, I hope you find her. As I said, she's a nice girl and doesn't deserve any of this."

"You never suspected she might be into something illegal?" Madison put it out there as delicately as possible, not wanting to insult him further. It was never easy when impressions steered a person wrong.

"None, and I'm still having a hard time believing it."

"We understand if you're not comfortable hanging around here any longer and need to get back to work," Madison said. "If you want to leave the keys to the apartment with us, we'll lock up and return them to you before we leave."

He pulled the bulky key ring out of his pocket and fished off a key. He placed it in Madison's palm. "Please do whatever you can to make sure Kayla's safe."

"You have my word."

. . .

The first thing Madison did after Hart left was go back to Kayla's bedroom. The space looked like a cyclone had passed through, but she hadn't made a fuss about what that might mean in front of Hart. Neither had Terry. It didn't appear as if a struggle had taken place, but dresser drawers were sitting open with articles of clothing dangling over the fronts.

"She was in a hurry to get out of here," Terry said. "Now what?"

She shrugged, made one suggestion. "We need to find out if Kayla has a phone we can trace."

"We'll see if we can find any phone bills, but my guess is if she had a phone, it's a burner like Nikitin's."

"Let's just see what we can find."

They spent a couple of hours rummaging around the apartment. No phone. No phone bills. But there was a very tiny amount of white powder on the floor of the closet. Maybe where Kayla set her backpack at night, some of the residue coming from it onto the carpet. They gathered what they could, which they'd take to the lab for testing.

They locked up and went to the neighboring apartment.

A woman in her sixties, Diane presumably, answered the door just as Madison went to knock. She was quite sure she saw an eye in the peephole just before the handle had twisted.

"Yes?" the woman said.

Madison and Terry showed their badges, and Madison made the official introductions. The woman told them she was Diane Butler.

"We have questions about your neighbor in 2B, Kayla Fleming. Could we come in for a moment?" Madison asked.

"You may."

The apartment smelled like canned tuna, and the reason for that was quickly made evident. Madison eyed the woman's lunch on the counter in the galley-style kitchen as she passed on the way to the dining table.

Everyone took a seat, and Madison started the questioning. "How well do you know Kayla?"

"Not at all really, but she seems like a pleasant enough girl. She always says hello when she sees me, asks how I am." Butler's blue eyes were sparkling as she spoke.

Madison smiled kindly, but her mind was preoccupied with thoughts of where Kayla might be and if she was still alive and safe. "When did you last see her?"

"Think it was, er…Monday morning. Yes, that was it."

Madison sat up taller. "You're sure?"

"Uh-huh."

"What time on Monday?"

"Ah, would have been around ten. Yep. Because I was just coming up from the laundry room after transferring the clothes from the washer to the dryer. She was in some sort of rush."

"She said that?"

"She did, but she didn't have to. She was breathing deep, but her backpack was bulging. She appeared to struggle with the weight of it. If I didn't know better, I'd say she was running away."

Exactly what she was probably doing… But if the bag was full of clothing and toiletries, what happened to the drugs she most likely had in the backpack Monday morning?

"Did she say where she was headed?" Terry asked.

"No, and not my business either." Butler tutted like that would have been crossing a line, though she apparently had no qualms about spying on her neighbor.

Madison found the woman's pastime amusing and useful. "Did Kayla ever have friends or a guy over?"

Butler pursed her rosy lips. "Nope, not that I ever saw. Truth be told, it makes me worry about her. A girl her age should have a hopping social life."

"So, no one came by to see her?" Madison asked again, pushing a little harder.

"Oh… There was a woman who came around Monday at noon looking for Kayla, but she was family."

Madison's gut clenched, telling her this was pertinent to the case. "Family?" she parroted.

"The woman said she was Kayla's aunt, but she didn't look anything like her. I told her that she'd just missed her."

"She was older?" Terry asked.

"Yes. Say about your ages."

Madison was thirty-six, Terry a few years younger.

Madison leaned forward, interested. "Had she come around for Kayla before?"

"No. And she had this, er, quality about her. Like she was trying to be nice, but she was being fake."

"What did she look like?" Madison asked.

"She'd be pretty, if not for her attitude. Fancy too. Dressed to the nines. Wouldn't say she's from this neighborhood. Brown hair, brown eyes, and she had a bit of an accent."

"Where was the accent from?" Dread crawled down Madison's arms.

"Oh, I've never been good at identifying that type of thing. But I'd guess Russian."

Madison went cold. The description of the woman, though somewhat generic, could fit Tatiana Ivanova. And whenever Madison had seen the woman, she'd always been impeccably dressed. Madison took a few seconds to gather her composure, and got up. She gave the woman her business card and said, "We appreciate your cooperation."

"No problem. Say, Kayla's okay, isn't she?"

"Hoping so."

The woman's face, which had been lit with hope, dimmed. Madison and Terry saw themselves out.

"It's her, Terry. I know it." Madison was moving as fast as her legs would take her. "The *aunt* was Tatiana Ivanova."

"You don't *know* it."

"Yes, I do." Madison didn't have solid proof, but she didn't need it—not when her intuition was screaming at her.

CHAPTER 24

Madison slid behind the wheel of the department car and keyed Kayla's name into the onboard computer. No phone number on file. No surprise. But there were a few useful tidbits. "She's only nineteen." Saying so burrowed an ache into Madison's chest. Even younger than Courtney had been when she'd disappeared. But this wasn't the time to get all sentimental and melancholy. She couldn't help Courtney, but she might be able to protect Kayla. "Her parents' names are listed…" Madison proceeded to type their names into the system. "Both dead, two years ago. That could explain why Kayla was vulnerable and ended up doing what she did." It lined up with her earlier thinking. Being part of the drug operation could have given her a sense of belonging.

"Broken homes, lost souls," Terry said. "It's a heartbreaking story on repeat."

Madison looked over at him, almost wondering if he was being sarcastic, but her partner's face was grim, his mouth set in a firm line. She went back to the database and frowned when her efforts met the result she'd been expecting. "Kayla didn't have any aunts. This confirms it for me. Tatiana was the "aunt." How much do you want to bet Tatiana also knows about Nikitin's murder—and that's what brought her here looking for Kayla? Well, that and presumably the missed delivery to Canada. Kayla couldn't have made it there with the drugs and got back to her apartment by ten AM to pack. We need to read through what canvassing officers got from Nikitin's neighbors and see if anyone can put Tatiana in his building. Either way, I'm quite sure the mob is onto the fact that the shooter from Monday took out their handler—and they're out to set things right. I'd bet on that."

Terry held out a hand as if to shake on one.

She batted it away. She wasn't in the mood for lightness. Who knew where Kayla was now? Was she even still alive? Because Madison was certain that once Tatiana caught up with her, she wouldn't be for long. Madison had to get to Kayla first. And while the shooter was likely in danger too, she didn't feel the same responsibility toward his safety. After all, he'd started this entire mess.

Madison's phone rang, and it was Cynthia. "What do you have?"

"Hello to you too."

"Sorry. Hi." She put the call on speaker. "Terry's here."

They said quick hellos to each other.

"Before you start," Madison said, "We have the girl's identity. Kayla Fleming. Now we just need to find her."

"That's great news you have a name. The facial rec databases weren't a help. All right, you're going to love me for delivering the news I'm about to and Mark for giving me something to relay. He's been scanning through hours of video—a couple of weeks' worth, to be more precise—and he's spotted the shooter. He's at least ninety percent sure. His stature and gait match the shooter's. Same height too, at six foot even."

Tingles danced over Madison's shoulders and down her arms. "We get a picture of his face?"

"Yep," Cynthia proudly announced. "It's running through facial rec databases as we speak, and I'll fire his picture over when I get off the phone with you. Just wanted to share the good news first."

"Great! Thanks."

"You're welcome. But you might also be interested to know that on some occasions, the shooter was seen trailing Vlas Nikitin through the train station, even following him to the exit."

"He probably didn't stop there and followed him home. That's how he knew where Nikitin lived," Terry said.

"Being at the station a lot would have also allowed him to familiarize himself with the rotation of police officers. He'd also have known about Kayla." Madison couldn't help but think what an elaborate scheme this was. Whoever was behind the murders certainly wanted the investigation to be complex and branch off in several directions. Mission accomplished. Except the shooter had messed up and shown his face. She could hardly wait to see his mug.

"See, so you...?" Cynthia's smile traveled the line.

"We love you guys!" Madison grinned. "Now send me that picture."

"You got it, boss." Cynthia chuckled and hung up.

Madison's and Terry's phones pinged. She held her screen up for the two of them.

The man was lean, almost scrawny—two things she picked up on first viewing of the shooting video. This picture was much more distinct though. Dark hair fanned out from beneath a baseball cap. He had brown eyes, a goatee, and a mustache. He had a long, narrow neck and a dominant Adam's apple. To the base of the throat was a red birthmark— just as Shannon had mentioned.

"Guess this gets the husbands off the hook," Terry said.

"Yes and no."

"Right. They didn't carry out the shooting themselves, but the possibility of a hit man is on the table. Or someone else with motive we're not seeing yet."

Madison nodded. "The amount of planning and legwork that he put in—at least two weeks' worth—and killing the handler too, that points me to a hired gun. But who hired him?"

"We just know the bullet caliber that killed Nikitin was the same one used in the train station shooting. We don't know if they were fired from the same gun."

"Really, Terry? What are the chances they weren't? Slim, I'd say."

"Fine. We look closer at the husbands to start."

It would be a good time to put their hands on the couples' financials. Another subpoena request would need to be made.

Madison and Terry proceeded to talk out the facts they had.

Shannon Brennan was still breathing, and Madison hadn't been notified that anyone had attempted to get past the officer and harm her, so it was likely she could be ruled out as the primary target. That would also take Russell Brennan off the suspect list.

Wayne Ridley was devastated by his wife's affair, but Madison believed his claim that he hadn't known about it. There went his biggest motive.

David Klein was untouchable for the moment. They didn't have enough against him to justify a request his financials.

Then there was the question of who had fathered Dana's baby—something her phone records would hopefully reveal. Maybe that man was the killer or he'd hired someone, but what was this theoretical man's motive? Was he married, too, and Dana had threatened to reveal the affair to his wife? All of this was conjecture.

Another loose thread was Shane Walker. That brought with it the enigma surrounding Morgan. Had she been Courtney Middleton?

"We're going to need to revisit every husband and see if they recognize this guy." She pointed to her phone where the shooter's face was still on the screen.

"If he was a hit man, though, it's possible even if one of the spouses had hired him, they might not have met face-to-face."

She sighed. "True enough, but a guy like this"—she nudged her head toward the shooter's face—"has a record. No way he woke up one day knowing how to do surveillance on a mark."

"He also got away with murder three times in the last two days."

"Not over yet, and if I have any say, he won't be getting away with anything. He'll be going to prison for the rest of his life." Her phone lit up with an incoming call. She groaned at the name. "Winston?" she answered.

A slight pause at her abrupt greeting, though he volleyed with one of his own. "Where the hell are you?"

Hello to you too…

"Knight, answer the question."

"Following a lead."

"You're looking for that girl with the backpack."

That stalled her for a second. How did he know? "Yes. We just found out the ID of the girl with the backpack. Kayla Fleming and…" She stopped there. There was no way she was going to bring up the mob to him again—not until she had more *and* not until she knew how Winston knew where they were. He would probably stress that her job was to apprehend the shooter, not set off on a wild chase after the mob again. And she wasn't in the mood to hear it.

"Good. Good. Now what? You guys really need to get your ass in gear. Reporters from the *Stiles Times* are harassing our media department, looking for answers."

She glanced at Terry, who was wincing. There was no way he wasn't hearing every single word Winston said, given the volume at which he was speaking.

"We just got the picture of our shooter's face, and our next stop will be to see if the husbands know the guy."

"Your thinking then? Let's pretend I have a penny."

She rolled her eyes. "The shooter isn't any of the husbands, and considering evidence leads us to believe he also killed Vlas Nikitin, we're entertaining the idea that he's a hired gun."

"A hit man."

"Yep." *Isn't that what I just said?*

"Good. Keep me posted."

And he was gone.

"Wow. That man is infuriating." She was gripping her phone, her knuckles whitening, as a realization hit. "How did he know we were tracking down the girl? Did you tell him?" She certainly hadn't despite Winston's numerous requests that she run things past him. There had been times in the past that Terry had filled their sergeant in without notifying her he was doing so.

"I didn't. Maybe he just assumed that because he heard we had a good shot of her face and knew a bit about her movements?" He shrugged.

She hoped that was all it was. One alternative was Winston was being swayed to downplay the importance of finding the girl for some reason. At the mob's bidding? Maybe she was being paranoid. It could have just been that the verbal warrant Judge McKinley had authorized made its way to Winston's ears.

She dropped her phone into the console and put the car in gear. She didn't say anything as she drove them to the Walker house. She figured she'd start there, as they hadn't spoken with Shane yesterday, and Madison was beyond ready to get some answers—about her old friend and the current investigation.

CHAPTER 25

The sky had turned a dark, murky gray as Madison and Terry stood on the front step of the Walker house. A storm was moving in. Madison found irony in how well the weather mirrored the case.

Tatiana Ivanova. It had to be her who had been at Kayla's apartment. Once Madison picked up Tatiana's photograph from home amid her surveillance pictures, she'd be taking it back to show Diane Butler, Kayla's neighbor. Madison would have to work Tatiana into a lineup to avoid accusations of leading the witness. They would have to do the same for any of Nikitin's neighbors who might have seen a woman of her description in the building.

Just more things to add to the growing list…

Madison knocked, and the door opened to a beautiful teenage girl who had a sprinkling of freckles across the bridge of her nose. The sight had Madison holding her breath for a second, flashing back to how Courtney had the same feature. She could see the freckles like yesterday and remember her friend complaining about how her fair skin would burn in the sun. Was this girl Courtney's biological daughter? For some reason, Madison had just assumed that the teenager was Shane's from a previous relationship. She racked her brain to remember how old the daughter was. Madison was quite sure Shane had told them she was fourteen. Could it be…? Courtney went missing just over fifteen years ago. Had she gotten pregnant shortly after?

"Ah, you must be Leanne Walker," Madison said, her badge in hand, her skin clammy.

The girl's eyes narrowed with suspicion. "How do you know who I am?"

"I'm sorry. I should have told you that I'm Detective Madison Knight, and this is my partner, Detective Terry Grant. We're here —"

The girl walked away, leaving the door wide open.

"Stiles PD," Madison called out into the home. "Shane Walker?" She just finished speaking when he appeared on the top landing of the staircase, off to the right of the front entrance.

"Detectives," he said as he jogged down the stairs. "Did you find the shooter?" If he was curious at all why they were standing on his front step, the door wide open, there was no sign of that—and no sign of Leanne.

"We're still investigating, but we're making some progress," Madison said. "Could we come in and speak with you for a moment? We have some questions."

"Yes, for sure." His eyes were bloodshot and heavily shadowed. Whether he was involved with hiring a hit man or not, he was obviously having trouble sleeping.

Madison and Terry stepped inside, and Shane closed the door behind them.

"Please make yourself at home in the living room."

They went ahead and did just that, sitting side by side on the couch. Shane dropped into a chair and crossed his legs.

Madison wasted no time pulling up the photo array that Cynthia had also included with the standalone picture of the shooter. The array was for questioning and included four other faces in addition to that of the actual shooter's. She got up, walked over to Shane, and handed him her phone. "There are five pictures I'd like you to look at. Please take your time and scroll through them one by one. Let me know if you recognize any of them."

Shane met her gaze as he took her phone. The understanding that one of these men had killed his wife was evident by the intensity in his eyes.

He studied each photograph but showed no visual reaction to any of them. When he'd finished, he gave Madison her phone back, hands shaking. "I've never seen any of these men before in my life. I wish I could say I did because then at least you'd have him... The man who stole my Morgan from me."

His pain and loss weighed heavily in his voice, and Madison felt a squeeze on her heart. She hated that she needed to ask him the next question. "How was your marriage, Mr. Walker?"

"You're probably not going to believe me, because most people wouldn't, but I'm not sure our marriage ever left the honeymoon phase." His lips and chin trembled.

"You told us on Monday that you were married for six years, is that right?" Terry asked, after allowing a few beats for the man to collect himself.

"Yes, and they were the best six years of my life."

"And the birth of your daughter...where did that rank?" Madison was certain that Leanne's birth would qualify as one of his best days.

"I'm not sure why you're asking me that..."

"Is Leanne your biological daughter?" Sometimes direct questions were more effective.

Shane shook his head. "Morgan's, but I treat her as if she's my own daughter because, to me, she always has been. She's a great kid, and I'm not sure how we're all going to get through this. She's absolutely heartbroken about her mother. Sorry she left you at the door like she did, but she's not really thinking straight."

"Completely understandable considering the circumstances," Terry said.

Madison could also empathize, but she wanted to remain objective with Shane Walker. There were some good actors out there, and he might be one of them. "What happened to Leanne's biological father?"

"Morgan was secretive about him, but I always got the feeling he died."

Madison nodded, not sure where that took the investigation or how it would satisfy all her questions about Courtney Middleton. "So you and your wife never had arguments or disagreements that may have gotten heated?"

"Heated? Never. But, yes, we had disagreements from time to time, but we'd talk things out. They were never usually about anything too serious."

"You told us you met in Comsey Park at a bar. Love at first sight?" Madison asked, tiptoeing into "Courtney Middleton" area, and she was doing her best to hide it so that Terry wouldn't pick up on it right away.

"Pretty much, yeah. She had such a confidence about her, and I knew if I wanted to stand a chance with her, I needed to make the first move. And as you can see, the gamble paid off." A rogue tear snaked down his cheek, and he wiped it away.

Terry was getting a little fidgety, and before he stood and bailed, she dropped back onto the couch. She wanted to get more out of Shane, just a little glimpse into Morgan Walker's past life to see if she could confirm her suspicion.

"It's nice when we find that person we just click with." Troy was that person for her. She'd been so afraid to give him a chance at first, but she felt this draw to him that she couldn't resist. "How well did you know Court—*Morgan*," she hurried out, "before you got married?" She could have slapped herself at the slip, and it wasn't missed by Terry, who flashed her a scowl. Shane's brow wrinkled.

"Enough anyway." He looked from Madison, to Terry, and back to Madison. "What does any of this have to do with finding the person who shot my wife?"

Madison bit her bottom lip, anxious. Terry was shaking his head. But she couldn't just walk away. Her desire to get answers was like a torrent bubbling within her. "Did she ever tell you about her childhood?"

Terry let out a deep sigh and said, "Detective, maybe we should get going."

"Just a few more minutes, and we will," she said firmly. She'd started trudging down this path, and she wasn't about to change course now.

Shane looked at Terry.

"Detective," Terry hissed at her.

It was now or never. "I have a reason for asking all these questions. And they very well might have something to do with why your wife was shot. So please tell me, did she tell you anything about her childhood?"

His face went dark, and he let out a deep breath. "She never liked talking about it. I gathered she didn't have a very good one, and I didn't want to push and upset her. But how could her childhood have anything to do with what happened to her now?" Irritation and curiosity marked his tone.

If Madison came right out with her suspicion, she'd run the risk of Shane filing a complaint with the police department. But wouldn't he want to know who his wife really was—especially if it ended up providing an explanation for why she was shot? Risks were sometimes worth taking… "This is going to sound very bizarre to you"—she nudged her head toward Terry—"as it did to my partner here, but I am quite sure that your wife was my old college friend. I knew her as Courtney Middleton. She disappeared just over fifteen years ago." She watched for any tells that he'd heard that name before, and there was nada.

"I'm not sure how that's even possible," Shane said. "And it makes no sense."

"That picture in the hallway of you and Morgan on your wedding day…"

"What about it?"

"In that picture, she looks more the way I knew her, with the bigger nose versus the more delicate features. And when I met Leanne, I noticed she has a dusting of freckles along the bridge of her nose. Just like Courtney."

"It's said everyone has a doppelganger. You know, people who really look like them. Maybe that's all this is? I'm sorry about your friend, but it's time for you to leave." Shane stood, and so did Terry. Madison stayed put.

"I can't promise that your wife's past will factor into the investigation and lead us to her killer, but don't you want to know who she really was?" Madison posed the question as tactfully as possible.

"I am well aware of who my wife was, Detective. Now, if you would please leave."

"If you're so sure, what do you have to lose if I look into this further?" She wanted him on board with her, but given the deepening scowl on his face, she highly doubted he could be swayed.

"Justice," he stamped out. "All the time you'd use chasing some theory of yours, my wife's—*Morgan's*—killer remains a free man."

"He is right, Detective Knight," Terry said. "And we should go."

"All right." She stood but didn't move for the door. She didn't want to leave this house without something of Morgan's to provide DNA. "Actually, Mr. Walker, before we go, could I use your bathroom?"

"Fine." Shane flailed his arms and directed her down the hall to the door on the right, which was located under the stairs.

"Thanks."

He mumbled something, and she was quite sure Terry did too. She tucked into the bathroom, wishing it had been the master en suite, but surely Morgan had a personal item in this room that could help Madison with her goal. Madison had a couple of days to think about how she could work around the system, and on the way here, she came up with a plan. She'd collect an article of Morgan's from her house and something with DNA on it from the Middletons when she visited them. Then she'd use one of those mail-in testing services. This would all be on the down-low, and no one would get into trouble—but it could put her mind at ease.

Now, where to look…?

The room was compact with only a toilet, pedestal sink, and a small cabinet. She opened the doors to the latter, doing so slowly in case they squeaked or made any noise that would alert Shane to her snooping. Even Terry could know nothing about what she was going to do.

She hunched down and peered inside. Rolls of toilet paper were stacked up, along with packages of feminine products. None of this would do her any good…

Shit!

She pulled them out and rooted to the back. A cosmetic bag—it would either belong to Morgan or Leanne—but either way the DNA would work for her purpose. That is, if Madison hadn't completely lost it. *And* if there was anything inside that could provide DNA.

She peeled back the zipper and found tubes of lipstick, powders, and creams. She pulled out one of the lipstick tubes, took off the lid, and twisted. It had been used. She pushed it into her coat pocket and returned everything else to its proper place.

She had her hand on the door handle, ready to leave the room, when she remembered her ruse. She spun, flushed the toilet with her foot, and proceeded to wash her hands. She had been rummaging in a bathroom cabinet, after all.

Madison came out and smiled at Shane. "Thank you again."

They left, and Shane closed the door a little heavier than warranted—in her opinion.

"What is up with you? Have you completely lost your mind?" Terry was breathing heavily. He pulled the passenger door of the department car shut, and the entire vehicle shook.

"Don't talk to me like that." She clenched her teeth, not even able to look at him.

"You shouldn't have told him all you did. This gets back to Winston and—"

"It's not going to." She leveled a glare at him.

"You don't know that."

"If he wants to know what happened to his wife, he won't say a word." Madison's mind was occupied with the fact she'd crossed a line in there—not just by telling Shane her suspicion but by lifting the lipstick. The only thing soothing her conscience was the fact that no one would be hurt by this. No one even needed to know.

"I hope you're right." He looked out the passenger window, and she got them moving.

They spent the next two hours visiting Wayne Ridley and Russell Brennan. Neither man recognized the shooter, but then neither would confess to it if they had hired him. And as it occurred to Madison and Terry before, any of the men could have hired the shooter sight unseen.

It was four o'clock by the time she and Terry were back at their desks, shuffling paperwork, and the lipstick was burning a hole in her pocket. She wanted to know—now more than ever—whether Morgan Walker was Courtney Middleton. But she only had one piece of the puzzle. She needed that other sample. She knew what she'd be doing tonight—visiting Bruce and Phoebe Middleton.

CHAPTER 26

Madison and Terry still didn't have authorization to be snooping through the victims' phones or their financials, but they weren't without next steps. It was around midafternoon, and they were back at Diane Butler's door armed with a photo spread that included Tatiana Ivanova.

Butler answered before Madison had a chance to knock. Either the woman lived with her eye to the peephole or their footsteps vibrated through the floorboards and alerted Butler to company.

"Detectives?" she said. "Did you find Kayla?"

Madison shook her head. "Could we come in for a minute? We'd like to show you some pictures to see if you recognize any of them as being her aunt."

"Certainly." Butler backed up and let them inside.

Madison brought up the image gallery on her phone and extended it to Butler. "There are pictures of five women. Please take a close look and let us know if one of them look like her."

Butler licked her lips and eyed the screen with intensity. She flipped from the first to the second, then the third, paused on the fourth, and raised her face. "This is her, Kayla's aunt."

Madison froze. *Tatiana Ivanova.*

"Detective…?"

Madison snapped out of her daze and took her phone back. "Thank you."

"Any time." Butler's face took on hard lines. "She's not Kayla's aunt, is she?"

"Sorry, but we're not at liberty to say."

"Hmm. I see."

Terry opened the door and walked out. Butler stayed at the threshold, watching them as they headed down the hall.

"Have a good day," Butler said.

"You too, Ms. Butler," Terry said. Madison was too preoccupied with thoughts of Tatiana to respond.

She didn't say a word as they went to the department car and loaded inside. She gripped the wheel and twisted her hand so tightly it tugged on the leather wrapping.

"You all right over there?" Terry asked. "I thought you'd be happy to know that."

"No. I'm not happy. If Tatiana came here, it tells me Kayla is on the run. And the mob isn't just going to let her go. There was that missed call on Nikitin's burner. He was probably supposed to update someone when Kayla got on the train and was on her way to Canada. When he didn't, Tatiana went to find out what the problem was and to deal with it accordingly. She found Nikitin dead. That made her eager to find the girl."

"If so, maybe someone saw Tatiana in Nikitin's apartment building."

"Our next stop is the police station to read the officers' reports, but even if no one commented on her, I bet she was there."

"Agree."

"What? You're— I'm shocked."

"Hey, there's enough that stacks up here to have me believing that the Mafia's behind the drug trafficking now," Terry said. "But it still doesn't get us any closer to our shooter—you know, the case we're actually investigating."

Terry was sounding much like Winston and the former police chief McAlexandar, who could turn a blind eye to crimes if they weren't directly related to the one being investigated. Madison couldn't do that. "We're still looking at the reports."

She took them back to the station, where they did just that. Terry also put in a request for the financials for the Walkers, Ridleys, and Brennans—just to eliminate any possibilities of them paying for a hired gun.

After an hour of reading tedium, which included repeated statements that no one heard anything, Madison finally found two leads worth moving on. "A Teresa Burton in apartment 511 saw a woman of Tatiana's description in the hallway the morning of Nikitin's murder. Around ten in the morning. Then there's a Kye Turner from apartment 503—across the hall from Nikitin's apartment. He described a young woman who could have been Kayla Fleming. Said he'd seen her a few times. Most recently was eight o'clock Monday morning when she let herself into Nikitin's apartment and left a few minutes later." Madison stood. "We've got to follow up on these. ASAP."

Madison and Terry settled in Teresa Burton's living room, and Madison got down to business.

"We'd like to follow up what you told Officer Tendum, and we also have some pictures to show you." She paused there while Burton soaked in Madison's words. When Burton nodded, Madison continued. "You saw a woman in the hall around ten AM on Monday morning?"

"That's right."

"And can you describe her to us?" Madison asked.

"Sure. Dark hair, pretty, around midthirties. She was dressed impeccably—very high-end. Let's see…what else?" She worried her lip. "Ah, she also had this huge purse, beige. It probably cost more than I make in a month."

"All right. Thank you." Madison brought up the photos that included Tatiana Ivanova and passed her phone to Burton. "There are five pictures. Please scroll through them and let me know if any of these women was her."

Burton nodded and proceeded to work her way through the pictures. She passed the fourth, which was Tatiana, glanced at five but went back. "This one." She pressed her finger to Tatiana's face.

"And you're sure?" Madison asked.

"Positive."

"Okay, great." Not that it was *great* by any means… Sometimes it would be nice to be wrong. "Now, I need to show you a few other pictures. Let me know if you've ever seen any of these women before." She brought up the folder on her phone that included Kayla Fleming and other similar-looking young women. "Five, as well. Take your time."

Burton hummed a little tune as she worked her way through the pictures. "Ah, she looks somewhat familiar." She handed the phone back to Madison, and Kayla Fleming's face was on the screen.

"Okay. Thank you. When did you see her?"

"I've seen her a couple times in the building."

"Visiting someone?" Terry interjected.

"I assume so. Don't think she lives here."

"Do you know who she came to see?" Madison asked.

"No. Sorry." Burton winced.

"No problem. You've helped a lot." Madison proceeded with one more photo spread, which included the shooter. Burton didn't recognize any of the men. "Thank you for your time." Madison got up, gave Burton her card, and led the way out of the apartment.

In the hallway, Madison leaned against the wall for a few seconds. "That's two people who have ID'd Tatiana Ivanova now."

"So Tatiana was here around ten on Monday morning, then at Kayla's place around noon."

"Thankfully Kayla was already gone." *But why would the mob leave Nikitin's burners…?*

Madison pushed off the wall, and they walked down the hall and knocked on apartment 503.

"Just a minute!" A man's voice called out from inside, followed by heavy-placed footsteps pounding toward the door. It almost sounded like he had shoes on, but he didn't when he answered the door. "Yeah?"

Madison had her badge up, and so did Terry. She gave the introductions and asked, "Are you Kye Turner?"

"The one and only." He smiled and winked. Turner was probably in his twenties with brown hair, brown eyes. There wasn't anything distinct about his facial features or body type, which was just slender and average height.

"We're here to follow up on the statement you gave Officer Tendum on Monday."

"Whatever you'd like." He swept an arm, inviting them to enter.

They ended up standing just inside the door.

"You told the officer that you saw a young woman in her twenties visit apartment 502 on Monday morning at eight."

"For sure. Think she was Vlas's girlfriend. She popped by at different times in the past. Cute thing too."

Madison had him run through the description again and then showed him the pictures in the spread that included Kayla Fleming. Turner pointed at Fleming's photo and added she had been wearing an orange backpack when he'd seen her on Monday morning.

"And that's unusual?" Madison asked.

"Yeah."

It sounded like Kayla may have come straight from the train station—between the bag and the time Turner had seen her. "And you said she went into Vlas Nikitin's apartment but didn't stay long?"

"That's right."

"Was she different when she left…?" Madison was thinking that after finding Nikitin dead, the girl would have, in the least, been shaken.

"Wasn't paying enough attention to know, really."

"Was she in a hurry maybe?" Madison pushed.

His brow tightened, then he nodded. "I guess…? I was down in the front lobby emptying my mailbox when she left. She didn't say hi or anything. She normally does." He shrugged, like it didn't matter.

But it did matter—just like her fast turnaround in Nikitin's apartment. It told Madison that Kayla Fleming had found Nikitin dead and had panicked. That, in turn, had led her to going home, packing up, and going on the run. She brought up the photo spread that included Tatiana Ivanova. "Tell me if any of these women look familiar."

"Okay," he dragged out. A few seconds later, he shook his head and handed the phone back to Madison. "Never seen any of these ladies."

"You're sure?"

"Ah. Yeah."

"Not even later Monday morning…?"

"I left for work at nine that day, so I wouldn't know if any of those chicks were hanging around after that."

Madison showed him the set of photos with the shooter, and Turner didn't recognize any of the men. She backed out of the photo gallery and put her phone in her pocket. "Thank you for your time."

"Sure."

They left him and ran the photos past the building manager. He confirmed that Kayla Fleming was the girlfriend of Nikitin's that he'd mentioned. He hadn't seen her this past Monday, and he'd never seen Tatiana Ivanova or the shooter before.

"Our shooter knows how to remain invisible, but we have both Kayla and Tatiana in Nikitin's building on Monday morning," Madison said as she and Terry exited the building. "Here's how I see it. When Nikitin didn't show up at the train station, Kayla came to check on him. When she found him dead, she freaked out, went back to her apartment, packed up her things, and ran."

"As you said before, and her backpack full of meth? What happened to it, assuming she had been carrying drugs at the time?"

Assuming? Apparently, Terry still wasn't convinced she was moving drugs Monday morning. "Maybe she left the drugs in Nikitin's apartment? Tatiana shows up, probably to follow up on the status of that morning's shipment. Tatiana finds Nikitin dead *and* the drugs. She's going to take them with her."

"That could explain the trace of meth that was found, and the timing works. Kayla's here around eight, gives her time to get home, pack, and run. Tatiana shows up around ten at Nikitin's apartment and is seen at Kayla's about noon. But if the girl left the meth, why go after her?"

"Because as far as the mob's concerned, they own that girl. They're not just going to let Kayla walk away. She knows too much. She'd know the location of the stash house and other players. Too much of a risk to them."

Terry blew out a haggard breath.

"And while Kayla may have left the drugs behind, Tatiana still wants answers—what happened Monday morning and why Nikitin was killed." Madison stopped talking as a chilling thought occurred to her. Tatiana might even think Kayla had killed Nikitin.

CHAPTER 27

Everything from that day was playing through Madison's mind as she drove to the Middletons' in Colton. It was a town forty-five minutes north of Stiles. It was going on eight o'clock at night, and she was still a few minutes out. From a quick look at their records, the couple had left Stiles after the memorial for Courtney, which was held about eight years after she had disappeared. Their reasons for moving Madison could only guess at, but she'd imagine it was for a fresh start.

This was a solo road trip. Troy knew where she was headed, but Terry didn't. After the mini blowup at the Walkers, she preferred to avoid discussing the subject of Courtney with her partner.

The GPS in her car announced the last turn. In two hundred feet, she'd be at her destination.

Her phone rang over the vehicle's Bluetooth system, and the display on the dash told her it was Cynthia.

"Mark's in the lab late tonight, and a hit came back on facial rec. We've got a name for the shooter."

"Great news. *Hit* me."

"The shooter's name is Justin McBride, thirty-three, and he has a record. He served a few years for armed assault in his twenties."

"Only a few…?"

"Yep. He must have had an extremely good lawyer. Anyway, I've got his address. I assume you're going to want to pay him a visit, slap on some cuffs…"

Madison was so close to the Middletons' home and possibly getting some answers about Courtney. In the least, she could get her hands on an item with DNA to compare to the lipstick she took from the Walkers' bathroom.

"Maddy? You do want the address?"

"Yes, of course, but..." She pulled up in front of the Middleton house and parked. Should she tell her friend where she was and what she was up to? She was torn. Should she turn around and postpone this visit? She'd called ahead, and the Middletons were expecting her, and she hated to break her word. Besides, she wasn't working the case alone. She did have a partner. Maybe she could release the reins a little. "Cyn, I'm out of town at the moment. Don't ask why. And everything's okay. Could you do me a favor and call Terry with this news? He can go over with backup. I'll be there as soon as I can."

There were a few beats of silence. "You're sure you're okay?"

Not really... "I'm fine."

"Okay, this is something you'd typically jump on."

"I know, but Terry can manage until I get back to Stiles." She'd put it firmly, not wanting her friend to sniff out any weakness in her resolve. She'd love nothing more than to put that McBride guy in prison for life for what he'd done. But she was here and Terry was right there—in Stiles, and more than capable of following up this lead.

"All right, as long as you're good. Night. Talk in the morning."

Cynthia hung up first, and Madison was left to question whether she was making the right decision—or one based solely on emotion. She turned the car off. And sat.

Lights were on inside and outside. She saw a figure moving through the window in the front door. Then it opened, and Phoebe Middleton stepped outside.

No turning around now that I've been seen...

Madison got out of the vehicle and hurried up the walkway, where Bruce had now joined Phoebe in the house's entry.

"My, Madison, it's been a very long time." Phoebe was all grins as she spread her arms wide and pulled Madison in for a huge hug. The woman had always been warm and affectionate.

"Bruce," Madison said as she left Phoebe and gave Bruce a brief embrace. He was more of a reserved man and preferred to keep his emotions in check. He always had a way about him that made Madison think he was suspicious of everyone. And that was before Courtney went missing. Courtney had resembled her father more than her mother. Her natural, dominant nose was a replica of Bruce's.

"Well, take off your shoes and coat and stay a while. Would you like a coffee, tea, water, wine?" Phoebe asked, her eyes wide and sparkling.

Seeing her happy drilled an ache in Madison's chest. It was good that Phoebe had moved on with her life, but Madison's being there would most certainly stir up the past and resurrect their grief.

"Dear, what will it be?" Phoebe prompted.

"Oh, water's fine."

"Coming right up. Just make yourself comfortable." Phoebe turned to Bruce. "Show her to the living room, would you?"

Bruce quickly shut the front door and threw the deadbolt. "This way."

Madison followed him and took in the features of the home. High ceilings, crown molding, marble flooring. It was a bungalow but with a spacious floor plan.

The living room was creams and shades of taupe, accented with blues and teals. Very beachy, but Phoebe had always loved the water. They used to live right on the lake in Stiles.

"Here you go." Phoebe handed Madison a glass of water. She was holding a wineglass for herself. "Please, make yourself comfortable," Phoebe said and took a sip of her wine.

"Thank you." Madison offered a small smile, trying to tamp down the bolts of guilt firing through her. When she'd called them, she said she'd be in the area and thought she'd stop by to see how they were doing, sort of for old times' sake. Not a lie, though not exactly the truth. The latter felt like something far better to address in person rather than over the phone.

Phoebe dropped into a plush chair, and Madison lowered into one very similar. Bruce was across the room seated in one that looked far more firm. On the table next to him was a beer bottle dappled with condensation. Madison smiled at that and pointed.

"Still like your beer I see."

"Some things never change." Phoebe laughed.

"And you're one to talk," Bruce said. "This woman would have been further ahead investing in a vineyard for the amount of grape *juice*"—he wrapped finger quotes around the *juice* bit—"she drinks."

Phoebe shot her husband daggers, but her expression quickly softened. Then she turned to Madison. "So, what has been going on with you?"

Such a loaded question. Madison started with the personal. She told them she was engaged and had a dog. She left out all mention of the baby she lost. On a professional level, she shared that she was now a detective in Major Crimes with the Stiles PD. Last they would have known, she was a uniformed officer patrolling the streets.

The Middletons said they'd moved out to Colton for "a fresh lease on life," and both were keeping busy in the community. Phoebe liked to help organize public events, and Bruce liked his bowling league on Tuesdays and playing darts on Fridays.

After a few minutes of catching up, the room fell silent, and in that space, grief moved in. The couple's excitement at seeing one of their daughter's college friends had faded. It was time for Madison to get to the point of why she came tonight. She didn't have the heart to come right out with it—that she felt sure Courtney had been shot on Monday morning at Liberty Station. Madison would work her way there. She licked her lips, considering how to proceed. Just coming out with it might be the answer—no matter how much it hurt.

The grief turned to tension, and Bruce set down his beer bottle, which Madison could tell was empty. His DNA would be all over it. She rushed to get up. "Would you like a new one?" Possibly a little presumptuous, given she hadn't seen these people for so long, but they had been so welcoming.

Bruce glanced at his wife as if seeking her permission, and then said, "Why not?"

Madison grabbed his empty bottle and, with a little direction, knew where to put it and where to grab a new one. Before tossing the bottle, though, she pulled out a DNA swab and vial from her pocket. She'd thought ahead to bring one from the station. She rubbed the swab around the lip of the bottle as quickly as possible, put the swab into the vial, and slid the sealed sample into her pocket.

She grabbed Bruce's new beer and returned to the living room. Both Middletons were staring into space, and they looked worn out. She gave Bruce his beer and sat down again. Bruce and Phoebe stared at her, and Madison could feel the question in their eyes. There would be no more delaying.

She cleared her throat and said, "Does the name Morgan Walker or Morgan Gardner mean anything to either of you?"

They looked at each other, hitched their shoulders.

"No." Phoebe raised her brows.

Bruce leaned forward. "Why do you want to know? Who is this Morgan?"

Madison wasn't a mind reader, but her gut was telling her by his leery tone that he was formulating his own ideas. Maybe it was cruel to hold off any longer, but first she'd lay some groundwork. "Recently, there was a shooting in Stiles at Liberty Train Station."

"Yes, I heard about it on the news," Bruce said.

Madison dipped her head and continued. "Two women died, and one of them was a woman named Morgan Walker."

"Don't remember the names of the victims. But what about this shooting has you bringing it up to us?" Bruce's new beer hadn't yet been touched, and he was watching Madison with keen interest.

"This Morgan woman looked a lot like Courtney." The admission came out on a rush of breath.

Phoebe and Bruce regarded her with skepticism and a touch of curiosity.

"They say everyone has a twin," Phoebe said casually but moved her mouth to the rim of her wineglass and drank, the level of liquid going down quickly.

"I really think it's more than that. Not that I can prove it yet, but things aren't adding up. I'm a person who needs all the answers." She paused, clearing her throat again. "The night Courtney went missing, I was one of the girls out with her. She met a guy there."

"Yes, and police exhausted all avenues trying to find out who he was," Bruce said stiffly.

"That's right."

Phoebe cradled her wineglass in her hands and inched forward on her chair. "Did you find him, Madison?"

She shook her head.

"Do you have a picture of this woman?" Phoebe's voice was small when she asked.

Madison showed her Morgan Walker's driver's license photo.

Phoebe leaned forward, not relinquishing her glass to take the phone, and looked closely. Tears pooled in her eyes. "She looks a bit like her, but it's not her, Madison." She gripped at the fabric of her shirt and let out a staggered exhale.

Madison was undeterred. "Focus on the eyes and chin. She had cosmetic surgery done on her nose."

Phoebe hesitated, but then put her gaze back on the photo. "Oh…" Her mouth opened, shut, opened. She put her glass on the table next to her. And sobbed.

Madison rubbed Phoebe's back. "It is her, isn't it?"

Phoebe nodded from behind her hands, which were now covering her face.

Bruce got up from his chair and walked over to them. "Let me see."

Madison gave him the phone, and shortly after, his legs buckled. She rushed to steady him and guided him back to his chair. She took her phone and returned to her seat as well.

"I appreciate how shocking all this must be, and I'm sorry for even bringing this up but—"

"Nonsense." Phoebe waved a hand. "You had to come to us." She hiccupped another sob and got up to snatch a tissue box from across the room.

"So she's been going by this Morgan name?" Bruce eventually said.

"Yes, I believe for some time. Does that name mean anything to you?"

"It was my sister's name, Courtney's aunt," Bruce said.

Madison searched her memory but didn't remember Courtney ever mentioning her aunt, but the last time they'd spoken had been over fifteen years ago. It was possible she'd just forgotten. "And the name Gardner?"

Phoebe dried her tears and returned to her chair, tissue box in hand. "Bruce, maybe we should tell her...everything."

Madison's stomach tightened. "Tell me what?"

"That has nothing to do with this," Bruce said firmly.

"You can't be sure, and our girl is dead. For real this time! All the years we missed out on, and why didn't she ever come back to us? Though I'm starting to think I know why she might have left in the first place."

Bruce leveled his gaze at his wife. "Phoebe, not a word."

"Please, Mr. and Mrs. Middleton, if you know something that might help me find who killed your daughter, tell me."

Bruce said, "We're talking over fifteen years ago, Phoebe. Nothing to do with now."

"We can't be sure that the past doesn't factor in," Madison countered. "Tell me whatever it is."

Bruce clenched his jaw, and fresh tears fell on Phoebe's cheeks.

Maybe a little detour... "There was another woman who died in Monday's shooting. Dana Ridley. A Shannon Brennan was also shot, but she survived her injuries. Do either of those names sound familiar? Maybe friends of Courtney's? Though they'd have had different last names." Madison wished she'd made a note of them before coming here, but her mind was all over the place with the findings from this afternoon. Now wasn't much better. Her thoughts kept skipping to Terry and what was happening with Justin McBride's arrest.

"No." Phoebe was shaking her head wildly.

"Haven't heard of them," Bruce said.

Madison addressed Phoebe. "Do you know why Courtney disappeared?" Rage and sadness were twisting inside her, ripping her apart. All those years of thinking her friend had been kidnapped, tortured, raped, then killed... Years of grief and guilt for leaving her at that bar, and Phoebe might have answers. "Mrs. Middleton," she prompted.

Phoebe gulped back the rest of her wine. "Gardner was my maiden name."

Madison shook her head. Such a random comment. "What am I missing?" She looked from Phoebe to Bruce.

Bruce clasped his hands in his lap. "What do you think prompted the shooting? It sounded random on TV."

No answer to her question, and Bruce had her whirling in another direction. "Evidence is starting to suggest it might not have been." That was as much as she dared say.

"Bruce. Please, we need to tell her. We'll be safe."

"How can you know that?" Bruce spat. "They could have gotten to Courtney!"

Madison stiffened. "Who could have gotten to her?"

He took a few heaving breaths, then spoke in a such a calm manner that it came across eerie after his outburst. "I know you can't tell us everything, but do you think her past might have gotten her killed?"

"As I said, we can't rule out the possibility."

Sweat was beading on Bruce's brow, and he wiped it away.

"Oh my goodness, Bruce." Phoebe gasped, and more tears fell. "You have to tell her. If it helps at all."

"We're in WITSEC," he eventually said.

"Witness protection," Madison whispered. "Why?" Memories were flooding back—how strange Courtney's parents could be at times, how they'd try to talk her out of different social events. But if the Middletons were in WITSEC, Courtney's fingerprints should be on record. They weren't. But before she asked about that, she'd let them answer the question she'd already raised.

"Surely, you can tell her, Bruce," Phoebe petitioned.

Bruce met Madison's eyes, and his expression pained her. She put a hand over her stomach, bracing herself for what he was going to say.

"I worked for a certain accounting firm and saw things I shouldn't have. I turned state's evidence."

Dread crawled over Madison like a thousand centipedes, their feet raising every hair on her body. "What firm?"

He gave her the name, and it took all her willpower not to gasp. Her entire body was trembling. "I've heard of it." Her voice came out returning to her ears as if it were from a million miles away.

"You should have. It was where—"

She held up a hand, stopping him there. "I know." Years ago, before she was born, her grandfather had been a police officer and had arrested a Mafia accountant. That had been the beginning of the end. The accountant's son had gunned down her grandfather, leaving her grandmother widowed and without the love of her life. The incident was why Madison became a cop. And when she'd heard the story, she had to know more. She'd made it her mission to take down the mob—and was still doing all she could in that regard. She'd studied the court records and knew the names of everyone who testified, both at the murder trial to convict her grandfather's killer and the trial against the corrupt mob accountant. "What is your real name?"

Bruce gave it to her.

"I don't remember that one."

"I never ended up being called on to testify, but the damage was done. The mob knew I was talking to the cops."

And the mob never forgets…

Phoebe had excused herself while Madison and Bruce spoke, and she now returned with a topped-up wineglass.

"But you stayed in Stiles?" Madison asked, not understanding. "Why didn't WITSEC put you elsewhere?"

"I only liaised with the firm in Stiles but worked at another branch a few hours out of the city. By putting us in Stiles, it made us close for the trial. And we were assured we'd be safe."

Guess the government was operating under the "can't see what's right under your nose" philosophy? "Wouldn't you risk being recognized?"

"Not when my wife and I weren't allowed out of the house, and the Russians didn't know about Courtney. She was born after we were already in WITSEC," Bruce explained.

"Why aren't her prints on file?"

"I couldn't bring myself to allow that, I just couldn't," Phoebe said. "She was going to grow up with enough restrictions. It was nerve-racking letting her go to college, not knowing if she was going to come home."

"But Courtney knew you were in WITSEC?" Madison asked.

"Yes. Probably why her disappearance was our fault," Phoebe muttered. "I should have known that she had run away. I'm her mother. She just hated it so much, found it like living in a prison. It was probably why she was so wild and carefree whenever she got the chance."

But maybe Courtney hadn't been entirely carefree and living in the moment. What if she hadn't just met that man the night she disappeared? What if she had already known him and had planned to run away with him? And was he Leanne's biological father? So many questions.

Phoebe shook her head. "If only we would have extended her more freedom."

"She might have been dead sooner, and us along with her," Bruce pointed out.

"There's no danger still, is there?" Phoebe asked. "Surely the mob have more important people to go after."

The Middletons looked at Madison, as if seeking assurance.

"From what I know of the Russian Mafia, they have long memories."

"Then do you think they killed Courtney?" Phoebe asked.

Madison would love to lay the murder on them, but the evidence didn't support that at all. While the mob could make an elaborate show of killing someone, they didn't usually do so publicly. And they certainly wouldn't have wanted to draw attention to the drug trafficking. "No." She shook her head to add emphasis and caught the time on the clock on the wall. *10:15 PM*. She still had a forty-five-minute drive back home, and she had to catch up with Terry and the shooter. But while she was here, she'd try one more thing. Even if it led nowhere, at least she'd sleep better for asking. "Does the name Justin McBride mean anything to either of you?"

The couple seemed to consider, then they both shook their heads.

Madison took it a step further and brought up the photo spread that included the shooter's face and asked them to look at the pictures. A few minutes later, it was confirmed that they'd never seen any of the men. She put her phone in her pants pocket and made a move to leave. "I should go."

"Wait," Phoebe called out. "Did she ever marry?"

"Yes." A sliver of apprehension ran through her at the thought of Phoebe reaching out to Shane Walker.

"Did she ever have children? Do I have…" She gulped, almost choking on her saliva. "Grandchildren?"

Madison wanted to tell her, but until she had DNA proof that Morgan was Courtney, she wouldn't. She'd probably done enough damage already. "Let me just continue with the investigation, and once I have more answers, I'll share all I know."

"Oh, okay." Phoebe wrapped her arms around herself. "I wonder if she ever gave us another thought."

Madison put a hand on Phoebe's arm. "She named herself Morgan Gardner. That wasn't random. It was to remember you and keep you both close. She probably knew she'd never be able to return to you for fear of putting you in danger."

"Bless you for saying that." Phoebe tapped a kiss on Madison's cheek.

Madison didn't make it to the car before her own tears fell. When Courtney had run away all those years ago, she'd left more than her family behind.

CHAPTER 28

The tears in Madison's eyes made it difficult for her to see during the drive home. Was there anything she could have done differently to get Courtney to stay?

Her phone rang, and it was Terry. "No idea where you've been but—"

"I'm only fifteen minutes out. You at McBride's, or have you picked him up yet?"

There was a huge sigh from the other end of the line. "I was at his place, only he wasn't."

"Was? You're gone already? We should sit on his place. Wait him out."

"He won't be coming home."

A feeling of dread spiked through her. "What do you mean?"

"He's dead. I'm looking at him right now. The guy was slashed from ear to ear."

They'd been too slow getting to him—and the mob had caught up with him first. *Had to be the mob.* "Tell me where, and I'll meet you there."

He told her McBride was found by the marina, and she pressed her foot harder on the gas. "See you very soon. Get officers to sit on his place, though. We'll want to get Crime Scene in to process it too."

"I understand all this, Madison." Terry clicked off.

So maybe she was sounding a bit like Winston with the micromanaging, but she just needed to get this case wrapped up before it ate her alive. She palmed her damp cheeks and turned up the radio, trying anything to drown out her past crashing into her present.

Eleven minutes later, Madison was parked at the marina and rushing toward Terry on the dock. He was waving her over and standing with Richards and Milo under a lamppost. That, a few halogens, and the pale moon were all that casted light. Past them was the inky darkness of the lake, and at their feet were the remains of Justin McBride.

Whitish-gray and bloated. The wound to his neck appeared quite deep, and if he wasn't supine on the dock, his head would probably lean back toward his shoulders. He had rope around his wrists and ankles—a lead weight attached to the latter, and his eyes were gone.

None of this was random, and it had all the markings of a mob hit—violent and dramatic enough to send a statement. "Where was he found? Who found him?" She rubbed her arms, the chill of the night and damp air seeping into her bones.

"He was found by a boater getting ready to take a midnight cruise," Terry said. "McBride was just to the side of the dock, weighed down, as you can see."

"Placed somewhere he could be found sooner rather than later."

"Yep. Now, I've already spoken with the boater and cleared the guy. He's just an innocent caught up in all this." Terry squared his shoulders as if daring her to challenge him on that point, which she might have at any other time—when the evidence didn't seem to clearly point to the Mafia.

She gestured toward the empty sockets and looked at Richards. "The eyes gone due to fish or...?" She swallowed roughly, barely able to stomach the alternative her mind spun.

Richards set his lips into a straight line. "From what I'm seeing, preliminarily I'd say they were cut out of his face, while he was alive."

She put a hand on her stomach. This was the work of the mob, likely Tatiana Ivanova herself. The torture was too barbaric to be anything else. "When did he...uh...time of death?" Guilt was snaking in on her from around the edges. *If only we'd been a little faster...*

"I'd say he's been in the water at least a couple of days," Richards said, "but I'll know once I have him back at the morgue and run more tests. Cause of death would quite obviously appear to be the slash to the neck. Guessing a large knife, and considering the damage I'm seeing, I wouldn't be surprised if the blade nicked cervical vertebrae."

"This *is* the mob, Terry," she punched out.

"We need to just step back, get all the evidence—"

"No. They don't get the luxury of killing people like this and walking away. That's not the justice system I work for." She went to leave, but Terry put a hand on her shoulder.

"We don't get to make our own version of justice."

"But they repeatedly get off," she snapped. "They've got money for the best lawyers." And she should know. One of them was an ex, but now wasn't the time to pile on even more self-judgment.

Terry added, "That's why it's integral to build a solid case against them, *then* go after them."

She gritted her teeth and stared out at the black surrounding her, darkness creeping into her soul. "Fine," she pushed out. "We do it your way."

Terry dipped his head.

They spent the next hour with the body, but at Terry's insistence, she left McBride's apartment for Crime Scene to process. She was beyond exhausted at this point. Though it was unlikely sleep would come, she had to try. She was of no use to the case or anyone if she made herself sick.

Still, all she could think about was retaliation. Sure, Justin McBride was a killer—and he deserved to pay for his crimes, but not the way he had. And her heart was aching at thoughts of Kayla Fleming. Was she still alive, or would they be finding her body next?

CHAPTER 29

As Madison had suspected, she barely got any sleep, and the amount she had was riddled with nightmares. Ones about her conversation with the Middletons, the fact that they were in WITSEC and the connection to her grandfather. Then there was Courtney telling Madison she had no choice but to stage her disappearance. Other dreams were about dead bodies, flashes of imagery layered one on top of the other in some sort of macabre collage. She had bolted awake at the sight of Kayla's face on McBride's body and decided she was up for good—rested or not.

A text on her phone confirmed her nightmares were based more on reality than she'd have liked. Richards told her the autopsy on McBride would take place today at noon.

She staggered out the door, stopping on the way to the police station to mail the DNA exemplars to a testing lab that guaranteed results in a week.

A week... And yet it takes police departments months... Sometimes the inconsistencies hurt.

Madison sucked back on an extra-large coffee as she checked her email for updates on what had been recovered from McBride's apartment. There was one from Mark, who told her they'd recovered a Smith & Wesson M&P M2.0 and 9mm ammunition. That was the same caliber used on the women at the train station and on Nikitin. Sam would still need to run ballistics testing to confirm if the weapon recovered was *the* gun used in both shootings. Mark had also found a phone in McBride's place.

Madison fired back a quick email to Mark and told him it was possible McBride was just a hired gun and to get his financial records. She also asked him to let her know if there was anything useful on his phone ASAP.

"Hey." Terry came in holding his own coffee and looked about as thrilled at the twist in the case as she was. *Not very.*

"Hi."

He dropped into his chair. "Guess it's case closed. We got the shooter, and I'm sure Sam will confirm the gun's a match for the murder weapon." He must have read Mark's email on his phone.

"Not exactly. We don't have motive and—"

"Sometimes we don't get all the answers."

She stiffened. "We don't have evidence to support why he shot the women. Until then, this case is wide open. We can't dismiss that McBride may have been a hired gun."

"He could have had a connection to one of the women and took all this on himself," Terry countered. "Either way, he's out of reach now he's dead."

"Uh-huh, but if someone paid him for the shooting, that person is likely very much alive. And I'm not about to let them get away with murder. Don't you think they deserve to pay for their role in all this?"

Terry sighed and grimaced. "Of course."

"All right, then. We keep doing our jobs. We get *all* the answers. Then, once we have them, the case is closed."

"You determined to get all the answers before you go after this Tatiana?"

"Don't feel like I have a choice." Madison would deal with her soon, but one investigation at a time. She recalled Richards's text. "McBride's autopsy is at noon today," she told Terry.

"Yeah, Richards messaged me too."

She nodded, her mind drifting to Kayla Fleming. Again, she wondered if the girl was even still alive.

An email filtered into her inbox and caught her eye. "Huh, and would you look at that? We have the approval to access the phone records for the three women from the train station—*and* their financials."

"It's like Christmas around here."

Even better. Unwrapped presents made a mess, but by the time she and Terry saw everything through, there would closure, and the victims would have justice. That was pretty much the only thing that got Madison out of bed that morning.

CHAPTER 30

Surely there had to be something in the phone records and financials. Otherwise, Madison wasn't sure of their next step. Confronting the Russian mob at this point wasn't a true option, even if there was a part of her that really wanted to. It was dangerous but debatably effective. Still, she had promised Troy that she'd watch her steps and her back.

If only she had contacts to help her find people, like Tatiana Ivanova had. Then maybe she could have found McBride sooner and she could get to Kayla now. But Madison didn't have people on every street corner, and Major Crimes wasn't exactly the unit designed for having confidential informants. It's not like their investigations took them back to the same people time and time again. The mob, excluded, but no one was snitching on them.

Terry was already at his desk starting on the phone records. She called Marsh. He answered on the first ring. She was quite sure he groaned when she announced who it was. "How is the investigation into a drug-trafficking ring at Liberty Station going?"

"Don't answer to you, Knight."

She shrugged, not that he could see. "Did you get the picture I sent?"

"Uh-huh."

She swallowed her initial reaction, which would have had her lashing out at him. "We have her name now, by the way. Kayla Fleming."

"I'll do all I can to help."

"Maybe you have CIs that have seen her around? Show her picture to them please."

"I'll take care of this."

"Please. She's in real danger."

"From?"

Madison hesitated. If she said the mob, then he might laugh at her. Even though her theories had a way of panning out most of the time, people often didn't want to hear that the Russians were behind anything. "Let's just say dangerous people, and last I knew, you took an oath to serve and protect, so—"

"Save the speech. I'll see what I can do."

"All I can ask. Thanks." She ended the call.

"Hey, so I found something you'd like to know." Terry lifted his gaze from his monitor and looked across his desk at her. "Dana Ridley's phone records don't indicate that she was sleeping with someone else other than her boss, but I came across something interesting, nonetheless. Five months ago, there were several calls between her and a place called Lotus Family Planning. I did a quick internet search. They're an insemination bank. Dana's baby may very well not have been her husband's or David's."

"Well, both men claimed they couldn't father a child."

"And without getting their medical records, we can't know for sure. We'd also have to get a warrant for Lotus Family Planning to give us information on Dana Ridley."

"Neither of which we'd get approval for."

"Right, but it occurred to me that if she hid her pregnancy from the two men in her life, what else might she have been hiding? Something that could have made her a target?"

"Good questions. You keep plugging, and I'll get started on Walker's phone activity over here."

And that's what she did—for the next hour or so. Morgan Walker had made calls to her husband, her work, companies who were supposedly clients. Madison made a list of these and would have Morgan's employer confirm whether or not that was the case. Morgan didn't seem to be hiding anything—except possibly her past life as Courtney Middleton. And, if so, that was a biggie.

She moved on to Shannon Brennan's phone records, and nothing exciting there. In that time, Terry had progressed to the financials, starting with the Ridleys' accounts. Nada.

"Nothing to see with the Walkers' financials either," she said. He didn't respond. "Terry," she prompted.

"I am quite sure I just found something."

Just the way he said it had the hairs rising on her arms. "What?"

"I'm looking at the Brennans' joint savings account. There were three cash withdrawals for fifteen hundred dollars over the last three weeks."

"None before that?"

"Nope."

The skin tightened on the back of her neck. "Money for a hit man? Looks like it's time to talk to Russell Brennan."

"Only thing is, if he ordered a hit on his wife, he never got his money's worth. Shannon's still alive."

She glared at him. "But two other women are dead, and Shannon, as far as I know, is still recovering in the hospital. Though, there could be complications." *Like this entire case.*

Madison sent over a brief text to Richards to inform him that she and Terry would be missing the autopsy on McBride. He acknowledged her message and promised to make good notes "as always."

Madison and Terry were sitting in the living room at the Brennan residence around noon. Shannon was still in the hospital, so they were face-to-face with Russell.

"Could we see your bank card, Mr. Brennan?" Terry asked. On the way over, they decided that Terry would start the questioning because the withdrawals were his find.

"Ah, sure." He fished his wallet out of his back pocket, and then handed the card to Terry.

He looked at the numbers and gave it back to him. "Thank you. Now can you tell us what these cash withdrawals were for?" Terry produced a copy of the statement with the transactions in question highlighted in yellow.

Russell took the sheet from him and looked down the page. He squinted. "I never took out this money."

"This is the statement for your bank account, isn't it?"

"It is, but that doesn't make sense. Shannon must have done it."

"I just saw your bank card, Mr. Brennan, and that's the last four digits of your card, right?" Terry pointed a finger to the page. The transactions were split by card number, then in date order.

"I don't have an explanation. It doesn't make any sense."

Madison settled back in her chair, relaxed, nonchalant, ready to become involved in the conversation. "Does the name Justin McBride mean anything to you?"

"No."

"You're sure?" she pushed.

"Positive."

"So you wouldn't object to us looking at your phone records or your computer?"

"Wait a minute. What do you think I'm guilty of? Because it's obviously something."

Madison gestured toward Terry for him to answer.

"A total of forty-five hundred dollars was taken out of your bank account—in cash. Unusual behavior, which you can't even seem to explain," Terry said.

"Shannon must have—"

Terry was quick to counter, "She uses your bank card?"

Russell pursed his lips and shrugged. "I don't see why she would."

"Then you can understand why we're here asking you about the cash withdrawals. You take out all this money, and then there's a shooting. Do you get where I'm going with this?"

"You think that I...*that I*..."

"It's looking quite possible that you hired someone to kill your wife, only they failed. The shooter did kill two other women, though, including one who was pregnant."

"No, you have this all wrong! And I wouldn't hire someone to hurt my wife. We didn't always see eye to eye, but we had a decent marriage."

"Decent?" Madison spat. "Sounds like a glowing review." Though it was an improvement over his first description that it wasn't a bed of roses.

Russell narrowed his eyes. "Shannon's still alive. You give that any thought? If I had hired someone to kill her, shouldn't she be dead?"

"You tell us, Mr. Brennan," she pushed out. "Maybe you hired someone to injure her. Maybe she survived but wasn't meant to."

"No. I didn't take out this money, and I certainly didn't commission someone to kill my wife."

"Having other victims involved was rather clever. Throws off the investigation," Madison said, and Terry was staring a hole through the side of her head.

"I didn't—" He clamped his mouth shut.

"You must be really disappointed that she's still alive." Madison just kept poking the gaping wound.

His chin quivered, and he shook his head. "I want a lawyer."

"Fine by us, but have him meet you down at the station."

CHAPTER 31

Madison and Terry spent the next hour and a half interrogating Russell Brennan and getting nowhere. Finally, she reached out to Cynthia and asked for help. "Could you contact the Brennans' bank to see if you can find out the location where the money was taken from? Then see if you can get access to security video from either the bank or the city—depending on what applies." They had to consider all the possibilities, but if it had been Shannon who withdrew the money with her husband's bank card, the question was why use his card? And for what purpose? It was entirely possible the cash had nothing at all to do with the shooting.

"I'll see what I can do," Cynthia told her.

"Also, I emailed Mark, and he's probably on it, but look at McBride's financials, see if there's anything there that furthers the investigation."

"We're all over it here." Cynthia laughed and hung up.

Madison and Terry boarded an elevator at Stiles General and spoke to the afternoon nurse on duty. She told them that Shannon Brennan would likely be released tomorrow if all her tests came back good. She certainly had fared much better than Ridley and Walker.

Shannon was sitting in her bed watching television and eating from a pudding container when they walked in. She had her color back, and she smiled when she saw them enter. "Detectives? Good news for me?"

"We're still investigating," Madison said firmly. "Do you ever use your husband's bank card?"

"I'd have no reason to. Why do you ask?"

Honestly, this was what Madison had suspected. Russell Brennan was the one with a secret to hide, and he was doing all he could to protect it, including sending them running all over the place, trying to shoot down his ridiculous claim of innocence. "There were three cash withdrawals from your shared account over the last three weeks. Do you have any idea what this could have been for?" Madison produced the printout of the statement.

Shannon set down her spoon and the pudding cup, pushed the wheeled table aside, and looked at the highlighted transactions. "None. Did you ask Russell about this? I'm sure he could tell you. Maybe he was trying to surprise me with something?"

Madison chewed on that. How could it be much of a surprise when the amounts were a regular occurrence for three consecutive weeks? Surely, Shannon would have noticed the money coming out of the account. "Did you see these transactions coming out—before now?"

"No. Wouldn't know the first step. Russell takes care of the budget. And you asked if I used his card to take out the money? I would never take out that much money without running it past him. Not to mention, why would I use his card? I have my own."

"Do you have any idea what your husband might need that money for?" Madison asked.

Shannon pressed her lips. "Nothing comes to mind except for a possible surprise."

"How is your marriage?"

"Good. Solid. Why?"

"Your husband told us you have your fair share of disagreements."

"Nothing more than any ordinary couple." Shannon's eyes narrowed. "Do you think that he—" She waved a hand, cutting herself off. "No. There's no way he hired someone to kill me. I'm right here. Alive. Besides, I thought this was some drug-dealer thing."

"Because…?"

"Well, that's what the paper made it sound like, and it wouldn't surprise me considering that girl with the backpack and the guy who shot at us. Smacked of a handler protecting something to me."

They'd first heard the rumor about a drug-trafficking ring operating through the train station from Julie Nelson. And during their first conversation with Shannon, she claimed not to have seen Kayla, the handler, or the shooter before. "And the paper is the only reason you said the shooting was connected to drug trafficking?"

"Ah, yeah. Not much else to do here but sleep and watch TV." She pointed to the one mounted on the wall across from her bed.

"Do you know Julie Nelson?"

"Is that the Julie that works at Just Beans?"

"Do you know her outside of Just Beans? Maybe you're friends?"

"Nope. She just gets my coffee." Shannon smiled.

"Does the name Justin McBride mean anything to you?" Terry interjected, speaking for the first time since they'd entered the room.

Shannon seemed to give it some thought. Eventually, she said, "No."

Madison and Terry saw themselves out, and in the hall, she said, "I'm just curious why Shannon is so certain now that the girl with the backpack—Kayla Fleming—was involved with a drug-trafficking operation."

"I don't know. I'm not making too much out of it."

"I can't help make something of it. Not that I know what. And just a gut feeling, but is there some way these women were connected that we're not seeing yet?"

"Don't know, but do we let Russell Brennan go for now?"

They had twenty-four hours to hold him without pressing charges, but it would take longer than that to get things moving with the bank. "I don't think we have a choice until we have more on him."

They loaded into the department car.

Terry snapped his seat belt into place. "What if we approached things from outside the box?"

"Okay," she dragged out.

"Let's consider that all the husbands are clean, even Russell Brennan, then where does that leave us?"

She gave it some thought. "We can rule out Dana Ridley and Morgan Walker."

Terry smiled. "Yeah, I think that's a safe bet. Guess my mind goes to who wasn't injured. The Just Beans employees."

"Shannon Brennan."

"Again, what would be her motive? Who was her target? And that doesn't explain the money coming out with her husband's bank card."

"Let's slow down. Just a little."

Terry raised his eyebrows. "Not used to that line from you."

"Yeah, yeah. I say let's dig deeper, see if the women may have crossed paths. Maybe through their jobs? Shannon's in advertising, and Morgan was a lawyer. Lawyer offices need advertising, don't they?"

"I think every business that wants to make money does. But you're suggesting Shannon took out the cash with her husband's card to pay a hit man?"

"Just a possibility."

"She paid someone to shoot her? And does she really hate her husband enough to frame him? Because that's exactly what it would do."

"Well, we know the marriage wasn't rosy."

"Okay, but there's a long leap between that and her killing people to frame her husband. There has to be more motive here."

"I agree. It only confirms to me that we need to see if we can uncover any connection between the Brennans and the victims of the shooting."

Terry paled. "You brought up a possible connection between Shannon and Morgan, but what about Dana Ridley? Could be that the environmental firm where she worked hired Spark Media."

"Could be." Madison just hoped they unraveled the riddle before more people died.

CHAPTER 32

The next morning, Madison and Terry were on the road for Braybury. She was armed with the list of companies she'd taken from Morgan's phone. She planned to run this by the manager there to confirm that these were clients of the law firm, then go from there, if necessary. They'd also ask if there were any dealings between the firm and Spark Media, where Shannon Brennan worked.

They made it to Peters, Hampton & Douglas by ten AM and were shown to a fancy conference room with a mahogany table and credenza and views of the city. The firm was located on the seventh floor of a high-rise.

"Ms. Holt will be with you shortly," said the woman who had shown them in.

"Thank you," Terry replied with a smile.

Madison paced near the table and stopped next to the window. If Courtney was Morgan as Madison suspected, she had graced the floors of this building, most likely the one right in this boardroom. And while she'd been alive and working, Madison spent those years worried that her friend had met with a horrible fate. She clenched her hands into fists. *How dare you do this to me, Courtney? To your parents?*

"Detectives?" A woman in a tight-fitting skirt suit opened the conference room door. "I'm Gabriella Holt. You wanted to speak with me? Such a shame about Morgan." Her face was blotchy, and so was her chest where her flesh showed in the vee of her blouse.

"It is," Madison said and gestured for the woman to sit. She made the introductions, then led with, "We have some questions for you."

"Certainly. Whatever I can do to help." Holt smiled pleasantly and clasped her hands on the table.

"Have you ever heard of the company Spark Media?"

"Yes, of course. They do the big billboards in the city. What about them?"

"Have you ever hired them to market for the firm?" Madison asked.

"Not that I'm aware of, and I need to sign off on all promotions."

There went that possible connection between Shannon and Morgan. Madison pulled out the list she'd culled from communications on Morgan's phone. "Do you know these company names?"

Holt eyed her suspiciously but took the paper. She scanned it and looked at Madison. "Where did you get these?"

"They were people Morgan had called from her phone," she said, still suspecting they were businesses the firm represented.

"Well, these are clients of the firm. All except for this one here…" She pushed a manicured fingertip to the page, and Madison read the name.

Innovative Creatives. "You don't know them?"

"I've heard of them, yes, but they're not clients of the firm."

If Madison remembered right, Morgan had been in contact with them often. "Do you know what they do?"

"They rent desks and office space to startup companies. They're usually very selective about the people they allow in."

"Seems like you know a lot about them," Terry said.

"My brother used to rent a desk for a few hours a week. He came up with some harebrained, get-rich-quick scheme. It didn't pan out, but no one can say my brother doesn't act on his ideas."

"Do you know why Morgan would have been in contact with them?" Madison asked.

Holt hitched her shoulders. "Not really sure, no. But maybe they were looking to hire our firm. Usually, in those type of situations, she'd have notified me. Maybe she just didn't get a chance." Her gaze dipped to the table.

"You were close with Morgan?" Madison asked, her insides jumping.

"You could say that. We worked together for five years."

"Were you friends outside of work?" Madison asked.

"We'd go out for drinks sometimes. More a casual friendship. But she was great. Always so out there, adventurous, you know."

Sounded like Courtney. "What was your impression of her marriage?" They hadn't fully ruled out the husbands yet and had only touched the surface with the financial statements for the three couples. The possibility was the money for a hit man was taken from an account they didn't know about—assuming the money withdrawals from the Brennans' account had nothing to do with the shooting.

"Oh, I think she and Shane were the perfect match. Meant to be." She grinned, but it faded fast into a frown. "He must be devastated. He has the kids too. I should really reach out. It's just so hard to know what to say in these types of situations."

"You should call him," Madison assured her. "He'd appreciate that."

Holt nodded. "I will. After this meeting, in fact."

"Please just leave out mention that we were here, though," Madison added. If Shane was somehow involved with the shooting, it could alert him and send him running.

"All right, I won't."

She was grateful Holt just accepted Madison's request without need for an explanation. "Do any of these names mean anything to you? Dana Ridley?"

"No."

"Shannon Brennan?"

"No, sorry."

"Justin McBride?" Might as well go for the trifecta.

"Nope."

"Courtney Middleton?" Madison figured *what the hell…*

Holt shook her head. "No, again."

"Are you aware of anyone who might have had an issue with Morgan?" Still a procedural question worth asking.

"Not that I know of, and I can't even imagine Morgan having enemies."

"What about cases she defended but lost? Any of those people make their displeasure known, possibly come after her?" Madison asked.

"You mean threaten her?"

Madison nodded.

"I suppose, but nothing drastic like showing up here. There have been some strongly worded emails over the years, and then delays in paying our billing department. All we can do is represent our clients to the best of our abilities. We can't guarantee them the outcome they want."

"Could you send a copy of any recent threats to me?" Madison pulled out her business card and handed it to Holt.

"I'll see what I can do."

"Thank you, and we're sorry for your loss." Madison stood. "Would we be able to see Morgan's office?"

"I don't see why not. Follow me." Holt led them to a brightly lit space with a nice desk and views of the city. A tropical plant stood in the corner.

Madison and Terry took some time to look around, including in drawers and cabinets.

"Detective Knight?" Terry said, sticking with formality, as Holt insisted on remaining as they did their search.

She went over to where he was standing, next to the desk, a slip of paper in his hand.

"Found this under her desk pad. It's a receipt for a coffee. The name on the top is Innovative Creatives."

Madison looked at Holt as if to seek an explanation.

"They have a small bakery there," Holt said.

"Detective Grant, I think we've seen enough for now." Madison turned to Holt and gave her a pleasant smile. "Thank you for being so cooperative and, again, we're sorry for your loss."

They left, and once on the sidewalk, Terry said, "Why was Morgan in touch with Innovative Creatives?"

"Not just in touch with them but *in the building.*"

"Was it simply a potential new client?"

"Could be. Whatever the reason, I intend to find out, though I'm not sure how much it will aid the investigation. But first, we're going to drop by Spark Media to speak with them about Shannon, see if they've ever heard of Morgan Walker or Dana Ridley." Madison just hoped she and Terry weren't hamsters going around on a wheel getting nowhere.

CHAPTER 33

It was after three when Madison and Terry left Spark Media. They had a short conversation with Shannon's boss, who didn't offer much. But Shannon was alive, so if she felt her employer's disclosures violated her rights, she could sue the company. Her boss did tell them that as far as he knew, Shannon and her husband had a decent marriage—whatever *decent* really meant. She'd guess that to mean no one was hiring a hit man to take out the other one, but the fact remained that forty-five hundred dollars was unaccounted for. Shannon's employer had never heard of Dana Ridley, Morgan Walker, or Courtney Middleton.

She and Terry just stepped onto the sidewalk when her phone rang with a call from Cynthia. Madison shuffled off to the side and ducked down an alleyway. Out of earshot of passersby, she answered on speaker so Terry could hear.

"Tracked down the withdrawals from the Brennan account," Cynthia said. "Each of them were taken out at the same ATM here in Stiles. I've got the request going through the proper channels to get the security footage from the vestibule where the machine is located."

"Great job, Cyn."

"Why, thank you."

"Have you or Mark seen McBride's financials yet or accessed his phone?"

"Yes, was just about to tell you. He deposited fifteen hundred dollars three times over the last three weeks. These came a day after each of the Brennans' withdrawals."

"That can't be a coincidence," she rushed out and turned to Terry.

"Do you have any leads on motive?"

"No, and right now we're in Braybury seeing if we can find a connection between the women in case it's relevant."

"How's that going?"

"So far...goose egg."

"Keep at it. I know if there's anything to be uncovered, you'll find it."

"Hey," Terry said.

Cynthia laughed. "I meant *you* as in both of you."

"Huh." Terry smirked at Madison; he was only pretending to be offended.

"What about McBride's phone? Anything useful?"

"Unfortunately, no."

"No communication between him and whoever paid him, then? Text messages, emails?" Madison mumbled.

"Again, that would be a no."

There was nothing in the phone records or communications they had, but they didn't have their hands on Russell's phone history. But with McBride depositing the same amount of cash as taken from the Brennans' bank account—with Russell's card, no less—any judge would approve a subpoena request.

"All right, well, stay safe."

"Thanks." Madison hung up, and she and Terry popped out of the alley. Her stomach rumbled at the smells coming from someplace nearby. She inhaled deeply. Charcoaled meat. And, God, yes, she could do a cheeseburger! "Time to eat."

"I was hoping you were going to say that." Terry rubbed his stomach. "It's been growling for an hour."

She noted the time on her phone as she went to put it into a pocket. *3:15 PM.* No wonder she was starving. The last thing she'd eaten was a bagel before leaving home that morning. She didn't even have a Hershey's bar on her. *What a shame!*

They followed their noses around the corner to a barbecue joint with sticker lettering on the windows and an animated LED flame sign. The place smelled even more intoxicating inside. She was practically drooling by the time she took her first bite, but the wait—and the torture—had been worth it.

They'd taken a corner booth next to the window that faced the sidewalk and watched the world go by, as Madison's grandmother liked to say. People passed in a constant stream, and the observation popped her back to Monday morning when she'd noted all the pedestrians on the sidewalk in Stiles. To think that was four days ago was hard to believe, as it felt so much longer. Even worse, it was four days *and* four bodies later—Ridley, Walker, Nikitin, and McBride. Was Kayla Fleming still alive? Madison wanted to save that girl so badly. She hadn't been able to save her friend, though it would seem she hadn't needed saving. Madison was still trying to come to terms with that—an especially hard thing to do after thinking Courtney had been dead all these years.

She and Terry left the burger joint about twenty minutes after going in. Their hunger was sated, and she was beyond ready to make some real progress with this case.

"All right, next up is Innovative Creatives..." She pulled out her phone and googled the place to get directions.

"Ah, Maddy, no need for that." Terry nudged her elbow and jutted his head toward a sign on a building a few doors down. They must have missed it before because they were so focused on getting something to eat.

"Not very far from Spark Media," she said, the comment essentially a throwaway. Did it mean anything to the case?

They entered the building and went to the front desk where three young women were working. One was on the phone, one looked up from whatever she was doing on a computer, and the third greeted them.

"Welcome to Innovative Creatives. How can I help you?" She offered a genuine smile that lit her eyes.

Madison flashed her badge quickly to get the point across, but not for long enough to allow her to see *Stiles* embossed on it. "We'd like to speak with the manager."

"Oh. One minute." She turned to the coworker who was on the computer. "Salma, could you speak with them?"

Salma regarded Madison and Terry with suspicion, but she tried to cover it with a smile as she stood. "What is this regarding?" Salma asked. "Sophie, the general manager, isn't in right now."

"We're here on police business. If she's not here, then whoever is next in charge will be fine," Madison said.

Salma squared her shoulders. "That would be me."

Madison resisted the urge to question that out loud. Salma barely looked old enough to have graduated high school, and she was in charge of the building? "Your last name, Salma? Just for the record."

"Washington."

"All right, Salma, would you be able to tell us if Innovative Creatives had any dealings with a law firm named Peters, Hampton and Douglas?"

"I've never heard of them. Why would we have dealings with them?"

"Since they're lawyers, I'd suspect legal issues that might arise." It came out a little sharp, but she'd asked a stupid question.

"I don't think so." Salma crossed her arms.

"And you'd know if there were legal issues?"

"I would have heard about it. Yes."

Madison had no choice but to take her word on it for now and move on. "What about the name Morgan Walker? Does it mean anything to you?"

"Yes, of course." Salma's exuberance faded. "Oh, you're the police…asking about her. Is she all right?"

"Unfortunately, she was killed Monday morning at a shooting in Stiles."

Salma's blue eyes pooled with tears. "At the train station?" Madison nodded, and the woman continued. "I heard about that but had no idea Morgan was…" She covered her mouth, blinked, dropped her hand, and took a deep breath. She cleared her throat. "Involved. What can I do? Anything?"

"Tell us how you know her," Madison said.

"She rents an office here."

"She held a job at that law firm I mentioned. But this place caters to startup businesses, is that correct?" That was what Holt had told them.

"Yes, we do."

"So, Morgan had a business of her own. Doing what?" Madison asked.

Salma winced. "It's not my place to say."

"But you know?" Madison recalled Holt saying this place was selective about whom they rented space to.

"Yes, but…"

"We'd like to see her office." Surely something there could explain Morgan's reason for renting a space.

"I can't allow that without a warrant."

Madison simply looked at Terry, and he was on the phone to request a verbal one.

"Coming shortly, I assure you," Madison said. "How long has Morgan been renting here?"

"A few months."

"Does she come with any sort of regularity? Is there a way for you to tell?"

"Absolutely. Everyone needs to sign in so we know who is in the building should there ever be a fire or other emergency. Carrie, could you…?" Salma petitioned the woman who had initially greeted them.

Carrie clicked on the keyboard. "Every Monday, Wednesday, and Thursday evening," she said.

"Time of checking in?"

"Within minutes of five thirty."

So Morgan worked at the law firm during the day and, afterward, made her way here three times a week. Whatever had her focus had her driven. They really needed to get into her office to see if they could figure out what that was.

"Detective Knight?" Terry motioned for her to step back with him. "It's a little messy, as this is out of Stiles PD's jurisdiction."

"Well, make it less messy."

"Wish I could, but a verbal search warrant is a no-go."

"Even though she's a murder victim?"

Terry pressed his lips as if to say, *Out of my hands.*

She clenched a fist at her side. "I'm not just turning around and heading home. Not when we've got this lead."

"I'm not sure there's much we can do about it."

She scanned his eyes and knew he was right, as much as she hated it. She took out a card and handed it Salma. "We'll have to come back, but if anyone comes looking for her, please get their information and let me know. But don't let them know I'm interested."

"Sure. Not a problem."

Madison detested being in a position where her hands were tied. But not all was lost. They didn't have authorization to access Morgan's office, but they did have approval to access whatever was on her tablet. That was waiting for them back at Stiles PD. Another option was to visit Shane Walker again and ask him about Innovative Creatives, but Madison wasn't going there just yet.

CHAPTER 34

Before leaving Innovative Creatives, they asked about Shannon Brennan and Dana Ridley, and no one had heard of them. They showed Salma and Carrie the picture of Justin McBride, in case he'd shown his face, but there was no recognition.

Madison pulled into the lot for the Stiles PD about six thirty.

"I can stay a bit longer, but I need to call Annabelle," Terry said.

They'd already discussed on the drive that they would scour Morgan's tablet that had been in her purse at the time of the shooting, and hopefully find out why she was at Innovative Creatives three times a week. If that included Google searches and a sleepless night too, so be it. They also planned to get the subpoena request underway for Russell Brennan's phone records now that they had more than enough to substantiate it. They had the cash taken out with his bank card and the corresponding amounts being deposited by McBride.

Terry went toward their desks, phone in hand, and Madison took a detour to find Troy. He'd texted to say he had gone home for Hershey but was back at the station. He had a desk, not that he was at it a lot—nor did he like to be, but the paperwork had to get done sometime. He didn't have a Terry.

Troy was blessed with actual office space, though he had to share it with five other detectives and officers with SWAT. The door was open, and he was the only one inside at the moment.

Madison knocked on the doorframe, breaking Troy's concentration from what he was working on.

"Hey there, beautiful."

"Hey." He was so gorgeous just sitting there. His blond hair, strong arms, lean, muscular frame.

"Close the door." He bobbed his head toward it.

"Oh, really?" She smirked.

"Get your mind out of the gutter, woman." He got up and went to her. He swept a finger through her hair, then kissed her with enough heat to make her toes curl. "I needed that."

"Was delicious." She licked her lips, savoring the display of affection.

"Sit if you want."

"No thanks. I just got back from Braybury. I've been sitting for hours."

"How are things going with the investigation?"

"We've got a lead and a suspect."

"And where are things with the mob?"

She'd told him about McBride's murder the morning after his body was found and that Tatiana Ivanova was her prime suspect. "Where they were before."

"So you haven't taken on any rogue missions?"

"No."

"There's just something about all this that isn't sitting well. Nikitin and McBride get taken out, but it's not like the mob or this Tatiana tried to cover their tracks at all."

She put a hand over her stomach, sensing what he might mean. "You think Tatiana's calling me out."

He took her hand into his. "We don't know that for sure."

"*But*...I sense there's one coming."

"Not exactly a but, *but* if she is the great assassin she's been made out to be, shouldn't she be good at concealing her presence?" He drilled his gaze into hers.

She dropped into the closest chair. He knew about the eyewitnesses at Kayla's and Nikitin's buildings. "You think she wanted to be spotted so I'd know she was out there."

"And possibly go after her. Just watch your back. Please. I know how cocky you can get and—"

"Hey. That's not fair."

He held up a hand. "I say that with love, okay? You can't take her on by yourself. And you don't have to."

She blew out a deep breath and nodded. It felt good to know he was by her side, but it also hindered her in some ways. Before, she would have acted far more impulsively; now she had him to consider. "All right, so what do you say we do?"

"We do this by the book. I'll talk to my sister, and we'll involve whoever we need to. We'll arrange a sting on the house."

Madison knew the house he referred to—the one registered to a numbered company that tied back to Roman Petrov. "I want to be there."

He peered into her eyes, concern written all over them.

"Oh no, you're not squeezing me out of this," she said.

"I don't know if there's another option."

She shot to her feet. "Of course there is!"

He put his hands on her shoulders, but instead of shrugging him off, she let him calm her down. "She wants you dead. I thoroughly believe that," he said. "She gets you on her property, then… Well, I don't want to think about it."

She touched his cheek, softened and distracted by his concern for her. But she didn't need it—not really. She'd gone up against the mob before and had lived to talk about it. She was a lot tougher than he was giving her credit for, and it chafed. She lowered her hand. "We're a team. That's what you're always saying."

"I do, and we are."

"Then we do this as a team."

He shook his head. "Sure. On the record. You want them to pay for their crimes, don't you? Or is it just about taking them down now?"

His question and accusation stung, as it held truth. So often the Russians escaped justice; they got off with barely a slap on the hand. They made bail and their trials met with either hung juries or an innocent verdict. Their money and power—the fear they put into people—went a long way. It seemed to hold sway over everyone but her. And maybe instead of seeking justice through the system, it was time to color outside the lines.

His face darkened when she didn't respond. "Don't tell me…"

"They always manage to slip through the justice system."

"So your answer is to take them all out?"

"No, of course not." She huffed and crossed her arms. "But how do you expect to get a sting authorized? Huh? That's what I'd like to know."

"That part I don't know. *Yet.*"

"See?"

"We're not just running in there, Maddy."

"If I find out that Tatiana has Kayla Fleming, I'm not waiting for everyone to get their shit together."

"Maddy, come on, that's not fair. We want to take her down the right way."

She met his gaze but said nothing.

"At least I thought we did," he mumbled.

She went to the door and turned around. "I've got to work late tonight. You headed home to be with Hershey soon?"

"Yeah."

"You be safe too, okay? Please."

"I will be." He blew her a kiss, and she sent one flying back at him.

CHAPTER 35

After leaving Troy, Madison went to the lab and found Cynthia still there but getting ready to leave. No one had the luxury of regular hours this week.

"Have you unlocked Morgan Walker's tablet yet?"

Cynthia laughed. "There is so much on my plate right now—and my team's. Quite sure Mark has the passcode, but that's as far as we've gotten."

"That's as far as I need. I'll take a look at it. Terry and I are thinking it might give us a clue about what she was up to at Innovative Creatives." Now might be a good time to tell Cynthia she suspected that Morgan Walker was her friend Courtney Middleton from college, but Madison decided against it. The fewer who knew, the better. At least for now—until the case was solved.

"Well, have at it. I can get it for you from lockup."

"Yes, please."

Madison followed Cynthia into secondary evidence storage. It resembled a locker room and housed items that were still awaiting processing. After that, they went to long-term storage.

Cynthia punched codes into a computer, and one of the compartments opened. Madison signed out the tablet, the chain of evidence falling to her now. That meant she was responsible for anything that happened to it until it was returned to its cubbyhole.

Cynthia locked the door again and studied Madison. "So, what's going on with you these days?"

"Nothing. Just have murders to solve." She turned to leave.

Cynthia touched her arm, stopping Madison. "You always have murders to solve, but there's something else. Something dark. Something personal. Everything all right between you and Troy?"

Except he doesn't know the secret I'm holding...that I really don't want kids. "Yes. Great."

"Then it's something else?" She made a show of tapping her chin.

Madison jacked a thumb over her shoulder. "Can this wait?" She lifted the tablet. "I have work to do."

"I'm pregnant," Cynthia blurted out, eyes wide.

"Wh-what? What d-do you mean?" Madison was stuttering. The room was spinning.

Cynthia smiled. "You're supposed to say congratulations."

"Congratu—" Madison hurried from the room; her torso arched forward as she wished her legs would move faster. She needed to get away from Cynthia, just for a few seconds, and compose herself. Deep breaths in. Deep breaths out.

She slipped into the restroom and locked herself in the first stall.

"Madison? What the hell?" Cynthia was standing on the other side of the door. "Come out and talk to me. What's going on?"

"I don't want to talk about it. I don't want to talk about anything." Why couldn't Madison just turn the clock back and never get pregnant in the first place? Then she wouldn't have lost the baby, and she wouldn't be in such a conflicted emotional mess."

"Oh, we're talking about whatever this is."

Cynthia was using her firm tone, one that Madison could rarely say no to, but she couldn't open up to her friend—not about everything. But she ended up unlatching the stall door and coming out. She hugged the evidence bag with the tablet to her chest. It served as an energetic barrier protecting her. But from what? The damage was done a month ago.

Cynthia was leaning against one of the sinks, arms crossed. "You're scaring me, Maddy. What's going on?"

"I lost a baby." The admission hurled out of her, and she wished like hell she could reel it back in.

Tears pooled in Cynthia's eyes. "I'm so sorry, Maddy."

"No, no, you don't have to be. I'm fine, Troy's fine."

"Oh, you're not fine." Cynthia wrapped her arms around Madison.

Madison trembled within her friend's warm hug. Tears wanted to release so badly, but she wouldn't allow them to fall. She went cold, and Cynthia, maybe sensing this, stepped back.

"Again, I'm so sorry, Maddy. You know I'm here for you?"

"Yeah, I…" Madison licked her lips. How was she supposed to speak the truth without sounding like some sort of monster?

"It's okay. Talk to me. It will remain between us." And it would. Cynthia always put whatever Madison told her in the "vault."

"I'm happy." The admission was at once freeing and restraining, not that Cynthia was yet aware of the context.

"You're…?" Cynthia seemed at a loss for words.

"I'm happy, Cyn. I didn't want a baby. It wasn't planned. But…" She sniffled and looked up at the ceiling. "But Troy was so excited."

Cynthia just stood there, facing Madison, silent, her hands on Madison's arms.

"You're probably thinking I'm a monster, not even grieving my unborn child. But I'm relieved! I didn't ask for a baby. *I didn't ask for a baby*," she repeated, and the tears fell in a warm stream. *Crap!*

"Oh, sweetie."

"No! Don't sweetie me, and don't think I'm in denial." The words struck her ears as hypocritical as pain bloomed in her chest. She kneaded a spot over her left breast and tried to steady her breath, but her heart was speeding up, and breathing was only getting harder. She pinched her eyes shut, wishing she'd never gotten into any of this with Cynthia. Terry was probably wondering why she hadn't joined him at their desks by now. "I really should go…"

"No way. Not right now."

"Do you think I'm a monster? I think I am."

"Not at all, and I do think you are grieving."

"You just want to believe that."

"No. You're still processing everything; otherwise, we wouldn't be here right now. And just because the baby wasn't planned or expected doesn't mean that some part of you didn't come to love it."

Love? "No, I can't go there!" It had taken most of the time she was aware she was pregnant just to come to grips with that fact, let alone celebrate it. She'd never had a real chance to do that. "And Troy, he wants to be a dad, but me…well, I have no plans of being a mother—now more than ever. But what if that lets Troy down? What if he…what if he—" She sobbed, and Cynthia hugged her and rubbed her back.

"Troy loves you, Maddy. He'd never leave you, no matter what. Just talk with him and be clear about your feelings."

Madison shook her head. "He can never know the part about me feeling relieved." Her heart and lungs were hurting so badly, it was hard to draw in a deep breath. She started gasping for air.

"Come on, sit."

"On the restroom floor? Not happening, no—" Her head spun. Cynthia's suggestion might not be that bad of an idea. "Maybe I should…"

Cynthia guided to her to the wall and helped lower her. Madison's breathing kept coming in desperate intakes.

"What the hell…is…"—her throat was tight, her chest heavy—"happening…to…me…"

"I think you're having a panic attack." Cynthia pulled out her cell phone.

"Who are you calling? What the—"

Cynthia held up her index finger and spoke into the phone. "Troy, it's about Madison."

Oh shit! This isn't happening! She leaned her head against the wall but quickly straightened out, her urgent hunger for air making it necessary. Her vision blurred.

Next thing she knew, Troy was hunched down in front of her.

"Madison, let's get you home."

"I'm fine. I…" She was so exhausted she could barely form words.

Cynthia took the evidence bag with the tablet from her. "I'll make sure this gets back to where it goes. You can sign it out again tomorrow." She tapped a kiss to her fingers and pressed them to Madison's forehead. "Call me later if you want. Take care of her." She patted Troy on the back and left.

Troy was looking at Madison with such a deep pain in his eyes, but there was also some confusion. She was mortified and embarrassed that he was seeing her like this. She felt like she'd been through a hurricane and barely survived it. She could sleep for a month straight with little effort.

CHAPTER 36

Madison had woken up with her head pounding, and it still was. She'd never had a panic attack before, and she wasn't in a hurry to *ever* sign up for another one. It was Saturday morning, and Troy had tried to talk her into staying home—without success. Kayla Fleming was still out there, either alive or dead, and there were questions about the shooting that still needed answers.

"I wish you'd tell me what set it off." Troy had said that numerous times, referring to her panic attack, throughout the night and this morning before she left the house.

She just couldn't bring herself to tell him. Not yet. She so feared that he'd think she was a horrible person. He was aware she hadn't had plans to be a mother, but the rest—the relief, her conviction not to be one—he didn't know. And how to tell him any of that? But maybe she wasn't as relieved as she liked to believe. Cynthia's words to that effect had struck a nerve.

It was just after nine AM when Madison settled at her desk. Richards had sent an email with a recap of McBride's autopsy, and there wasn't anything too telling that they didn't already know from the scene. *His eyes were removed while alive… His neck was slashed with a sharp knife with a blade at least two inches in width, non-serrated. No hesitation marks. TOD was Wednesday.*

Madison had also taken out Morgan's tablet from evidence. Mark was in, not Cynthia, so at least Madison hadn't needed to face her yet. She felt horrible for last night. Her friend and her husband were expecting their first child—and so happy about it. Madison had ruined Cynthia's moment with her own feelings. How selfish.

Madison fired off a quick text to Cynthia: *So happy for you guys. :)*

She stared at the smile emoji, feeling like a fraud and doing her best to separate her personal emotions from Cynthia's situation.

"Hey! For you." Terry arrived, holding up one of two cups from a tray. "Venti caramel cappuccino."

She appreciated the thought but found his exuberance tough to swallow. She had no desire to be viewed as a delicate flower, and she likely had Troy to thank for this treatment. He had probably told Terry what had happened. "Don't treat me like I'm fragile."

"Wouldn't dream of it. So, that's Morgan's tablet?"

"Who else's would it be?" she slapped back with a smirk.

"Sarcasm is alive and well. Guess you are all right." Terry smiled at her. "Glad to see it."

"You might not be happy to learn I'm operating at peak efficiency, because I'm determined that we solve this case today. So get ready."

"It's always good to have high ambitions." He dropped his jacket on the back of his chair and walked back to her desk.

"I woke up with an epiphany," she started. "So far we haven't had any luck connecting Shannon Brennan to Morgan Walker. But I wonder if we can connect Shannon to Courtney Middleton."

"Oh, here we go."

"Listen to me. I have no idea what Courtney has been up to these last fifteen years or the enemies she may have made."

"You also don't know for sure that Morgan was your friend."

"Just play along for once."

"Fine. Let's say you're onto something with this. Shannon and Morg—*Courtney?*—knew each other. And Courtney did something to Shannon years ago. Then why come after her now?"

"Don't know yet, but maybe the two just recently interacted and something triggered Shannon."

"Except they often saw each other at the train station where they've been commuting for months."

"Okay, but Courtney changed her nose. Maybe it was just one look that had it all clicking and Shannon seeking revenge."

"Oooh, so many hypotheticals."

She struggled to find something that would open her partner's mind but couldn't come up with one thing. Sometimes faith was called for. "Just do some internet sleuthing and see what you can find out about Morgan Walker, Morgan Gardner, Courtney Middleton, and Shannon Brennan. Also try Shannon's maiden name."

"Will do."

His eager acceptance to do as she'd asked had her going silent for a few seconds. *Guess he* is *playing along...* "While you're doing that, I'm going to look around her tablet and see if I can find any explanation for what she was doing at Innovative Creatives."

"What about a search warrant for her office there? Do we just back off on that?"

"For now. Before we waste hours getting the paperwork together—"

"You mean before *I* waste hours."

"Very funny."

"Very *accurate*." He laughed, and she narrowed her eyes at him. "I'll get to work."

"Thanks." She tipped back her cup, testing the brew with a small sip. Perfect temperature. A few big gulps, and she was ready to study the tablet.

She keyed in the passcode, and a slew of app icons appeared onscreen.

Her phone pinged with a message from Cynthia. *Thank you. Hope you are feeling better this morning. Let's talk soon. XO*

Madison sent back a quick *You got it* and proceeded to scour the tablet. The device was loaded with various apps, but she went for the email one first. She started reading through the inbox. Good thing she had the cappuccino, because from the looks of it, she was going to be here for a while.

After being at it for half an hour, there was still nothing there to indicate the purpose of Morgan/Courtney's office at Innovative Creatives. It would be so much easier if they just asked Shane what he knew about it, but she had to be careful not to push him too hard right now. She didn't want to give Shane a reason to complain to Winston. In fact, she was surprised he hadn't already.

She opened an email from a Lucy Jefferson, subject was *Investment*. That had Madison sitting up straighter. After all, if Morgan was looking to start a business, she'd need the money to do that. Madison opened the message and read. She plucked out the business name. *Safe Haven*. Whatever that was. But some clues were in Lucy's response. It appeared to be a charity.

"Ah, Terry, I think I might have found something."

"Good thing because I'm not making much progress over here. Only time Morgan's name comes up is in relation to court cases she worked."

"I think Morgan was trying to start up a charity called Safe Haven. From the looks of it, she was seeking investors."

"Sounds like it would be something for abused women and children. Possibly animals."

"I don't know what it's for yet, but people don't usually start a charity unless it means something personal to them. We need to find out what the motivating factor was for her."

"Let me google the name. One second…" The clicking of keys, then, "Nothing coming up for that name. Maybe it's time to see Shane and find out what he knows."

That might be the easiest way, but as she'd thought a moment ago, she wasn't going to risk everything by showing her face there again unless it was absolutely necessary. The last thing she wanted this late in the investigation was to be removed from it. There was one possible solution. "I can't go, but you can. Just give me another hour here to see if I can find anything."

"All right." He put his gaze back on his monitor.

Terry was treating her differently today, and while she didn't need pity, his cooperation was refreshing.

She left the email app and poked around other files on the tablet. She found some Word documents and opened them one by one until she struck gold. The filename had been rather obscure, but the title in the document was *Business Plan: Safe Haven*. "Bingo!"

"What?" Terry called out.

"I have her business plan." She read down and shared the gist of it. "Safe Haven was to be a charity group to support families who lost loved ones to drug overdose."

"Let's assume that Morgan was Courtney. Do you remember Courtney losing someone in that way or knowing someone who did?"

"Not that I know of." *But I haven't known her for over fifteen years—if I ever really did!* "You're not finding anything on Google regarding her and Shannon?"

"Answer is still no."

Why had Morgan been starting a charity, and why one that focused on this particular mission? Could the reason be connected in any way to her death? One of the most common motives for murder was revenge. "Was Morgan trying to atone for something?" she pushed out.

"Wouldn't know. Had she caused someone to OD?"

"When I knew Courtney, she was up for pretty much anything. I know she tried experimenting with different drugs. Maybe she gave someone bad drugs or too much, then did nothing to help them?"

"Huh. If that person's loved one found this out, that could be motive for murder."

"Yep. Basing it on the money trail, I'd say that person was either Shannon or Russell Brennan, but which one?"

"Okay, let me try searching another way." He started tapping away on his keyboard, and she rounded his desk and stood next to him. He'd keyed in *Morgan Walker Gardner Courtney Middleton Brennan drug overdose.*

A few results filled the screen with all the words crossed out but *Brennan* and *drug overdose*. One of these was an obituary for a Scott Brennan from eleven years ago.

"Click on that," she told him.

He did, and a picture of Scott Brennan was staring back at them.

It can't be…

Her legs buckled beneath her, and Terry rushed to help her stay upright.

"Here, take my chair." He helped her to it, and she gratefully accepted his offer. "What is it? You know this guy?"

"Kind of. When I last saw Courtney, it was in the Roadhouse Bar just outside of Stiles. That guy—Scott Brennan—was who she was with that night."

Terry rubbed the back of his neck. "Okay…so we can put Courtney and this guy together, but how does that help us now?"

"Is he a relative of Russell's?" She looked at the screen and scrolled down the article, plucking out words as she went along. "No mention of cause of death. He'd died at the age of twenty-seven and left behind his parents and older brother… Russell. What the—" Madison snapped her mouth shut. "Go to the articles that came up. What do we have?" She quickly scanned the screen. "Pick that one."

Terry clicked a piece entitled "Killer Drugs: What You Need to Know."

"Read it. Apparently, the name Brennan is in there somewhere."

Terry used the "Find on the Page" function and went right to it.

> *The latest victim, Scott Brennan, twenty-seven, was found dead in his apartment over the weekend. An autopsy will be conducted, but drug overdose is the medical examiner's preliminary ruling as to cause of death.*

A look at the rest of the article put that statement into context. There was a batch of contaminated cocaine circling Comsey Park.

"Comsey Park is where Shane said he'd met Morgan. Had Courtney lived there for a time and made a home with Scott Brennan?"

"Well, his death would have been investigated. We could look that up, at least."

"We'd have to contact the police in Comsey Park."

"Not a huge deal."

"No…" Not that she had the desire to put things on hold to jump through that hoop just yet. "Theorizing here. Let's say Russell blames Courtney for his brother's death. Then more recently he runs into her and begins scheming how to kill her and get away with murder. He had his wife, Shannon, shot to make the shooting appear random. Dana Ridley was just collateral damage. It's time to bring Russell Brennan in for more questioning."

"I agree. I think we have more than enough justification."

"You can say that again." Her mind was still sorting out all the pieces as they headed to the station lot.

Terry was already making the call, trying to wrestle up a verbal court order to seize Russell's phone and computer.

Maybe they would have their answers by the end of the day.

CHAPTER 37

"Russell Brennan, we have some questions we need to ask you." Madison sat across the table from the man and his lawyer.

Now the four of them, including Terry, were all cozy in interrogation room three. Meanwhile, Mark had Russell's laptop and his phone in the lab—the authorization had come through.

"When we first spoke, Mr. Brennan, we had asked if you knew Morgan Walker. Do you remember your answer?" she asked.

"Sure. I've never heard of her."

"So you never knew this woman?" Madison pulled a photo of Morgan from the folder she'd brought. She set it on the table and pushed it across to Russell. "Go ahead, take a close look."

He glanced down. "Nope, I don't know her."

"Imagine a bigger nose. Take your time."

Russell lifted the photo and went through the motions, but the tell was in the way his eyes grazed over the picture. He knew her, and Madison would wager he blamed Courtney for his brother's death. Had Morgan/Courtney also blamed herself, and that was why she had been starting the charity?

Eventually, Russell shook his head. "No, never seen her before." He tried to hand the picture to her, but she wouldn't take it, and he let it fall to the table.

"Your brother, Scott," she began, and it had Russell locking his gaze with hers. "He died eleven years ago. Drug overdose."

Russell scowled. "What does he have to do with any of this?"

"Apparently, there was a bad batch of cocaine going around at that time, and your brother took some and didn't survive," she said.

"Stop talking about my brother."

"Your brother"—she pulled his obit photograph from the folder and pushed it across with the one of Morgan again—"and this woman were together. They had a daughter." She was stretching the truth and making assumptions, but she was inclined to believe Leanne was Scott Brennan's child. Also that when Courtney had run away, she'd done so with Scott.

"So what?"

That response confirmed her suspicions. "*So what?* She's dead."

"Nothing to do with me."

"And your brother's dead." Madison was being insensitive on purpose, to elicit a reaction, and it was working.

Russell scowled and balled up his fists. "How dare you talk about him! He has nothing to do with any of this."

"I think he does." Cool, calm, unaffected. "What happened? Did she give him the drugs that killed him?" She pressed a finger to the photo of Morgan/Courtney.

"Detective," the lawyer interjected, "what does any of this have to do with—"

She held up a hand. "Tell us, Mr. Brennan."

"She left him to rot!" Snot was bubbling in Russell's nostrils. "He was in his apartment one week before anyone found him."

Madison certainly couldn't entertain that Courtney had killed him intentionally. She tried to place herself in her friend's situation. Courtney watched on as the man she loved overdosed. Or maybe she found him dead, panicked, and ran? Not that she must have run far as Comsey Park was where she'd met Shane Walker. Either way, the hypothetical situations she'd conjured would have been terrifying for Courtney. Not to mention Courtney would have had a daughter to worry about at that time too. Had it played out in life as Madison imagined? "She was scared," she said, concluding it likely had.

"No. Even if she was, that doesn't give her the right to leave him like that! She could have called for help. Maybe he could have been saved."

"Is that why you hired someone to kill her?" Madison pressed a finger to the photograph again.

Tears were pouring down Russell's cheeks, but pure rage filled his eyes.

"May I advise you to say nothing more at this time," the lawyer said calmly to his client.

"You hired someone to kill Morgan Walker. At the same time, was he to take out your wife or was she just to be injured?"

The lawyer cleared his throat—loudly—and said, "Enough, Detective. Until you have something to back up these allegations, this meeting is over."

"It's over when I say it is." She leveled a glare at the lawyer. "Mr. Brennan, I just want to know, why after all this time?" There were many other questions to cover, but one at a time.

"Don't answer that." The lawyer stood and prompted his client to do the same.

"Mr. Brennan's not going anywhere," she stamped out. "We'll be holding your client under suspicion of commissioning a murder."

"Ridiculous."

She ignored him and returned her focus to Russell. "Can you explain why the shooter, Justin McBride, deposited fifteen hundred dollars into his account every time the same amount came out of yours?"

"What? No idea."

"Huh. Well, you better get comfy, because we're not done with you yet." She stood, and Terry followed her into the hall. She notified a uniformed officer that Russell Brennan was to be taken to a holding cell.

"What are you doing?" Terry asked her.

"The guy needs to cool off for a while. In the meantime, we're going to the lab to see if Mark has made any progress on Russell's phone and laptop."

When Madison and Terry reached the lab, they found Mark hunched over the computer.

"Tell us you have something," she said.

Mark turned to look at them, his expression grim. "Can't find anything to indicate Russell Brennan ordered a hit on Morgan Walker and/or his wife. Not on his phone or his computer."

"How can there be nothing there? Did he wipe everything out? Isn't there a way to bring back deleted files?" Every bone in her body was telling her Russell Brennan was behind the murders now.

"I've tried everything, and I'm sorry, but there's nothing here."

She growled. "The money trail can't be a coincidence. We're missing something. Have to be." She paced, thinking through what they knew so far, and sadly, it wasn't a lot. Questions lingered. One, why after all these years had Russell sought revenge? It would suggest that he'd just recently run into Courtney/Morgan—but where and when? Two, how did he know how to contact McBride? Three, how could he know where the hit man might find Courtney to kill her? Four, did Russell have help?

That was a chilling thought, but maybe Russell passed the cash onto someone, who then arranged the hit with McBride. But who would take that risk for Russell and why? A person who had a close relationship with him, and possibly also had something against Morgan?

A close relationship... That really didn't seem to apply to the Brennans' marriage. "Any evidence that Russell Brennan was cheating on his wife?" she asked Mark.

"Not that I've found."

She raked a hand through her hair. "Why isn't any of this coming together?"

"Maybe it's not him," Terry kicked back.

"Oh, it is. We just need proof." *Someone who helped him hatch the entire scheme...* "Mark? Could you bring up the video of the shooting?" Maybe she'd spy something this time she hadn't seen before. Fingers crossed.

"Ah, yeah, sure."

She snapped her fingers a couple of times. It just felt like it was taking him forever to get moving.

"Seriously?" Terry raised his brows at her.

"We're right on the cusp of solving this thing, Terry. I feel it."

"By all means then, be rude to those who are trying to help you."

She rolled her eyes. "Mark knows this isn't personal. Video?" she prompted, and Terry shook his head.

The train station surveillance video popped up on a wall-mounted TV. "Ready?" Mark asked, and just as she was about to respond with something sharp, he smiled and hit the Play button.

Someone else has found their sense of humor...

Madison watched it closely. Kayla sweeping by, the conversation between Shannon, Dana, and Morgan, the shooter confronting them, him pulling his gun, the women ducking... "Wait! Go back just a bit."

Mark did.

"There! Right there!"

Mark hit Pause.

"Tanya Murray, one of the Just Beans workers... She ducks just before the shooting starts."

"Could be nothing more than her intuition telling her where the situation was headed," Terry said, a thinly veiled dig at her for her myriad of gut feelings.

"Don't be smart. Why would she anticipate things would turn violent? They never have in the past. She said she didn't know the guy, but did she?"

"What are you getting at?" Terry asked.

He and Mark were watching her closely.

"I think Russell Brennan didn't concoct the shooting all by himself. Maybe he and this Tanya Murray are connected. We'd never asked if he knew her. We never had a reason."

"Oh, dear Lord." Terry looked up at the ceiling. "Now we have something else to prove."

"Mark, go back and replay the video slowly," she said. "Both of you will see what I'm talking about."

Mark did as she'd asked. As the scene played out again, she waited for a reaction. She didn't have to wait long.

"She did seem to anticipate the shooting," Terry said.

"Yep. She's in the middle of ducking when he's just going in his pocket for the gun. How did she know he was going to pull a weapon? I'll tell you how: she knew because she was in on this."

"Fine. How do we prove it?"

"Tanya Murray may be a little more willing to talk if she thinks Russell Brennan is turning on her."

"But he's not."

"She doesn't need to know that." Madison was banking on the fact that there was a relationship between Russell Brennan and Tanya Murray, and she hoped she wasn't wrong.

CHAPTER 38

Madison banged on Tanya Murray's door like her house was on fire.

"What the—" The door swung open. "Detectives?"

"We need to speak with you. And it's rather urgent. I assume we can come in?" Madison looked past Murray and took a step to go inside.

"Ah, sure." Murray closed the door behind them. "You find the shooter?"

"We did." Madison led the way to the kitchen table and sat down.

"Oh. That's good." Murray smiled, but it faltered. She slid into the chair across from Madison. Terry remained standing in the doorway between the hall and kitchen.

"It is," Madison said. "At least there will be some justice for the victims of Monday's shooting."

Murray laid a hand over her heart. "So happy to hear it."

"You wouldn't happen to have known him? A Justin McBride?" Madison was trying to get a feel for the situation, as she didn't have it all stitched together in her head yet.

Murray frowned and shook her head. "Never heard of him."

"All right. And Russell Brennan?"

The subtlest of flickers danced across Murray's eyes.

"You know him," Madison said with confidence. "And your relationship with him?"

Murray rubbed her arms. "There is no relationship."

"Interesting." Madison tossed in the hook.

"Why interesting?" Murray bit.

"He's downtown telling us this whole thing was your idea."

"He what?" Murray spat.

"You set this all up for him, didn't you?" Madison pressed, still unsure of the depth of Murray's involvement or motive. On the latter, she only had her suspicion. There was no evidence of an affair on Russell's electronics. There also wasn't a digital trail that confirmed he'd hired someone, but the unexplained withdrawals of cash couldn't be ignored. Madison was going to continue rolling with her theory. "You love Russell and would do anything for him—including hiring a hit man to kill his wife and a woman he blamed for his brother's death."

"I don't know what you're talking about."

"I'm quite sure you do. How did you know when to duck?"

"Excuse me."

"The day of the shooting. You crouched down before the shooter had even pulled the gun, like you knew it was coming. He was reaching into his pocket. He could have been going for a pack of gum or cigarettes."

"I wasn't taking any chances! The guy was yelling at those women. He was caught up in that drug-trafficking operation too."

Hearing her say that made Madison appreciate the poetic justice of how they'd orchestrated the murders. Not only had they taken out the target—Morgan Walker—but the shooting had managed to expose the drug-trafficking operation. It didn't matter that the Russians may not have been the ones to supply the bad batch of cocaine that killed Scott Brennan, the ring was representative of the drug epidemic afflicting the world. "Ah, it all makes a little more sense now."

"What does?"

"Just why everything played out the way it did. I just want to know why you'd risk your freedom to help Russell. Was it because of love? Let me guess. His wife was supposed to die and then you two could finally be together? But she didn't die. Not sure where that leaves you…"

Murray's eyes filled with tears, but her scowl communicated rage not sadness. "Whatever Russell is telling you is a lie."

Madison didn't say a word, playing the power of silence.

"What exactly is he telling you?"

Madison shrugged.

Murray's eyes darted around the room. "Shannon was never supposed to die, okay? Just that Morgan woman," she spat with vehemence. "But none of this was my fault. He's the one who paid for it!"

"But you helped facilitate the crime. You hired the hit man." Madison was running with the assumption to gauge Murray's reaction.

"Is that what he's telling you? He's a…" She pursed her lips. "A liar. I want a deal."

"I'm listening." Not that Madison was in the habit of extending deals; it just wasn't in her nature. If someone did the crime, they should pay to the full extent of the law.

"Russ told me about this Morgan woman and what she did to his brother."

"What even made him bring her up?" Terry asked.

Murray gave a tiny shrug. "Guess he ran into her in Braybury when he went up there about a month ago, to have dinner with his wife at some burger joint."

Madison glanced at Terry. It quite possibly could have been the same place where they had eaten. The restaurant was close to both Innovative Creatives and Spark Media.

"Okay, go on," Madison encouraged.

"He just *knew* it was the girl who his brother had been with. I wanted him to let it go, but every time he brought her up, he became angrier. Then I saw him following her in the train station while I was working. Later he told me he wanted her dead for what she'd done."

"Can you prove any of this?" It all sounded so conclusive, but it would be nice to have something more tangible. She supposed they could always watch the train video for any sign of Russell Brennan.

Murray shook her head. "You have my word."

"Okay, then what? You knew someone who would be able to take care of her?"

"Did he tell you that? What an ass."

"You facilitated the murder. Russell Brennan took out the money, gave it to you, and you handed it to McBride and set out the details of the hit."

Murray pinched her eyes closed.

"Ms. Murray, you're under arrest for commissioning murder," Madison began and motioned for Murray to stand. She proceeded to snap on cuffs and run through the Miranda rights.

CHAPTER 39

Madison had Russell Brennan hauled from holding into the interrogation room. "We have your girlfriend, Mr. Brennan, and she told us everything."

"I don't have a girl—"

"Save it. We know everything."

"I'm telling you. I don't have a mistress!"

"Tanya Murray." Madison slapped a color photo from the DMV on the table. "She works at Just Beans. She knew Morgan Walker went there on a regular basis, and when she found out about your beef with her, she helped put you in touch with Justin McBride."

"I don't know what you're talking about," he said through heaving gasps for breath.

"You're not amusing me, Mr. Brennan. As I told you, Tanya told us everything we need to know. You wanted Morgan Walker dead." It was niggling for Madison, though, why he hadn't paid to have his wife taken out too. That way he'd be free to move on with Tanya Murray. Was it just a matter of money? From what she could tell by looking at their finances, that shouldn't have been an issue. Then it struck that Shannon would have been released from the hospital yesterday, but they hadn't heard a word from her. And she wasn't at the house when they brought in Russell. Goosebumps raced down her arms. "Where is your wife right now, Mr. Brennan?"

"Shannon? She's at home. Probably resting."

"While you're here facing murder-for-hire charges?"

"She's recovering from a gunshot wound, Detective. She needs her rest."

Madison stood. "Detective Grant."

They both went into the hall. "I have a bad feeling. Something's not right. We should have thought of it when we were at the house earlier. At least checked in on her."

She couldn't get to the lot to sign out a department car fast enough. Then she swore they hit every red light. *Screw it!* She flicked on the lights and sirens.

"What are you doing?"

"Trying to make up for lost time." She pushed the gas pedal to the floor and got them to the Brennan door in ten minutes. She barely had the car in park when she jumped out. She banged on the door a couple of times. "No answer," she informed Terry when he finally joined her on the front step. She tried the handle.

"What are you doing? We can't just go in."

"She could be in trouble in there, Terry, and I'm not going to stand around and do nothing." She tried to peek through the window in the door, but the etched glass made that impossible. She stepped off the front step and rounded the house, looking in every window she could.

"I can't believe I'm following you," Terry grumbled behind her.

"No one said you had to." She made it to the back of the house, and there was a patio door. The blinds were open, and she could see inside. A figure was standing there. Madison hurried toward the glass.

The slider opened, and Shannon eyed them skeptically. "Detectives? What are you doing back here?"

"Sorry to disturb you, ma'am," Terry began.

"We were worried about your well-being," Madison rushed out.

"How sweet." Shannon smiled at her. "But I'm fine."

Dread tingled through Madison. She was rather chipper for a woman whose husband was suspected of ordering a hit on her. "You're sure you're fine?"

"Yeah, I mean it's shocking about Russ. I don't know what I ever did to make him want me dead."

The words clawed at Madison. *Want me dead...* Only she was standing there very much alive. The only people in graves were Morgan Walker, Dana Ridley with her unborn child. And Murray had made it sound like Shannon was never supposed to die. If Shannon had though, Tanya Murray and Russell Brennan would have been free to be together. Why wouldn't they have wanted that? There must be something that Madison was missing.

"Could we come in just for a moment? I could use a glass of water." Madison was trying to buy more time to figure out what exactly was going on.

"Ah, sure..." Shannon smiled and let them inside. She asked Terry, "You?"

"No thanks," he said.

Shannon grabbed a water bottle from the fridge for Madison, but there was something off about Shannon's energy. Her movements were quick, and she was being overly accommodating and easy with her dispensing of smiles.

Madison drank some water and set the bottle on the counter. "You must have been afraid to come home to the man who tried to have you killed."

"I was terrified."

Madison studied the woman. Shannon crossed her arms, then winced due to her gunshot injury that would still be healing. "How did you know he tried to kill you?"

"The money you told me about. You said he took out forty-five hundred dollars."

"We thought it was suspicious, yes."

"You don't think he paid a hit man now? What was the money for, then?"

Madison didn't like how Shannon kept trying to putt the narrative back to Madison to direct. It was shifty. "We obviously suspect your husband, Mrs. Brennan. That's why we have him downtown. The only reason we're here was to check on you." *And now it's to see through a budding hunch…*

"Okay."

"Why did you come home to a man who tried to have you murdered?" Madison was slowly pacing around the kitchen as she spoke, her hand ever cognizant of where her holster and gun were. She made brief moments of eye contact with Terry, who gave the slightest of nods. He'd received her unspoken message of her suspicions and to watch himself.

"Well, where else would I have gone?"

"Guess I wouldn't know." Madison offered up a fake smile, hoping it passed as genuine. "A friend's maybe?"

"I don't have that many friends, unfortunately."

Madison's mind had been tossing around everything Russell had said, his claims he didn't have a mistress. Then there was the lack of evidence on his electronics. And the video. The way Murray had ducked preemptively. And something that just hit Madison now from having watched the surveillance video again. At the time of the shooting, McBride had been wearing a hoodie zipped up tight to his neck and the hood itself covered most of his face. There was no way Shannon could have seen the red birthmark on McBride's neck—at least not then. She'd seen it some other time. "Not even Tanya Murray?"

Shannon's eyes widened in shock, and she reached for a knife from the block on the counter. Terry moved to stop her, but he wasn't quick enough. Shannon had the blade to Terry's throat.

"Stop right there!" Madison yelled, her gun now drawn and aimed at Shannon.

"I will kill him!"

"No one else needs to die." Madison caught the fear in Terry's eyes, but she needed to stay focused on the mad woman with the knife. "What did Dana Ridley ever do to you?"

"Dana? Oh, the other woman? Nothing."

"She was sixteen weeks' pregnant with her first child." Madison searched Shannon's face for any sign of remorse, but she was too absorbed in her own fabricated justifications.

"She was in the wrong place at the wrong time." Thrown out nonchalantly.

"What about Morgan Walker? She did nothing to you."

There was just the trace of a smile. "She was for Russell. A parting gift. Or she should have been. He was the one who was supposed to go to prison for all this! He had reason to want her dead. Not me!"

"She left behind a husband, a teenage daughter, and a five-year-old son." Even as Madison put it all out there, it was clear by the woman's blank expression the words fell on a dark soul.

"This isn't on me. It's all Russell's fault." A tear fell as if on cue, and Madison didn't care for the sudden shift in energy—or the unsteadiness of Shannon's hand that held the knife to Terry's throat.

The chick is certifiably crazy! And sometimes there was no choice but to play along with crazy. "Tell me. I'm listening. How is it Russell's fault?"

"He wouldn't let me go! I didn't love him anymore!"

The fog was beginning to clear. Murray had confessed, not to clear her conscience but to protect Shannon. "You and Tanya Murray are in love."

"Yes. Russell was to go to prison, and she and I were going to be together."

"You thought that was the only way out. And you made sure Morgan died because you knew we'd find motive against him?"

"Yes," she hissed. "He told me about bumping into her and wouldn't stop talking about her and what she'd done to his brother."

Madison's stomach churned. All of this because of some antiquated viewpoint on the sanctity of marriage. If only Russell had given Shannon the divorce she had wanted, then maybe Morgan and Dana and her baby would be alive. All this ran through her head while Madison was laser-focused on Shannon and Terry. He was so scared. "You need to let Detective Grant go. Please, Shannon."

"Why should I?"

"You're not an evil person. You just did what you felt you had to in order to be with the woman you love." It was making Madison ill speaking these words, but she had to get through to Shannon somehow, and the best way was to present herself as an ally, a person who understood her side.

Tears made a wet mess of the woman's face. "You could never understand. And I'm not going to prison!" She shoved Terry away and took the knife to her wrist. Blood sprayed everywhere.

Vomit shot up the back of Madison's throat. She swallowed the bile back down and turned away. She called 911 while Terry did what he could to staunch the woman's bleeding.

CHAPTER 40

Shannon Murray was dead before paramedics arrived. Madison and Terry had returned to the station to lay out everything for Russell and to let him and Tanya Murray know that Shannon had killed herself. Murray would be going to prison for her role. She'd admitted that her initial confession had been to shield Shannon.

But they didn't need Murray's confession. The ATM video came to Mark while Madison and Terry had been with Shannon. Murray was at the ATM at the time the money was taken out of the Brennan account. Shannon had given Tanya Murray Russell's card.

"I'm going home for a stiff drink." Terry looked like he was about to collapse.

"Things could have gone a lot worse today."

"Trying not to think about it. Failing miserably."

"Go home and hug Annabelle and Danny."

He waved a hand over his head as he walked away.

At least Terry was okay, but there was still more blood spilled. She didn't want to dwell on that, though. She blamed herself, like she always did in such cases. Now the shooting at Liberty Station could be put to rest except for one thing—Kayla Fleming.

An offshoot to that was McBride's murder, but she needed sleep more than anything right now. The mob wasn't going anywhere, and she knew where to find them tomorrow. Plus, her heart had a harder time finding empathy for a hired gun.

She hung around and did some paperwork. It was about nine o'clock when she shut down her computer and headed home. She planned to spend the night tucked in with Troy and Hershey, grateful she had them and happy she'd be able to provide some closure to the Ridley and Walker families. Possibly the Middletons too. But one thing at a time.

She called Troy on the way, and he answered on the second ring. "You home?" she asked him.

"Could be in five minutes."

"Well, that's where I'm headed."

"You sound happy. You solve the case?"

"Yep. Got a lot of my questions answered too."

"Good."

They ended the call, and twenty minutes later, they were both at home petting Hershey. Troy grabbed himself a beer from the fridge and poured her a glass of wine. He brought it to her on the couch.

"Oh, do I need this after today." She took a long sip, sank into the couch, and put her feet up on the coffee table.

"Thought it was a good one."

"Turned out that way, but it was a little iffy there for a bit." She told him about Terry being held at knifepoint.

"Wow. Lucky little bugger."

"You could say that. I don't know if I could have saved him. Even if I shot her in the hand to make her drop the knife, would I have been quick enough?" She'd been squeezing the thought from her mind since the incident had taken place, and she was so worn out from thinking about how things could have turned out—with Terry dead.

"Shoot her in the hand...you?" Troy laughed.

She shoved him.

"Hey, you're a good shot, but..." He teetered his hand side to side.

He had a point. She was taught to aim for center mass. Someone more skilled with a gun, like Troy, would have had a better chance of pulling off the shot she was talking about.

"But you don't need to worry about any of that now." Troy put his arm around her and clinked his bottle to her glass. He'd always been big into making toasts. "To brighter days ahead."

"Yeah." She drank some wine, then said, "Cynthia's pregnant." She slowly turned to face him.

"Wow. She and Lou must be excited." He smiled, sharing the expression that was so rare for him.

She winced inside. Why would he assume they'd be excited? Was it a foregone conclusion with every parent-to-be? Was there something wrong with her?

"They are, right?"

"Yeah." She gave him a tight smile. If they weren't, they would be monsters. Like her…

"It's starting to make sense now." He was peering into her eyes with those knowing green eyes of his. "Is that news what set off the panic attack the other night?"

She considered her next words carefully. "Is having children really important to you?" The question barely squeaked from her throat.

"They'd be nice, but it's not the end of the world. No rush."

She pulled away from him, shifted her body to face him. "But you definitely want children someday?" Fear of losing him was starting to tighten its grip around her throat.

"Madison, the most important thing to me is you and I. *Us.* If a baby comes along, then great. But I'm not attached to some image of us being a perfect family with two-point-five kids and a white picket fence."

She laughed, finding humor in his wording. "Well, good because two-point-five would be hard to muster."

He caressed her cheek affectionately. "All I'm saying is, I love you, and I have the feeling you're not really sold on having kids. We have touched on this before."

She nodded. But they hadn't discussed the depth of her relief after losing the baby. As Cynthia helped Madison see, though, that didn't mean she didn't feel any grief. Rather, she was just bottling it up. "Yeah, and about the two-point-five kids, I don't really see myself with, uh, even one." She felt the need to be very clear so her words couldn't be twisted.

"I understand."

She stood. "I feel like I'm letting you down."

He moved closer to her. "Ridiculous."

"What if you look back years down the road and regret not having them? You're going to take off with some hot young thing who wants you as her baby's daddy."

He laughed.

She nudged him in the shoulder. "I'm being serious."

"I realize that, and I'm a big boy too, yes?"

She skimmed down his torso...farther down... "Oh, yeah."

"Then trust me. Whatever life has in store for the two of us—together—I'm in. I just want to do life with you."

"I felt relief after..." The words spilled out, and his green eyes widened. She swallowed roughly. "After the baby was gone, I was relieved. I've been fighting with my guilt over feeling this way. I didn't even know how to tell you. I must be some sort of monster."

"No. Not at all. A baby would have meant a lot of changes. They do tend to flip things upside down."

"You don't judge me for feeling relief? That was our baby..." She choked on that word.

"I'd never judge you." He tapped a kiss on her lips.

After holding on to this secret for a month, conjuring up images of Troy not understanding her viewpoint, of thinking less of her... And now he knew, and he was nothing but loving and accepting. How had she ever been so lucky to draw Troy into her life?

She tugged on him, bringing him even closer. She put her mouth on his and was ready to disappear into his arms for the rest of the night.

Her phone rang.

"Shit!"

"Just leave it," he said.

The ringing continued. She thought of Kayla. Maybe it was Detective Marsh with news about her. She pulled away. "I've got to get it." Caller ID was Unknown, but she answered anyway.

"Is this Detective Knight?"

"Yes."

"Word is you're looking for some girl named Kayla?"

"Who is this?"

"Name's not important, but I'm one of Marsh's CIs."

The skin tightened on the back of her neck. "You have info on her?"

"I do."

Something about this wasn't right. Marsh should be calling her, not his CI, and how did he get her number? But she couldn't just ignore what this guy was saying either. "Where is she? Is she all right?"

"Far as I know."

She was quickly tiring of his short, clipped answers. "You've seen her. Tell me now. Where?"

"Down near the docks. There's an abandoned warehouse there."

That was the area where Cynthia had tracked the one number from Nikitin's burner. Was that a coincidence? "When did you see her?"

"Looking at her right now."

"Don't go near her or spook her."

"I won't."

"And where did you get my number?"

The line went dead.

"Maddy?" Troy said. "Everything all right."

"No. Something is really *not* all right." She met his gaze. "That was supposedly a confidential informant of Detective Marsh's. I'd asked Marsh to talk to his CIs in case any of them had seen Kayla Fleming."

"The CI called you directly?"

"Yeah." She was still puzzled by that.

"That's hinky."

"I agree. But maybe Marsh just gave the guy my number, to cut himself out?"

"Nah. I don't see that."

"Fine, but it is a possibility, a reasonable explanation for this guy calling me directly."

"Call Marsh and ask if he's been handing out your number."

She tried calling Marsh, but there was no answer. She hung up without leaving a message. "Can't get him."

"You do realize this could be a trap," Troy pointed out.

"It could be...."

"Where did he see her?"

This would likely be the point where he'd insist that appropriate hoops be jumped through and everything done to protocol. She shook her head. "She could leave the area. I can't take that chance. I've gotta go."

Troy grabbed her arm. "Not without me, you're not."

She put her hand over his and nodded.

CHAPTER 41

The sun was gone, and night had moved in. Ten o'clock was not exactly the most cheery time to be down at the docks, mingling among vagrants and druggies—and she and Troy were trained and armed. They were also wearing vests.

"Surprised you didn't want to go in with warrants and loads of backup," she said to Troy.

"You don't have the patience."

"Just be careful, okay?" She'd never forgive herself should something happen to him because she'd dragged him into this mess.

He nodded, and she loved him for his sacrifice in this moment. She'd always admired his courage and his strength and his drive to find justice. She envied his ability to step back and gather intel before moving in—an aspect he was letting go to support her. It could be because he didn't feel he had much of a choice. She would be going with or without him.

They entered the warehouse, and shadows slithered and crept. Fires burned in metal drums, and there were sleeping bags and shopping carts, cardboard boxes, crates. People were in small cliques around the building and didn't pay her and Troy any attention.

She leaned against Troy. "I'm getting a bad feeling." Her heart was beating rapidly, but she could already feel the familiar warmth of adrenaline moving in.

"Just now?"

Then Madison saw her—Kayla Fleming. She was about thirty feet in front of them. Madison called out her name, but the girl held up a hand and yelled, "Stop!"

"We're here to help you." Madison kept walking slowly and, getting closer, noticed the girl was crying, but there was also something strapped to her chest.

Fuck this day!

"She's rigged with explosives," she said to Troy, but he must have already noticed himself. He had his phone to an ear.

"No signal," he said.

"That's a good thing, right? Then the bomb can't be detonated."

"Bombs go off without cell phones. Could simply be on a timer."

"Shit."

"Yeah, shit."

"Kayla, remain calm, okay?" Madison approached the girl cautiously.

The small red digits came into clarity. Two minutes and counting down...

She spoke to Troy over a shoulder, keeping her voice low. "Please tell me you know how to disarm this thing."

"Bombs aren't my area of expertise."

Shit! Shit! Shit! "We're going to see if we can get you out of this thing, Kayla." Madison holstered her gun.

"I don't want to die." Kayla was crying and hysterical.

"I know, sweetie. We'll do whatever we can to help you."

"She said if you tamper with the vest, it will explode. There's nothing you can do." Kayla trembled.

She... This was a trap, one set by Tatiana. Her seeming disregard for whether she was spotted at Nikitin's or Kayla's buildings. Then leaving McBride's mutilated body where it would be found. All of it was part of her tactic to draw Madison out. The call from a fake confidential informant had been the cherry on top. *Son of bitch!*

"You sure we can't just—"

Troy pulled on her arm. "Madison, we've got to get away from her now."

"We can't just let her die." This was another cruel trick by Tatiana. She, no doubt, remained at a distance watching this situation unfold. There was probably a camera in the rafters pointed on them right now. She was probably having a good laugh over this.

"Madison!" Troy screamed. "We have to go!"

The timer is down to thirty seconds. Twenty-nine. Twenty-eight...

"I'm so sorry." Tears fell down Madison's cheeks as she turned to run, Troy pulling her along with him. She felt like a doll blowing in the wind.

Along the way she yelled for others to leave, but they looked at her and Troy wide-eyed and uncomprehending.

Madison and Troy made it to the doorway of the warehouse when the explosion thundered, rocking the night and the ground beneath their feet. The concussion blew her and Troy forward, and the next thing she knew, she was flying. Her arms reached out, trying to brace herself, but there was nothing but air.

Then she landed.

The impact forced the air from her lungs. "Tro—" That's all she could get out before her vision went black.

CHAPTER 42

Madison's head pounded and spun. Her ears felt like they were stuffed with gauze. Still, she heard a woman's voice, a Russian accent.

"Huh. Not much of a challenge for me. I should have never bothered sending them after her," the woman said.

Madison was nudged with a shoe in her ribcage. It took all of Madison's willpower not to scream out and open her eyes, but the woman thought she was dead. Right now, that was to Madison's advantage.

What is she talking about? Madison was having a hard time concentrating, but it was obvious this woman was talking to someone. She opened her eyes just a slit and made out two figures. One male, one female. Tatiana Ivanova.

I should have never bothered sending them after her... The statement pinged around in her head. Then Madison deciphered the meaning. The car accident last month. It hadn't been an accident at all. The corrupt cops hadn't acted of their own accord. They'd tried to kill her because the Russians, specifically this woman, had ordered them to kill her!

Madison wriggled her fingers, doing so cautiously, and it seemed to go unnoticed. She reached for her holster, every movement excruciating. Her fingertips danced over the handle of her weapon. *I can do this!* A deep breath in, and she yanked her gun out and fired off two shots in quick succession.

Madison rolled onto her side, her body moving on sheer willpower fueled by adrenaline, and she got to her feet. One shot had found purchase in the man, who now lay on the ground bleeding out from a wound to his throat.

Tatiana was standing back with a gun in hand, but she hadn't returned fire. "Detective, glad to see you're alive. Now, I can kill you myself."

Madison managed to duck and roll behind a dumpster just as Tatiana squeezed off a round. The bullet pinged off metal. Madison returned fire. Tatiana screamed, and her gun went flying from her hand. Madison inched out, her gun trained on the woman. She'd struck her in the shoulder, but Tatiana wasn't cradling it. Rather she was leaned forward, arms open, like she was summoning her opponent in a wrestling match.

"Heard you ended up losing your baby. Probably not good mother material anyway."

How did she know that? But it took everything for Madison not to pull the trigger and end this woman's pitiful life. Anger was coursing through her body, and all she could see was red.

"What? Nothing to say to that?"

Madison got closer to her. "You're under arrest for the—"

Tatiana chortled loudly and, with a swoop of her leg, threw a high kick, knocking Madison's gun out of her hand. She shuffled trying to go for it, but Tatiana pulled her back.

Madison spun and landed a punch square in the woman's face, but she laughed like she hadn't felt a thing. They threw punches and juked, each taking turns dominating. But Madison couldn't keep going like this for long. She felt her energy draining. She could have been bleeding internally from the blast and the fall.

"Ah, tiring out, are we?" Tatiana smiled down at her.

Madison refused to go out like this, to have this Russian's face be the last thing she'd ever see. She potshot her in the nose, the cartilage giving way under her fist.

Tatiana howled in pain but only gave a fraction of an inch.

Maybe this is how I die…

She turned her head to avoid a direct blow and spotted Tatiana's gun. It had slid just under the front edge of the dumpster. If she could get to it…a foot away.

Madison kept fighting back and did her best to shift closer to the weapon.

Six inches away.

She reached out, her fingers longing to grasp the handle.

More scuffling.

And enough of the distance was closed.

Madison grabbed the gun, and as Tatiana drew back her fist, getting ready to strike again, Madison pulled the trigger.

Tatiana's face exploded with the impact of the bullet, and her blood rained down over Madison just before she started to fall forward. Madison quickly pushed the woman's body from her and puked on the pavement.

Troy!

She pulled herself off the ground, stumbling, searching. "Troy!" She called out his name as loudly as she could.

She walked around, becoming frantic. Why wasn't he answering her? Why couldn't she see him?

The warehouse was ablaze and lighting up the sky, but it didn't seem like enough. She pulled out her phone, turned on the flashlight, and aimed it over the area.

Then she caught a glimpse of his boot…his jeans…

"Troy!" She ran toward him. He was pinned under a steel beam that must have been thrown out of the warehouse when it exploded.

She dropped down next to him. "No. Please, dear God, let him be alive." She felt for a pulse, and it was so small and thready that she almost missed it. She went to dial 911 but heard roaring sirens and, soon after, flashing, colored lights filled the sky.

"Hang in there. Please." Madison kissed Troy's forehead.

CHAPTER 43

Four days later

The sun was shining like nothing bad ever happened. Only it did.

Madison looked down at where she held Troy's hand. How could she ever say goodbye? Warm tears splashed her cheeks, and she sniffled. He appeared so peaceful.

His eyes fluttered open, and she kissed his lips and pulled back, palming her cheeks and acting tough. "Don't ever scare me like that again."

"Guess now you know how it feels." He squeezed her hand.

He had stayed vigil by her bedside for two days while she'd been in a medically induced coma after the car accident. Right now, they were in his hospital room, and the sun was beating through the window. He was just waking from a nap.

"I'm so sorry, Troy."

"None of this is your fault. Big boy, remember?" He winked at her.

She smiled at him. "Of course I do."

According to the doctor, Troy was going to be fine. He'd cracked his femur and had two broken ribs, but if the beam's weight hadn't been supported somewhat by other pieces of debris, it was quite possible that she could have lost him.

Madison had a bunch of scratches and bruises but no broken bones—a miracle in itself. She was suffering mentally more than physically. The body tended to heal much faster than the mind. She couldn't help but chastise herself that if it hadn't been for her, Troy wouldn't be in that hospital bed.

And poor Kayla. Tatiana had used that girl as bait to draw out Madison. And it wasn't just Kayla's death that rested on her conscience, but a total of thirty-one people died in that warehouse.

All because Madison couldn't let things go—Kayla, the Mafia—Tatiana had been able to use this weakness against her. "I'm done, Troy."

"Done what?"

"Going after the mob. It's time to let them go."

"You're only saying that because you killed their star assassin."

Tatiana. Madison had also taken out the man who had been with her. A phone recovered from his pocket confirmed he had been the one to call Madison to get her to the warehouse. "No." She shook her head. "There will be more that rise in her place. This vendetta I have against them has gone on for long enough. I've almost gotten myself killed more than once, and I've put others in danger. You, Terry, our baby…"

"You don't know they're to blame for that."

"They didn't help things." She'd told him about what Tatiana had said and that she'd ordered the cops to ram her car, and he hadn't had much to say to that. She had a feeling he was too angry to speak. She went on. "And maybe life will improve for all of us if I just leave them alone." If there was anything this case had taught her, it was that grudges were deadly. Even though Russell Brennan hadn't ordered the death of Morgan Walker, he'd still spent years with hate in his heart. "It's just not worth it. One day the cost could be too high." She'd been warring against the Russians for far too long. She held them responsible for killing her grandfather, but he was gone. There would be no bringing him back. And by clutching to the memory of him, she was bound to turn herself into a martyr at some point, and that wouldn't be what he would have wanted. It was time to relinquish the vendetta before it ate her alive—or took everyone from her who she held dear.

"You're just going to let them go?"

She shook her head, feeling the tug of a smile on her lips. "They killed a lot of people in that warehouse, and the Feds are far better equipped to weed through the evidence and hold the mob accountable once and for all. I've already called them in, and they're going to make sure justice happens. I should have called them in years ago."

Troy squeezed her hand. "I'm so proud of you."

A few seconds ticked past before he spoke again.

"But what about corrupt cops…?"

"I'll still expose them whenever I can."

"Yeah, that's my woman." He pulled her to him for another kiss. When they parted, he said, "I'm sorry about that girl. I know you really wanted to save her."

"Yes, I did. Kayla Fleming." She said her name because she wanted to always remember it. The girl had a horrible life with a horrid ending, but there were more like her who Madison might be able to save. That was the part she had to focus on or risk losing her sanity.

"You have the funeral today, right? For Courtney?" Troy's eyes shot toward the clock on the wall. "You don't want to be late."

"I won't be." She smiled at him.

When it came to Morgan Walker/Courtney Middleton, there was closure and an extra twenty dollars in her pocket from winning the bet she'd made with Terry. The DNA test had come back in two days, and the results were a match. She'd driven up to see the Middletons to let them know what she'd done and shared the findings. She thought they might be angry with her for crossing that line, but they weren't. They thanked her for caring about them and their daughter so much. When they were told they had two grandchildren and that their daughter had set up a charity, they showed enthusiasm about taking over from where she'd left off.

Madison had also confessed what she'd done to Shane Walker. He didn't take it quite as smoothly, and there was some resistance, but eventually he conceded that he understood why she had done what she had. It had only been motivated by love and a drive to find the truth.

Now everyone had closure. And she and Troy had a fresh start.

What would tomorrow look like? Only one way to find out—release the past and move forward.

A LETTER FROM CAROLYN

Dear reader,

I want to say a huge thank you for choosing to read *Girl on the Run*. If you enjoyed it and would like to hear about new releases in the Detective Madison Knight Series, just sign up at the following link. Your email address will never be shared, and you can unsubscribe at any time.

CarolynArnold.net/MKUpdates

If you loved *Girl on the Run*, I would be incredibly grateful if you would write a brief, honest review. Also, if you'd like to continue investigating murder, you'll be happy to know there will be more Detective Madison Knight books. I also offer several other international bestselling series and have a number of published books for you to savor—everything from crime fiction, to thrillers, to action adventures. Please visit my website to browse all my available titles.

Often as a writer, I'm asked what inspired a book and for this one, I pulled from a real-life experience. They say real life is stranger than fiction, and sometimes that's true. I was in a train station, much like the one I described in the book, and went to get a coffee. There was a girl with a backpack who grabbed food items from the refrigerated unit. I was in line with a few other women, and we started talking among ourselves. We couldn't believe what we just saw. We were trying to get the attention of the clerks, and this man came over. He was all hopped up. He raised his voice and told us to mind our own business, and what were we, a bunch of Good Samaritans? He even went so far as to claim he was a cop. I wanted to contest that, but a strong instinct told me to stay quiet and hope he went away. Thankfully, nothing came of this confrontation, but I think all it would have taken was for one of us to really stand up to him. The clerks at the counter seemed to shy away as if they were oblivious to the situation. I walked away that day, but I was shaken. In the deepest part of me, I know something was going on in that train station. I even reached out to a police friend of mine and ran the scenario past her, and she said that it sounded like drug trafficking to her. She told me that I did the right thing by staying quiet. It was this event and the questions of *what if* and *what's going on* that led me to create the story you just finished reading.

I want to give a shout-out to Officer Rebecca Hendrix, who served with the Quinton Police Department. She reached out to me years ago to tell me how much she enjoyed the Detective Madison Knight Series because she saw herself as Madison. We've remained in contact, and Rebecca has always been there if I have a procedural question. For the writing of this book it was no different. Thank you, Rebecca, for your experience and insights.

As always, I want to mention my husband, George, who is my best friend. He's believed in me and my writing from the start and has remained by my side for over twenty-six years. Love you, George!

I also want to voice my appreciation for the editors who worked on this book and helped push me to make it the best it could be.

Last but certainly not least, I love hearing from my readers! You can get in touch on my Facebook page, through Twitter, Goodreads, or my website. This is also a good way to stay notified of my new releases. You can also reach out to me via email at carolyn@carolynarnold.net.

Wishing you a thrill a word!
Carolyn Arnold

Connect with CAROLYN ARNOLD Online:
CarolynArnold.net
Facebook.com/AuthorCarolynArnold
Twitter.com/Carolyn_Arnold

Read on for an exciting preview of
Carolyn Arnold's FBI thriller
featuring Brandon Fisher

ELEVEN

CHAPTER ONE

Nothing in the twenty weeks at Quantico had prepared me for this.

A crime scene investigator, who had identified himself as Earl Royster when we'd first arrived, addressed my boss, FBI Supervisory Special Agent Jack Harper, "All of the victims were buried—" He held up a finger, his eyes squeezed shut, and he sneezed. "Sorry 'bout that. My allergies don't like it down here. They were all buried the same way."

This was my first case with the FBI Behavioral Analysis Unit, and it had brought me and the three other members of my team to Salt Lick, Kentucky. The discovery was made this morning, and we were briefed and flown in from Quantico to the Louisville field office where we picked up a couple of SUVs. We drove from there and arrived in Salt Lick at about four in the afternoon.

We were in an underground bunker illuminated by portable lights brought in by the local investigative team. The space was eleven feet beneath the cellar of a house that was the size of a mobile trailer. We stood in a central hub from which four tunnels spread out like a root system. The space was fifteen feet by seven and a half feet and six and a half feet tall.

The walls were packed dirt, and an electrical cord ran along the ceiling and down the tunnels with pigtail light fixtures dangling every few feet. The bulbs cut into the height of the tunnels by eight inches.

I pulled on my shirt collar wishing for a smaller frame than my six foot two inches. As it was, the three of us could have reached out and touched each other if we were so inclined. The tunnels were even narrower at three feet wide.

"It's believed each victim had the same cuts inflicted," Royster began, "although most of the remains are skeletal, so it's not as easy to know for sure, but based on burial method alone, this guy obviously adhered to some sort of ritual. The most recent victim is only a few years old and was preserved by the soil. The oldest remains are estimated to date back twenty-five to thirty years. Bingham moved in twenty-six years ago."

Lance Bingham was the property owner, age sixty-two, and was currently serving three to five years in a correctional facility for killing two cows and assaulting a neighbor. If he had moved in twenty-six years ago, that would put Bingham at thirty-six years old at the time. The statistical age for a serial killer to start out is early to mid-thirties.

The CSI continued to relay more information about how the tunnels branched out in various directions, likely extending beneath a neighboring cornfield, and the ends came to bulbous tips, like subterranean cul-de-sacs.

"There are eleven rooms and only ten bodies," Jack summarized with impatience and pulled a cigarette out of a shirt pocket. He didn't light up, but his mouth was clamped down on it as if it were a lifeline.

Royster's gaze went from the cigarette to Jack's eyes. "Yes. There's one tunnel that leads to a dead end, and there's one empty grave."

Jack turned to me. "What do you make of it?" he asked, the cigarette bobbing on his lips as he spoke.

Everyone looked at me expectantly. "Of the empty grave?" I squeaked out.

Jack squinted and removed the cigarette from his mouth. "That and the latest victim."

"Well…" My collar felt tighter, and I cleared my throat, then continued. "Bingham had been in prison for the last three years. The elaborate tunnel system he had going would have taken years to plan and dig, and it would have taken a lot of strength. My guess would be that Bingham wasn't working alone. He had help and, after he went to prison, someone followed in his footsteps."

Jack perched the unlit smoke back between his lips. "Hmm."

I wasn't sure how to read *Hmm*, but the way his gaze scrutinized me, I was thinking he wasn't necessarily impressed.

"Anyway, you'll want to see it for yourself." Royster gestured down one of the tunnels and took a step toward it. "I know I haven't seen anything like—" Royster didn't catch his sneeze in time, and snot sprayed through the air.

Ick. I stepped back.

More sniffles. "Again, sorry 'bout that. Anyway, this way."

Jack motioned for me to follow behind Royster, ahead of him.

I took a deep breath, anticipating the tight quarters of the tunnel.

Sweat dripped down my back, and I pulled on my collar again.

"Go ahead, Kid," Jack directed.

He'd adopted the pet name for me from the moment we'd met, and I wished he'd just call me by my name.

Both Jack and the CSI were watching me.

The CSI said, "We'll look at the most recent victim first. Now, as you know, the victims alternated male and female. The tenth victim was female so we believe the next is going to be—"

"Let me guess, male," Jack interrupted him.

"Yeah." Royster took off down the third tunnel that fed off from the bottom right of the hub.

I followed behind him, tracing the walls with my hands. My heart palpitated. I ducked to miss the bulbs just as I knew I'd have to and worked at focusing on the positive. Above ground, the humidity sucked air from the lungs; in the tunnels, the air was cool but still suffocating.

I counted my paces—five, six. The further we went, the heavier my chest became, making the next breath less taken for granted.

Despite my extreme discomfort, this was my first case, and I had to be strong. The rumor was you either survived Jack and the two years of probationary service and became a certified special agent or your next job would be security detail at a mall.

Five more paces and we entered an offshoot from the main tunnel. According to Royster, three burial chambers were in this tunnel. He described these as branches on a tree. Each branch came off the main trunk for the length of about ten feet and ended in a circular space of about eleven feet in diameter. The idea of more space seemed welcoming until we reached it.

A circular grave took up most of the space and was a couple of feet deep. Chicken wire rimmed the grave to help it retain its shape. With her wrists and ankles tied to metal stakes, her arms and legs formed the human equivalent of a star. As her body had dried from decomposition, the constraints had kept her positioned in the manner the killer had intended.

"And what made them dig?" Jack asked the CSI.

Jack was searching for specifics. We knew Bingham had entrusted his financials to his sister, but when she passed away a year ago, the back taxes had built up, and the county had come to reclaim the property.

Royster answered, "X marked the spot." Neither Jack nor I displayed any amusement. The CSI continued. "He etched into the dirt, probably with a stick."

"Why assume a stick?" Jack asked the question, and it resulted in an awkward silence.

My eyes settled on the body of the female who was estimated to be in her early twenties. It's not that I had an aversion to a dead body, but looking at her made my stomach toss. She still had flesh on her bones. As the CSI had said, *Preserved by the soil.*

Her torso had eleven incisions. They were marked in the linear way to keep count. Two sets of four vertical cuts with one diagonal slash through each of them. The eleventh cut was the largest and was above the belly button.

"You realize the number eleven is believed to be a sign of purity?" Zach's voice seemed to strike me from thin air, and my chest compressed further, knowing another person was going to share the limited space.

Zachery Miles was a member of our team, but unlike Jack's reputation, Zach's hadn't preceded him. Any information I had, I'd gathered from his file that showed a flawless service record and the IQ of a genius. It also disclosed that he was thirty-seven, eight years older than I was.

Jack stuck the cigarette he had been sucking on back into his shirt pocket. "Purity, huh?"

I looked down at the body of the woman in the shallow grave beside me. Nothing seemed too pure about any of this.

"I'm going to go," Royster excused himself.

"That's if you really dig into the numerology and spiritualistic meaning of the number," Zachery said, disregarding the CSI entirely.

Jack stretched his neck side to side and looked at me. "I hate it when he gets into that shit." He pointed a bony index finger at me. "Don't let me catch you talking about it either."

I just nodded. I felt I had just been admonished as if I were his child—not that he needed to zero in on me like that. Sure, I believed in the existence of God and angels, despite the evil in the world, but I didn't have any avid interest in the unseen.

Zachery continued, "The primary understanding is the number one is that of new beginnings and purity. This is emphasized with the existence of two ones."

My eyes scanned Zachery's face. While his intelligence scoring revealed a genius, physically, he was of average looks. If anything, he was slightly taller than Jack and I, probably coming in at about six foot four. His hair was dark and trimmed short. He had a high brow line and brown eyes.

"Zachery here reads something once—" Jack tapped his head "—it's there."

Jack and I spent the next few hours making our way to every room where Jack insisted on standing beside all the bodies. He studied each of them carefully, even if only part of their remains had been uncovered. I'd pass him glances, but he seemed oblivious to my presence. We ended up back beside the most recent victim where we stayed for twenty minutes, not moving, not talking, just standing.

I understood what he saw. There was a different feel to this room, nothing quantifiable, but it was discernible. The killer had a lot to say. He was organized and immaculate. He was precise and disciplined. He acted with a purpose, and, like most killers, he had a message to relay. We were looking for a controlled, highly intelligent unsub.

The intestines had been removed from nine of the victims, but Harold Jones, the coroner—who also came backed with a doctorate unlike most of his profession—wouldn't conclude it as the cause of death before conducting more tests. The last victim's intestines were intact, and, even though the cause of death needed confirmation, the talk that permeated the corridors of the bunker was that the men who did this were scary sons of bitches.

Zachery entered the room. "I find it fascinating he would bury his victims in circular graves."

Fascinating?

I looked up at Jack, and he flicked his lighter.

He held out his hands as if to say he wouldn't light up inside the burial chamber. His craving was getting desperate, though, which meant he'd be getting cranky. He said, "Continue, Zachery, by all means. The kid wants to hear."

"By combining both the number eleven and the circle, it makes me think of the coinherence symbol. Even the way the victims are laid out."

"Elaborate," Jack directed.

"It's a circle which combines a total of eleven inner points to complete it. As eleven means purity, so the coinherence symbol is related to religious traditions—at minimum thirteen, but some people can discern more, and each symbol is understood in different ways. The circle itself stands for completion and can symbolize eternity."

I cocked my head to the side. Zachery noticed.

"We have a skeptic here, Jack."

Jack faced me and spoke with the unlit cigarette having resumed its perch between his lips. "What do you make of it?"

Is this a trap? "You want to know what I think?"

"By all means, Slingshot."

There it was, the other dreaded nickname, no doubt his way of reminding me that I didn't score perfectly on handguns at the academy. "Makes me think of the medical symbol. Maybe our guy has a background in medicine. It could explain the incisions being deep enough to inflict pain but not deep enough to cause them to bleed out. It would explain how he managed to take out their intestines."

Was this what I signed up for?

"Hmm," Jack mumbled. Zachery remained silent. Seconds later, Jack said, "You're assuming they didn't bleed out. Continue."

"The murders happened over a period of time. This one—" I gestured to the woman, and for a moment, realized how this job transformed the life of a person into an object "—she's recent. Bingham's been in prison for about three years now."

Jack flicked the lighter again. "So you're saying he had an apprentice?"

Zachery's lips lifted upward, and his eyes read, *Like* Star Wars.

I got it. I was the youngest on the team, twenty-nine this August, next month, and I was the new guy, but I didn't make it through four years of university studying mechanics and endure twenty weeks of the academy, coming out at the top of the class, to be treated like a child. "Not like an apprentice."

"Like what then—"

"Jack, the sheriff wants to speak with you." Paige Dawson, another member of our team, came into the burial chamber. She had come to Quantico from the New York field office claiming she wanted out of the big city. I met her when she was an instructor at the FBI Academy.

I pulled on my collar. Four of us were in here now. Dust caused me to cough and warranted a judgmental glare from Jack.

"How did you make out with the guy who discovered everything?"

"He's clean. I mean we had his background already, and he lives up to it. I really don't think he's involved at all."

Jack nodded and left the room.

I turned to Zachery. "I think he hates me."

"If he hated you, you'd know it." Zachery followed behind Jack.

CHAPTER TWO

Salt Lick, Kentucky was right in the middle of nowhere and had a population shy of three hundred and fifty. Just as the town's name implied, underground mineral deposits were the craving of livestock, and due to this, it had originally attracted farmers to the area. I was surprised the village was large enough to boast a Journey's End Lodge and a Frosty Freeze.

I stepped into the main hub to see Jack in a heated conversation with Sheriff Harris. From an earlier meeting with him, I knew he covered all of Bath County which included three municipalities and a combined population of about twelve thousand.

"Ah, I'm doing the best I can, Agent, but, um, we've never seen the likes of this before." A born and raised Kentucky man, the sheriff was in his mid-fifties, had a bald head and carried about an extra sixty pounds that came to rest on his front. Both of his hands were braced on his hips, a stance of confidence, but the flicking up and down of his right index finger gave his insecurities away.

"It has nothing to do with what you've seen before, Sheriff. What matters is catching the unsub."

"Well, the property owner is in p-pri-prison," the Kentucky accent broke through.

"The bodies date back two to three decades with the newest one being within the last few years."

Harris's face brightened a reddish hue as he took a deep breath and exhaled loud enough to be heard.

Jack had the ability to make a lot of people nervous. His dark hair, which was dusted with silver at the sideburns, gave him a look of distinction, but deeply-etched creases in his face exposed his trying past.

Harris shook his head. "So much violence, and it's tourist season 'round here." Harris paused. His eyes said, *You city folks wouldn't understand.* "Cave Run Lake is manmade but set in the middle of nature. People love coming here to get away. Word gets out about this, there go the tourists."

"Ten people have been murdered, and you're worried about tourists?"

"Course not, but—"

"It sounds like you were."

"Then you misunderstood, Agent. Besides, the counties around here are peaceful, law-abidin' citizens."

"Churchgoers?" Zachery came up from a tunnel.

"Well, ah, I wouldn't necessarily say that. There are probably about thirty churches or so throughout the county, and right here in Salt Lick there are three."

"That's quite a few considering the population here."

"S'pose so."

"Sheriff." A deputy came up to the group of them and pulled up his pants.

"Yes, White."

The deputy's face was the shade of his name. "The in-investigators found somethin' you should see." He passed glances among all of us.

Jack held out a hand as if to say, *By all means.*

We followed the deputy up the ramp that led to the cellar. With each step taking me closer to the surface, my chest allowed for more satisfying breaths. Jack glanced over at me. I guessed he was wondering if I was going to make it.

"This way, sir."

The deputy spoke from the front of the line, as he kept moving. His boots hit the wooden stairs that joined the cellar to the first floor.

I inhaled deeply as I came through the opening into the confined space Bingham had at one time called home. Sunlight made its way through tattered sheets that served as curtains, even though the time of day was now seven, and the sun would be sinking in the sky.

The deputy led us to Bingham's bedroom where there were two CSIs. I heard footsteps behind me: Paige. She smiled at me, but it quickly faded.

"They found it in the closet," the deputy said, pointing our focus in its direction.

The investigators moved aside, exposing an empty space. A shelf that ran the width of the closet sat perched at a forty-five-degree angle. The inside had been painted white at one time but now resembled an antiqued paint pattern the modern age went for. It was what I saw when my eyes followed the walls to the floor that held more interest.

Jack stepped in front of me; Zachery came up behind him and gave me a look that said, *Pull up the rear, Pending.* Pending being the nickname Zach had saddled me with to remind me of my twenty-four-month probationary period— as if I'd forget.

"We found it when we noticed the loose floorboard," one of the CSIs said. He held a clipboard wedged between an arm and his chest. The other hand held a pen which he clicked repeatedly. Jack looked at it, and the man stopped. The CSI went on. "Really, it's what's inside that's, well, what nightmares are made of."

I didn't know the man. In fact, I had never seen him before, but the reflection in his eyes told me he had witnessed something that even paled the gruesome find in the bunkers.

"You first, Kid." Jack stepped back.

Floorboards were hinged back and exposed a hole about two and a half feet square. My stomach tossed thinking of the CSI's words, *what nightmares are made of.*

"Come on, Brandon. I'll follow behind you." Paige's soft voice of encouragement was accompanied by a strategically placed hand on my right shoulder.

I glanced at her. I could do this. *God, I hated small spaces.* But I had wanted to be an FBI special agent and, well, that wish had been granted. Maybe the saying, *Be careful what you wish for, it might come true,* held merit.

I hunched over and looked into the hole. A wooden ladder went down at least twenty feet. The space below was lit.

Maybe if I just took it one step at a time.

"What are you waiting for, Pending?" Zachery taunted me. I didn't look at him but picked up on the amusement in his voice.

I took a deep breath and lowered myself down.

Jack never said a word, but I could feel his energy. He didn't think I was ready for this, but I would prove him wrong—somehow. The claustrophobia I had experienced in the underground passageways was nothing compared to the anxiety squeezing my chest now. At least the tunnels were the width of three feet. Here, four sides of packed earth hugged me, as if a substantial inhale would expand me to the confines of the space.

"I'm coming." Again, Paige's soft voice had a way of soothing me despite the tight quarters threatening to take my last breath and smother me alive.

I looked up. Paige's face filled the opening, and her red wavy hair framed her face. The vision was replaced by the bottom of her shoes.

I continued my descent, one rung at a time, slowly, methodically. I tried to place myself somewhere else, but no images came despite my best efforts to conjure them— and what did I have waiting for me at the bottom? *What nightmares are made of.*

Minutes passed before my shoes reached the soil. I took a deep breath when I realized the height down here was about seven feet and looked around. The room was about five by five, and there was a doorway at the backside.

One pigtail fixture with a light bulb dangled from an electrical wire. It must have fed to the same circuit as the underground passageways and been connected to the power generator as it cast dim light, creating darkened shadows in the corners.

I looked up the ladder. Paige was about halfway down. There was movement behind her, and it was likely Jack and Zachery following behind her.

"You're almost there," I coached them.

By the time the rest of the team made it to the bottom, along with the deputy and a CSI, I had my breathing and my nerves under control.

Paige was the first to head around the bend in the wall.

"The sheriff is going to stay up there an' take care of things." The deputy pointed in the direction Paige went. "What they found is in here."

Jack and Zachery had already headed around the bend. I followed.

Inside the room, Paige raised her hand to cover her mouth. It dropped when she noticed us.

A stainless steel table measuring ten feet by three feet was placed against the back wall. A commercial meat grinder sat on the table. Everything was pristine, and light from a bulb reflected off the surfaces.

To the left of the table was a chest freezer, plain white, one owned by the average consumer. I had one similar, but it was the smaller version because it was only Deb and me.

My stomach tossed thinking about the contents of this one. Paige's feet were planted to where she had first entered the room. Zachery's eyes fixed on Jack, who moved toward the freezer and, with a gloved hand, opened the lid.

Paige gasped, and Jack turned to face her. Disappointment was manifested in the way his eyes narrowed. "It's empty." Jack patted his shirt pocket again.

"If you're thinking we found people's remains in there, we haven't," the CSI said, "but tests have shown positive for human blood."

"So he chopped up his victim's intestines? Put them in the freezer? But where are they?" Paige wrapped her arms around her torso and bent over to look into the opening of the grinder.

"There are many cultures, the Korowai tribe of Papua New Guinea, for example, who have been reported to practice cannibalism even in this modern day," Zachery said. "It can also be involved in religious rituals."

Maybe my eyes should have been fixed on the freezer, on the horror that transpired underground in Salt Lick of Bath County, Kentucky. Instead, I found my training allowing me to focus, analyze, and be objective. In order to benefit the investigation, it would demand these three things, and I wouldn't disappoint. My attention was on the size of the table, the size of the meat grinder, and the size of the freezer. "Anyone think to ask how this all got down here in the first place?"

All five of them faced me.

"The opening down here is only, what, two feet square at the most? Now maybe the meat grinder would fit down, hoisted on a rope, but the table and the freezer? No way."

"What are you saying, Slingshot?"

My eyes darted to Jack's. "I'm saying there has to be another way in." I addressed the CSI, "Did you look for any other hidden passageways? I mean the guy obviously had a thing for them."

"We didn't find anything."

"Well, that doesn't make sense. Where are the burial sites in relation to here?"

"It would be that way." Zachery pointed at the freezer.

We connected eyes, and both of us moved toward it. It slid easily. As we shoved it to the side, it revealed an opening behind it. I looked down into it. Another light bulb spawned eerie shadows. I rose to full height. This find should at least garner some praise from Jack Harper.

"Nothing like Hogan's Alley is it, Kid?"

Also available from
International Bestselling Author
Carolyn Arnold

ELEVEN

Book 1 in the Brandon Fisher FBI series

Eleven Rooms. Ten Bodies. One Empty Grave.

When Brandon Fisher joined the FBI Behavioral Analysis Unit, he knew he'd come up against psychopaths, sociopaths, pathological liars, and more. But when his first case takes him and the team to Salt Lick, Kentucky, to hunt down a ritualistic serial killer, he learns what nightmares are truly made of.

Beneath a residential property, local law enforcement discovered an underground bunker with circular graves that house the remains of ten victims. But that's not all: there's an empty eleventh grave, just waiting for a corpse. The killing clearly hasn't come to an end yet, and with the property owner already behind bars, Brandon is certain there's an apprentice who roams free.

As the FBI follows the evidence across the United States, Brandon starts to struggle with the deranged nature of his job description. And if the case itself isn't going to be enough to push Brandon over the edge, he's working in the shadow of Supervisory Special Agent Jack Harper, who expects nothing short of perfection from his team. To make matters even worse, it seems Brandon has become the target of a psychotic serial killer who wants to make him—or his wife—victim number eleven.

**Available from popular book retailers or
at CarolynArnold.net**

CAROLYN ARNOLD is an international bestselling and award-winning author, as well as a speaker, teacher, and inspirational mentor. She has several continuing fiction series and has many published books. Her genre diversity offers her readers everything from police procedurals, hard-boiled mysteries, and thrillers to action adventures. Her crime fiction series have been praised by those in law enforcement as being accurate and entertaining. This led to her adopting the trademark: POLICE PROCEDURALS RESPECTED BY LAW ENFORCEMENT™.

Carolyn was born in a small town and enjoys spending time outdoors, but she also loves the lights of a big city. Grounded by her roots and lifted by her dreams, her overactive imagination insists that she tell her stories. Her intention is to touch the hearts of millions with her books, to entertain, inspire, and empower.

She currently lives near London, Ontario, Canada with her husband and two beagles.

CONNECT ONLINE

Carolynarnold.net
Facebook.com/AuthorCarolynArnold
Twitter.com/Carolyn_Arnold

And don't forget to sign up for her newsletter for up-to-date information on release and special offers at

CarolynArnold.net/Newsletters.

CPSIA information can be obtained
at www.ICGtesting.com
Printed in the USA
BVHW050241261022
650294BV00001B/67